Perceptions
&
Secrets

by
Jessica Gold

Perceptions & Secrets by Jessica Gold
Copyright © 2022. All rights reserved.

Published by Pen It! Publications in the U.S.A.
812-371-4128 www.penitpublications.com

ISBN: 978-1-63984-261-2
Edited by Nicole Mullaney, Leah Pugh
Cover by Donna Cook

Contents

6

Dedication

To my mom. Thank you, Mom, for teaching me to love and appreciate writing.

Acknowledgements

To my husband and children, thank you for the support, always.

To Judy, Mike, Elaine, Wayne, Scott and Stefanie, thanks for the cheers.

To Ros, Rich, Mary, Melissa, Jocelyn, Susan, Linda, Sue and Tricia, Alice, Allen and Chris, Jodie and Bill. Thank you.

Big thank you goes to Nicole. You are an amazing editor and teacher. I am very appreciative.

To my readers, enjoy the journey. May this book leave you laughing, crying, smiling and wanting more.

Prologue

The midday sun's brilliance captivated every beachgoer on a scorching July day at Shreeland Beach. Its rays shone down in endless beams, causing the white frothy tops of the waves to look even brighter. Chad Harper stood in the distance, on the boardwalk, in a light blue golf shirt and khakis, taking in the scenery.

Lost in a simple moment, a woman with auburn hair, wearing a white one-piece bathing suit, with a light tan and pearly whites captured in the sun's ray caught his attention. She looked stunningly beautiful dancing in the waves and smiling at the children playing nearby. He was fascinated by her beauty, the sun highlighting her hair. Her face was one of an angel, personifying pure happiness. He needed to meet her and simply couldn't keep his eyes off her.

His phone rang, interrupting his perusal. He glanced down at his screen and seeing the name, knew he had to take the call. He took another look at Wave Girl, sighed in frustration, and prepared to deal with the business at hand.

****

Down the road in the rustic brick Southampton courthouse, Rick Lynch, a seasoned lawyer stood clenching his jaw, quietly seething as he made mincemeat out of his adversary. The witness to the accident squirmed in his seat, wondering what explosive words would be catapulted at him next. Rick considered his trials to be an art, and himself to be Picasso. His dark haired, polished good looks drew the jurors in, and yet his silver-tongued trial tactics seem slick and questionable, no one ever quite knew when he would throw a curveball.

This man's magnetism always drew eyes to him. The men appeared to be awed by him, sitting a little straighter in their seats when he looked their way, while he believed every woman wanted him and tried to meet his turquoise eyes. Today was no different than any other. Looks like these were often exchanged, while conversations about his rapport took place in the breakroom at his firm, in restaurants, and in restrooms. He was well aware. Knowing it was one thing, but unlike many, Rick also knew how to use it to his favor. In every situation, every encounter, he was there for the kill; he was there for the win.

Chapter 1

Two weeks later

Gorgeous blue-eyed Chad Harper stretched his long, muscular legs while sitting on the wooden porch of his grandmother's sprawling Hampton white Tudor home enjoying his visit, until inevitably she brought up what he dreaded most. He came here to eat hotdogs on a stick over a bonfire, toast marshmallows with his niece and nephew, not to have his future dissected. But, being around Cecilia, it was bound to happen.

Frustrated, he ran his fingers through his sandy blonde hair, preparing for her to push him in a way only Cecilia can. She has the look on her face that means business. Her intelligent green eyes focus in his direction like lasers and lock him in a pointed stare, her lips tightly clenched and her chin tilted upward. She greeted him warmly with her hugs when he first arrived, but now it's time for her discussion with him, for her it is all about mentoring and directing. Chad squirms just a little knowing he's sitting in her hot seat, and there's absolutely no way to avoid it. When Cecilia wants to discuss politics, it's best to give her your ear.

"It is your time, Chadwick, I feel it," she proclaimed with conviction, looking up at him proudly from the white wicker chair on the porch with her eyes bright.

Her tan crochet bag sat next to her, with her white hair pulled up in a bun, and her long blue linen skirt blowing in the breeze, she looked like the proverbial Norman Rockwell painting. She portrayed the quintessential lady from head to toe and the proud matriarch of the long line of Blue Blood politicians. She's a true lady alright, but she could throw you a zinger.

Her sons worked as proud federal judges, real estate lawyers, and a senator thrown into the mix, and she expects her grandchildren to follow the same path. Her son Zane was a Federal Judge in Manhattan, her son Damian, a Family Court Judge in Brooklyn, her daughter Elana, a successful real estate lawyer based in Connecticut and Thaddeus, a senator. Cecilia was proud of them all.

Chad deeply respects his grandmother. She may be eighty-five years old, but her wisdom and wit are still there and when Cecilia doesn't get what she wants, she packs a punch. He has seen her in action, bringing six-foot men to their knees with her laser all-knowing eyes and sharp tongue.

Chad, now thirty, had been groomed from the minute he was born to follow in the footsteps of his father, Thaddeus Harper, Thad to those who know him well. After leading what many deem a successful three-term seat as a popular senator, he's ready to enjoy golfing everyday down in sunny Boca. The whole family expected to pick up where his father left off and fulfill the legacy.

He smiled at his grandmother. "I suppose so."

Chad knows this is his destiny, what he's expected to do. It's the reason he endured all the years of private schools, tutors and law school being put in front of him, to follow this path. Only in reality, all Chad wants is to be out on his sailboat, on the water, taking in the beauty of the ocean and the peace that only comes from the wind on the water.

Chad would have been happy just driving a ferry from Sayville to the tourist island. He did that for his summer job all through school and to be honest, for him that was the happiest time of his life. He longed for the feeling of being carefree again, no family pressure, being who he was. Unfortunately, it's not meant to be.

He turned back to his grandmother as she insisted, meeting his eyes in a deadlock. "I know, so, this is your time." Chad clenches his jaw as he looks away, breaking the stare. He didn't want to let her see what he was really thinking. It wasn't worth debating Cecelia. She's a stubborn force, and when she had an idea in her head, there was simply no budging her. She directed her sons and daughter to their careers and now she was working on her grandchildren.

"So, what are you two talking about so intently?" asks a pretty blonde walking up the paved and landscaped driveway carrying her aqua tennis bag across her shoulder and drinking a bottle of Perrier.

Chad's older sister stands before them smiling. Jillian is thirty-one years old, married with two toe-headed gorgeous children ages six and eight. She lives on Columbus Avenue in Manhattan with her lawyer husband, two kids and their cats. Jillian, a former accountant, was the rebel of the family, turned stay at home mom. She's all sunshiny and fun. She is happy in her life and confident in her skin. Jillian loves her family and treasures these weekends at Cecelia's Hampton home.

"We are discussing Chadwick's future," Cecelia announced with a nod, smiling at her granddaughter.

"I am sure he is thrilled," Jillian commented, only loud enough for Chad to hear, while stepping up to her grandmother. Jillian leaned over giving Cecelia a kiss on her slightly wrinkled cheek. Cecelia smiled back at Jillian, her eyes sparkling at the sight of her beautiful granddaughter.

Jillian turns her attention back to Chad who meets her eyes and laughs. At only eighteen months apart, they had always been partners in crime as well as each other's biggest supporter. Jillian used to help Chad with his math homework, and Chad used to always help her with her social studies. They would spend their childhood days playing tennis and squash with each other, and both truly had each other's backs.

"Oh, that is wonderful," Jillian remarked, smiling at her grandmother. She knew how seriously Cecilia took her politics and her family's lineage. She also knew her brother and his feelings about being a legacy.

Cecilia took in her grandchildren and admired them as only a matriarch would. She possessed immense pride for who they've become, but she also had high expectations of keeping their family regime intact.

"Chadwick has much to do, after all he needs those signatures on the petitions. Get to it, Chadwick." Cecilia dismissed them with a back handed wave, and picked up the scarf she was crocheting, continuing her work.

Chad and Jillian met each other's eyes again, knowing they've been gratefully dismissed. As they walked back into the house, Jillian whispered to Chad, "If I were you, I would take the boat out and run away now."

Chad smiled and nodded in agreement. "Sounds like a plan."

He knows Jillian means for him to escape for the rest of the day. Chad wishes he could escape the rest of his life.

Chapter 2

A few minutes later…

Chad had noticed a lot of activity on the private wooden dock behind his grandmother's house as he approached a few minutes later.

"Coast Guard rescue," revealed his grandmother's middle-aged neighbor, Pat, who stood watering her hibiscus plants, looking concerned. She turns off her hose and gives her attention to Chad.

"Looks serious," she added, her voice shaky, sounding worried. "Someone needs to do something quickly."

Chad could see the flames coming up from the sailboat and the frantic waves of the woman on board. Chad narrowed his eyes, seeing the woman wearing a blue bathing suit and white shorts screaming, "Help me," her cries loud enough for them to hear from the dock.

"Oh, my goodness, I see flames," Pat gasped, pointing towards the soon to be wreckage.

Chad watched the woman perch herself on the edge of the boat, about to jump from the fifty-foot Sloop. Looking around, he spotted the Coast Guard boat heading towards it, but not close enough. He knows he needs to take action. The dark water is rough due to a storm off the coast out to the east, making it more difficult for the Coast Guard to get there quickly. He can't stand by doing nothing, watching this unfold.

Without further thought, Chad grabbed his white wave runner, jumped on it with his muscular legs and guns it to start it up. He looks behind him and motions for all the curious onlookers to move back. Returning his focus to the scene in front of him, he takes off like someone's life depended on it, and maybe it does.

The dark water churned around him and the wave runner bobbed like a child's toy in the rough sea. Chad watched closely as he neared the woman who jumped helplessly into the water. He found her clinging to a fairly useless red floatation device in the rough waters. The boat behind her glowed, now a mass of red flames and black smoke. She struggled against the waves, desperately trying to move further from the boat.

Chad hustled, instantly soaked in the spray. As he got close enough to her, he began coughing from the smoke. Reaching up, he wiped the salty water and ash from his eyes, took a deep breath and prepared to dive in just as she went under.

Years of boating and lifeguard training served him well as he dove off of the wave runner perfectly. He opened his eyes in the turbulent water, searching his surroundings to get his bearings. Quickly, he spots her holding her breath with all her might as she begs for help with her eyes. As he assessed her, he suddenly noticed that her foot appears to be caught in the floatation device's rope and it keeps pulling her under as she tries to surface.

Chad has one brief moment of panic and then without hesitation, he ripped his keys from the snapped pocket of his denim shorts, extracted the corkscrew/ switchblade he keeps on the keychain, and sliced the thick, frayed rope in one swift move. Her blue eyes go wide with gratitude as they both swim with all their might to the surface, gasping for air.

At that moment, the Coast Guard boat pulls up and a man swiftly reaches down, pulling the choking woman out of the water. One man covered her with a blanket and began tending to her needs as another reached out a hand, motioning for Chad to come onboard, too.

"I'm okay," he sputtered. Nodding towards the woman, he proclaimed, "Take care of her."

Then he turned, and swam over to his wave runner, thankful it didn't drift too far and climbed back on, exhausted but grateful he got there in time. The adrenaline rush propelled him to race back to the dock. He glanced back, exhaling his worry and tension, feeling pure relief flooding his body, knowing the woman was alive.

When he returned to the dock, he was greeted by neighbors slapping him on the back and celebrating his fast and heroic action. Chad smiled and mumbled his appreciation when someone handed him a blue beach towel. "Thanks." Wiping his face, he expressed his gratitude. With one last glance at the burning boat, he turned, heading back to his grandmother's house. All Chad desired after that was a hot shower and a good burger. He's just happy she's okay.

Chapter 3

An hour later at County General Hospital

Marissa Lynch lay in the hospital bed hooked up to a saline IV drip wearing a hideous white and pale blue hospital gown and wanting nothing more than to be released. The whole thing was a nightmare. How did a late afternoon 'get away from it all sail' turn into an explosion and an overnight observation hospital stay?

The gray blood pressure monitor made a beeping noise. That's not a good sign. She knows she better calm her thoughts if she wants to be released anytime soon. She overheard the issues the doctor had revealed to her sister about her condition, "Swallowed water, lung infection from smoke inhalation, and blood pressure elevation."

She heard Hailey's concern as she asked, "Will she be okay?"

Holding her breath, she awaited the doctor's response. "Yes, but she needs to rest, and she needs to be watched carefully."

Marissa nervously winced knowing her husband would normally be here and not wanting to be watched. She doesn't want Rick there with her. She didn't even tell the hospital to call him. He's the one she needs to get away from. It was his boat she had been on. It was his boat that exploded after their fight. He warned her, "If you try to leave me, things could happen."

Had he been behind the explosion? She doesn't know but she is afraid of the answer. Right now, she needs to get as far away from him as possible. He's a dangerously unpredictable and powerful man.

In her ten years of marriage, five had been good and five had been filled with mental abuse and control. Marissa was done. Rick would flatter her one day and tell her how much she means to him and the next day he would ghost her, leaving her sitting up all night worrying, wondering if he were dead or alive. It's always all about Rick, he was the star of the show and everyone else merely the extras.

She and her daughter Emily deserve a fresh start. Thank goodness Emily had been with her sister during the boat explosion. Marissa found sailing to be calming and had gone out for a jaunt alone to think, knowing Emily was being entertained by her sister, Hailey. Marissa was an experienced sailor and had never encountered problems before. She had left Emily with Hailey and was looking forward to emotionally detoxing on the water., but things certainly didn't go as planned.

Hailey has always been great with children and became a music teacher. She's like a child whisperer, while Emily loves spending time with her aunt. Hailey's angelic voice and incredible musical talent make her a favorite amongst her students. Marissa is grateful for her twin sister and the bond they share. She's even more thankful her daughter gets to be part of that close bond.

Marissa called Rick from Hailey's house to tell him it was over after she had safely gotten Emily out. Rick had predictably exploded and threatened to destroy her.

"I will find you and you will lose Emily. You both belong to me. I warned you the last time that you pulled this that it wouldn't work. You have nowhere to go where I won't find you."

"I need to go for my sanity. You have already destroyed me!" Marissa had screamed back at him and slammed the phone down.

Although Rick was a top lawyer, Marissa was sure he would try something. But this time she was armed. She had evidence of his ongoing affair with his partner's wife. She wanted him gone and now she had a means to help make it happen.

Chapter 4

"Chad, you have gone viral," Harding, Jillian's husband, announced as he woke him up the day after the rescue. Only Harding, Chad's best friend, could get away with waking him. He was so fond of him, he introduced him to his sister, Jillian and they couldn't be happier. He had been best man at their wedding and was thrilled to have welcomed his best friend into his family. Now Harding stood before him, waking him up. He better have a good reason.

"What?" Chad questioned, looking up at Harding with sleep in his eyes as he tried to focus. "What are you talking about?"

"That rescue," Harding proclaimed, holding up his phone displaying a YouTube clip of his bravery. "You are on Instagram, SnapChat, YouTube and every other social media platform out there. You have 500,000 hits already and a few marriage proposals from some very attractive women." He winks.

"I'm telling Jillian," Chad quips, and grabs the phone from Harding. Harding laughs at his friend.

Chad takes in the YouTube clip of the rescue and reads the comments below, 'Now that's a man', 'Bring that one home to mama', 'He can rescue me anytime' and laughs, shaking his head. One comment catches his eye, 'Isn't he about to run for senator?' Chad groans; the media would be all over this now that he's recognized.

Chad liked to separate his personal life from his professional life. He knew he had an obligation to be public at some point, but this was his week of vacation at the beach house with his family and the last thing he needed was the press here.

"Harding," he groans, "please don't tell me the press found out already?" Chad sat up and pulled a t-shirt on as he climbed out of bed in his shorts. His sandy brown hair sticks out in every direction as his eyes go wide.

"Well," Harding began, dragging out the word, "that's why I am here doing the wakey wakey thing. Jillian told me to break it to you gently that Sean is on his way over to discuss how to navigate this with the press. Dad felt it best if Sean handles it. Sorry, Mr. Hero, it's your time to shine."

Down the road…

Rick stormed into the lobby of the hospital with a presence that had all the nurses looking up. They all know who he is. Some look at him with awe and some with fear. His reputation as a lawyer was ruthless and no nonsense. He puts up with nothing. He represents crime bosses, CEOs and keeps many Wall Street Tycoons from seeing the inside of Club Fed.

He's on TV monthly and sought after by the media. They love to interview him. He flirts just enough with the interviewers to make them feel important and attractive, but he never crosses the line. Many have tried to get to him, but he has held steady.

He has Marissa at home, mother to his most cherished possession, his daughter, and a blonde, chic, gorgeous, sexy mistress of almost a decade. He has been with her for his entire marriage and the duration of the time he has spent as a partner in his law firm. Two women are more than enough for him. One is his Madonna figure and the other remains his plaything and stress reliever.

He has only slipped up twice, and those mistakes cost him handsomely. The young actress wanted to talk, and he had to silence her. She mysteriously disappeared on a hiking trip in Yellowstone, along with her brother. Nobody ever threatened Rick Lynch. It cost him a pretty penny to solve that problem, but he did, and he learned his lesson.

Fortunately, his mistress had much more to lose than he did, so he considered her a stalemate and expected it to stay that way.

Chapter 5

S ean, the public relations executive, a dark-haired polished man in his forties wearing blue suit pants, blue shirt, and red tie, sat pensively in the living room formulating a plan with Chad's dad Thad. Dressed in khakis and a blue golf shirt, Thad nervously tapped his pen on a notepad. Beside him sat his wife Sara wearing a lilac sundress, and Cecilia in her formal dress of a linen skirt, collared white shirt and pearls. Harding sat within earshot listening intently, while Jillian mouths, "I'm sorry," to a petulant Chad.

It seems his vacation was over even before it even started.

"Can't we just give the press a quote and move on?" Chad asked, towel-drying his hair still wet from the shower.

"No," answered Sean, pushing his brown hair out of his eyes with a sweep of his hand and giving Chad a stern look. "You did a good thing, and we need to showcase it."

"Chad," his dad begins, looking him square in the eyes, making sure he's paying attention. "Any press is good press. You need signatures on those petitions, and you need to have your name known. This is the perfect launch for you. Proud of you, son. You've got this."

Chad knew they were right, but he hated the attention, he just likes to do what's right. At that moment, it was right to save the woman. His thoughts drift back to her, hoping that she is okay. He still pictures her frantic turquoise eyes under the water, signaling him with panicked motions that she was stuck in the rope. That moment would forever be emblazoned in his mind.

He couldn't let someone just die. He knew in his heart he would have done anything, including putting his own life in jeopardy, in order to save hers. It was just who he was. Why did everyone have to make it such a big deal? A quote to the press would have been fine, and then he could have taken his niece and nephew out on the boat and enjoyed his time. This was supposed to be a family vacation.

Instead, he hears, "Let's set up a press conference at the hospital, see if we can get the rescued woman to interview. And we need to get her doctor on camera, too if the woman will allow her to tell us and the public anything. I have her name right here, are you ready for this?" inquired Sean, arching his eyebrows. "The woman is Marissa Lynch."

———————————————

Meanwhile...

Rick doesn't listen when the nurses inform him Marissa is sleeping following an emergency procedure to remove some debris that was irritating her left eye. It had felt increasingly painful and the swelling around it had been getting worse. Doctors moved her into the OR and extracted some ash and debris. Thankfully, her eye would be okay, but she would have to wear a bandage and eventually a patch for a few weeks. Other than that, Marissa had minimal scarring and her lung infection appeared to be responding well to antibiotics.

She was still sleeping off the anesthesia when Rick burst into the room urging her awake with a loud, "Marissa, Marissa, wake up."

"Sir," a pretty red headed young nurse interrupted Rick, "she needs to sleep. Please keep your voice down." She didn't give two hoots who Rick was, she cared about her patient's health and found Marissa to be kind.

Rick turned away from Marissa while clenching his jaw, as he crossed his arms over his chest and glared, sizing up the young nurse. "Wake her," he asserted in his stern, no nonsense voice.

"I can't do that," she insisted, and straightened, rising to her full five-foot two height. "Please, leave." Her face turned red with determination as she stared Rick down with her piercing brown eyes.

Rick turned away from her when he heard Marissa stir, both him and the nurse looking over. "Get him out of here," she stammered sleepily and promptly threw up.

Rick scrunched his nose and curled his lip, looking at her in disgust. Turning to the nurse, he demanded, "Clean her up, I will be back." Without another word, he spun on his heel and stormed out of the room.

Chapter 6

Chad stood at the podium outside River Hospital in Northampton, New York, just wanting to get this all over with. Sean had arranged a press conference with Marissa's doctor to update everyone on her condition, and Marissa was supposed to be wheeled out to meet her hero.

He was a bit taken aback when he heard the name. Everyone knew who Marissa and Rick Lynch were. They were New York elite. He was known to be a ruthless, heartless lawyer, and she was his silent sidekick, famous for her charity work.

It could not have been easy being married to a man like Rick. Chad's cousin Scott was one of the associates in his firm. Chad often questioned Scott's choice to be there, but he had known Rick from their college days and swore there was actually a heart in his body. No one else would believe it.

In addition to being ruthless, Rick was cunning and charming wrapped in a good-looking package. One could sense power and danger in him, and no one would dare to get too close. Marissa was stunningly beautiful with her gorgeous silky hair and her put together style. She was always the quiet one on his arm, or she was holding the hand of their pretty auburn-haired daughter, Emily.

Chad scanned the crowd noticing the press had arrived. The media networks had sent their heavy hitters to be here for this. Rick Lynch's name attached to the story would be top selling news. This was the media's lucky day, Chad, and Marissa Lynch in the same press conference. They couldn't do better than this.

"Ready, Chad?" Sean questioned expectantly.

"Let's get this over with," Chad mumbled, covering the mic so he couldn't be heard. He smiled at the press and nodded for Sean to begin.

Sean stepped up to the mic, and even though he was well known in the political and press arenas, he introduced himself. "Sean Castleton, Island Media C.A.S.T.L.E.T.O.N. Welcome and thank you for coming down today."

"Marissa Lynch, wife of Rick Lynch, Trial Attorney is fortunate to be here today. She was extremely brave in escaping the explosion on her family's Schooner, and was lucky to be rescued by Chad Harper, Esquire. Chad will now make his statement." Sean moved aside at the mic and brought Chad up to the podium.

Chad hated this with a passion, but he had been trained from a young age how to do it right. He looked 'GQ' model handsome in his light-colored sports jacket, khakis, and light blue shirt. Taking a deep breath, he began, "Ladies and gentlemen, I thank you for being here."

Shouts of, "Hero! Hero!" came from the crowd.

Chad smiled and continued. "I have to ask you all two questions: How many of you would let another person die? How many of you would help another in need?"

Murmurs went through the crowd.

"Exactly," Chad agreed, nodding. "All of us would do the right thing for our neighbors and community. I happened to be at the right place at the right time, and I'm just happy to see that Mrs. Lynch will be okay. And I thank my brother-in-law for filling the tank of my wave runner after he used it, so I was able to get there quickly."

The crowd laughed as Harding, who stood off to the side of the podium, took a bow.

"Now, that being said," Chad began after the laughter died down, "I think we should hear from Mrs. Lynch's doctor, the real hero in this story. Thank you." Chad nodded and exited to a round of applause from the press.

Done, finished, now off to the boat in a few. I just want to get out of here, into a pair of shorts and out onto the water going wherever the wind and sea take me.

After the doctor finished his update, Sean stepped back up to the mic, announcing, "Mrs. Lynch will be coming out shortly. We are going to dim the lights a bit due to the injury she suffered to her eye. We ask that you please don't use any flash photography or bright lights while she is speaking."

Murmurs from the press soon followed and Doctor Stein nodded his approval of the request. Chad stood off to the side, drinking a bottle of water. Bring her out already, so I can get out of here.

Suddenly, a hush overtakes the crowd and all eyes veer towards Marissa as she's wheeled in by the red headed nurse. She looked stunning and manicured, her chestnut shoulder length hair highlighted and lowlighted. She's wearing perfectly done makeup, despite wearing an eye patch over her left eye which matched her turquoise silk robe. Marissa was breathtaking in person, and Chad, like every other man in the room, couldn't take his eyes off her. She looked frail and vulnerable, as though she needed a knight in shining armor to protect her. Marissa had the attention of everyone in the room.

Sean lowered the microphone and Marissa looked at him and murmured her appreciation, "Thank you."

Turning towards the crowd, she gulped, attempting to swallow her nerves. "Hello," she mumbled, speaking quietly into the mic. "I am a little hoarse from the smoke, so I am going to talk quietly. I would like to thank the nurses and Dr. Stein for their amazing treatment of me, they have been incredible. I would also like to thank Chad Harper for being in the right place at the right time."

The press laughed, all of them knowing the quote would be one heard often, and forever connected to Chad.

"Chad, please come over here," she urged, waving him over, her smile holding his gaze. She was mesmerizing.

Chad grinned and struck by the pull Marissa seemed to have on him, he momentarily forgets about his hate of public meetings, his hate of getting the attention, and walked right over to beautiful Marissa. He knew she was Rick Lynch's wife and therefore, unavailable. But for that moment, he wanted what every man in the room desired, attention from Marissa.

"Chad, please sit down next to me," Marissa requests, motioning to the chair to her right.

Chad smiled again and nodded, taking the seat. Marissa turned to him, looking at him with her good eye. She smiled   at him, licked her lips and whispered, "Chad," in a seductive voice that caught him off guard. She took his face in her hands, as the press wildly began taking pictures, and promptly kissed him on the lips with quite a bit more than a peck, taking him by surprise.

"Now that," declares Marissa, "is what a hero deserves."

A shocked Chad sits facing her, wide-eyed and speechless for once. He has no idea what just hit him.

Rick Lynch tightly clenched his fists, watching from a discrete distance. Furiously, he reached for his phone and started making a few phone calls. He needed his people to quiet this down and minimize the damage that Marissa had just done to their reputation in seconds.

Chapter 7

The media attention finally died down following the hospital press conference. Marissa's doctor quickly wheeled her away after that spectacle and blamed it on the effects of the painkillers and anesthesia. People began wondering if Marissa Lynch had a substance abuse issue. These high-profile families were known to have their secrets. Maybe Marissa has been hiding this?

Rick Lynch put out his own statement asking for privacy while his wife recovered from this tragic accident. Marissa was nowhere to be seen for the past two weeks by the media, and little Emily was driven by a nanny to an upstate sleep away camp to give Marissa the chance to recover.

Chad sat at the desk of his Manhattan law firm, grateful for the peace and quiet that came at last. The media had been hounding him for weeks and he was exhausted. He was even followed into the men's room by a female reporter desperate for a quote and apparently a date. Chad rejected her advances on both accounts and did his best to offer a smile and a quick, "No comment," whenever he was approached.

He didn't want to make the media his enemy, but he didn't want to fuel the obvious Lynch scandal fire either. He hoped his life could return to some sort of normalcy. Well, as normal as it could be with the campaigning he was expected to do now that he was the official candidate for senator.

He wasn't thrilled about the campaigning part; it was way too much attention on him. But he knew if elected, he would step up to the plate and do the job well. His heart just wasn't in it, but what choice did he have?

Chad looked out his office window taking in the Manhattan view. The skyline is spectacular with the Chrysler Building, and the majestic Empire State Building, while Lady Liberty carrying her torch could be seen in the foggy distance. Chad marveled every day at the enormity of seeing the Freedom Tower designed in remembrance to those lost on 9/11. He took it all in, never taking it for granted. New York is an amazing city, a city that he adores. He's proud to work here, and hopefully represent its people.

He turns his black rolling chair from the window, flips on his laptop, and looks up the file on a case he's working on pro bono. The city of New York vs. Hatting Construction Corp. He finds it an interesting case. A local theater group had basically taken over an abandoned downtown warehouse that used to belong to a shoe manufacturer and turned it into a makeshift art gallery/theater spot. The city had granted them temporary use of the facility pending sale of the property. Hatting Construction bought the property all around the warehouse, but not the half acre of property the warehouse sat on. The city refused to give it up.

The theater crew had a big connection to the Planning Department and somehow managed to get him to write up the sale, minus the theater property. Hatting Construction felt conned and they were filing a suit. Chad represented the City of New York in this case.

He had an appointment with the head of the theater company, Hailey Everson and she was due to arrive in ten minutes. He found out she ran the company pro bono as well, so he was very interested in meeting someone who would give their time gratis. She might be an asset to him in some capacity when he campaigned. It was always good to have like-minded people help you out when running for office.

The last decade of Chad's life had been spent working on his dad's campaigns. He knew what it took to run for office and if he had to do it, he might as well assemble a good team. Harding and Jillian had agreed to be his campaign managers, and Sean signed on as his public relations manager. He now needed to assemble a good working crew. He was looking forward to meeting this Hailey Everson and seeing what she was all about, hoping she might be a good fit.

His intercom buzzed, grabbing his attention. "Chad," his secretary, Maria states, pressing the button on the silver intercom as she gave Hailey who stood before her a shy smile.

"Yes?" he prompts.

"Hailey Everson is here."

"Send her in. Thanks."

Within a minute Chad looked up to see chestnut-haired Hailey standing in his doorway, wearing a green sweater matching her bright green beautiful eyes. She has delicate features and to him, looked like a model. He had an instant reaction to her, his heart beat so fast, as he sensed her confidence and took in her beauty. She was stunning and she seemed somehow familiar. Where had he seen her before?

He cleared his throat and pulled himself out of his momentary stupor. "Come in," he murmurs, and motions for her to take a seat in the leather chair across from him. "It's nice to meet you, Hailey."

She glanced at Chad from across the room and smiled. Her smile was beautiful, reaching her eyes, taking his breath away. "Nice to meet you, too, Chad,"

Hailey commented, looking at him as she lowered herself into the seat as directed. He was a very attractive man, and she felt herself instantly drawn to Chad.

"First, I have to thank you for rescuing my sister. You saved her life."

Chad took a minute to process the fact that Hailey was Marissa's sister. His
eyes widened at the realization as he pushed back his sandy hair with a brush
of his hand, slightly taken aback. He had found Marissa to be a bold, glitzy
beautiful woman, while Hailey seemed to be a more subtle, natural beauty. Yet,
he realized they had the same perfect face, only Hailey's eyes were green and
Marissa's blue.

"Twins," Hailey declared in answer to the question in his eyes. "She is older
by two minutes."

Chad almost hesitated in asking the next question because he was so tired of
the Lynch scandal, but he knew he needed to for the sake of manners. "How is
your sister doing?"

Hailey grimaced and sighed heavily. "Rick sent her off to a spa. I get a text
a day, but that's about it." Forlorn, she looked as though she wanted to tell him
more, but hesitated.

Chad took in the worried look appearing on her beautiful face wanting to get
rid of it for her.

"Thank you," she murmured, in a soft voice. "Thank you again for saving
her."

Chad cleared his throat. He's incredibly attracted to Hailey and if he didn't
change the subject quickly, he might do something uncharacteristic of him and
hop over the desk to comfort her. At that moment she looked so vulnerable and
sad. He knew there was so much more to the Marissa and Rick story, and to be
honest he didn't want to know. The media circus had been enough for him.

He better get down to business with Hailey, or else her pull on him could
quickly become dangerous. Anyone associated with Rick Lynch spelled trouble.

Chapter 8

Rick stands over the sleeping Marissa in their dark bedroom. The shades had been drawn for two weeks, and Marissa had been knocked out for just as long. Every time she stirred, Rick would knock her out with another dose of painkillers. He forced her to eat protein shakes when she was conscious enough, and could handle drinking it down, and had the night aide he hired clean her up. He paid her enormously well. She didn't ask questions and claimed to buy the explanation that Marissa was resting and healing from her accident. For the sum of money she was paid, she didn't ask any questions.

He wanted Marissa punished for hurting him. He didn't want to kill her, but he wanted to control her. Her absence had been easily explained by a press release claiming that the family needed their privacy. Her friends and her sister were told she was resting comfortably at a spa. People believed Rick Lynch. People hung onto his every word.

Rick took one last disgusted look at Marissa, picked up her cell phone, and typed a text to her sister. "The spa is wonderful, feeling better every day." Without a feeling of hesitation or guilt, he pressed send.

Down the road….

"So, the plan is to somehow convince Hatting Construction that there is a community need to save the theater," Chad began, looking across at Hailey from the other side of the table.

They had moved into the conference room at this point and were discussing the case in detail. To be perfectly honest, Chad found it hard to concentrate. He loosened his tie a bit and positioned himself as far away from Hailey as politely possible. He was close enough he could still smell her vanilla scent from where he was sitting and her green, expressive eyes drew him in without even trying.

Chad felt like a middle school boy with a crush on a girl in his math class. Normally, he was not awkward around women at all. He's had his share of relationships and ended a two-year one six months previously. But Hailey had quite the effect on him, and he had to constantly remind himself to focus.

"Do you think it's possible to save the theater?" Hailey inquired sincerely, her eyes so full of hope. "The kids come every day after school for play practice and chorus rehearsal. They need this, Chad. Many come from homes where there isn't much of an opportunity for the arts." She looked into Chad's blue eyes and saw compassion and kindness reflecting back at her. Her chest tightens, feeling very attracted to him making her grateful he moved far away to the other end of the table. Although, she could still smell his delicious aftershave and attempted not to react.

Focus, Hailey, focus. She did not come here for a date; she came to save the theater.

She could definitely understand why her sister, numb with painkillers, impulsively kissed him. Hailey felt her phone vibrate in her pocketbook. Reaching into her bag, she took it out, and glanced at the screen, seeing a text from Marissa. "Excuse me, are you okay if I just take a moment? It's a text from Marissa," she advised holding her phone up as proof.

"Of course," agreed Chad, smiling at her.

"She is enjoying the spa apparently," she muttered, failing to hide her grimace.

Chad noticed her voice was flat and her face fell, looking sad once again. But she quickly straightened, cleared her throat, and pulled herself together, going back to talking about the kids and the theater after responding to the text messages. Taking a deep breath, Chad attempted to do the same, doing his best to focus on the case and not on Hailey.

Chapter 9

Hailey left Chad's office with another appointment set to meet up with him next week, same time, same place. They had awkwardly made some headway on the case in between staring into each other's eyes. Hailey was embarrassed by her behavior. She bordered on flirty at times, which was totally not her style. He's so attractive making it hard to focus. She had recently broken off her relationship with Steven after it had run its course, which might explain the wow factor Chad seemed to have on her.

Her heart beat faster at just the thought of him. He was so compassionate, so caring, so gorgeous. Hailey's mind drifted back to their conversation a few minutes prior, and that look in his eyes when he spoke. He was all fire and passion. He wanted to save the theater as much as she did, and for that she was grateful.

She and Steven were trying to remain friends. They were both music teachers in the same school district, making it awkward at times. They were bound to run into each other at school events. Steven had been the one to say it was over, but they had both known it for the past year. Hailey didn't want to get engaged and Steven, at thirty-one years old, wanted to settle down.

He came home one night, kissed her on the forehead, and packed his things he kept at her apartment and left.

"Hailey, I love you, but this isn't working for me anymore," he began, looking at her intently, his eyes welling up and his jaw locked tightly. "I want marriage, kids. We don't want the same things right now. We have grown apart."

"I am sorry, Steven," she replied, staring at him, caught off guard by him. "Time apart might be good." She didn't say anything after that. He looked at her with a long sad gaze and went into their bedroom. She heard the loud zip of the suitcase being closed and knew then that it was over.

Hailey felt only a tiny bit of remorse about it ending, but knew it was the right decision. She was twenty-eight years old, and knew he wasn't the one. They had been arguing too much lately and even their time together just wasn't fun anymore.

Steven was her past and she needed to focus on her future. After the meeting with Chad, Hailey walked the seven blocks home since she loved walking in Manhattan. She truly enjoyed the energy and the hustle and bustle of the people on the street. She loved the smells from the colorful food trucks and vendors lining the streets of Central Park. There were hot dogs being sold, hot pretzels, gyros, funnel cakes, roasted nuts. The delicious aroma of the food trucks met her nose as she walked by. She stopped for a cup of lemonade and drank it right down enjoying the sweet taste and the refreshing coolness of it on this beautiful day. Hailey felt truly invigorated by her meeting with Chad and was lighthearted. She sat for a moment on a wooden bench in Central Park taking it all in. Children were playing tag nearby and laughing, an elderly couple walked by, the man dressed in a proper gray suit and black tie and the woman dressed in a floral sundress. Hailey couldn't help smiling at them.

"We're on a date, married sixty years," the gentleman exclaimed as they walked past Hailey arm in arm.

"Congratulations!" Hailey responded smiling after them. "That is wonderful!"

The man turned back smiling at Hailey and the woman waved, giving her husband's arm an affectionate squeeze. Hailey admired them and hoped she would someday find a love like that, someone to enjoy life with and grow old with. Steven was definitely not the one, and she was ready to open her heart to new love. Her thoughts went immediately to Chad, and she smiled. She left the bench and headed in the direction towards her apartment.

After leaving Central Park, she stopped at a street market and picked up some fresh flowers to put in a vase in her apartment. There was a mix of bright red zinnias, yellow sunflowers, and blue carnations. She smiled her thanks at the elderly woman wearing a purple wrap around apron when she handed her the money, and the woman commented, "You have a smile that lights up a room."

"Thank you so much," Hailey replied blushing. She took a moment to smell the flowers and walked the last three blocks home until she arrived at her modern brick apartment building.

She let herself into her Columbus Avenue apartment, her Shih Tzu, Cleo instantly greeting her. Cleo jumped excitedly at the sight of Hailey, her little paws clicking on the light wood kitchen floors, her tail wagging. Hailey opened the white wood cabinet and took out a treat for Cleo. Cleo's tail went wild.

"Hi, girl." Hailey smiled down on her, lifting her up. Hailey hands her the treat which Cleo takes excitedly from her hand and drops it on the floor to save for later.

Cleo kissed her on the chin, making Hailey laugh. She had a dog walker who had just been there an hour before, so Hailey knew Cleo could wait to go out. Hailey promised her a walk later. "We'll find your favorite fire hydrant and see your doggy friends in a few," she remarked. Kissing Cleo on the top of her head, Hailey put her down in her pink dog bed. Cleo grabbed her bone and gnawed on it while wagging her tail and looking at Hailey.

Hailey picked up her black tote bag and set it on her dark blue microfiber couch. She found a crystal vase in her wooden kitchen cabinet and filled it with fresh water from the tap. Placing the flowers in the vase made her happy. They definitely brightened her place with their vibrant red, yellow and blue colors, their sweet fragrance reaching her nose.

She stepped into her living room and picked up one of the light blue pillows Cleo knocked over in her puppy excitement. Hailey turned on her Maovesa Floor Lamp she found at a secondhand shop. It did the job well and shined on her Steinway piano she had received as a gift from her parents when she moved into the apartment. She enjoyed playing on it at night to relax. Hailey loved to play classics like Cannon, and Bach. She would hit the keys tonight before bed. She had a new piece to learn for her choir.

Hailey tiredly plunked down on the couch and looked through her mail, seeing lots of junk. She was always hoping for something from Marissa, a card, a note, anything. All she got was the once-a-day text and no response to any of her messages. Marissa was like that sometimes when she traveled, but she was supposed to be recovering now and it just seemed odd. Her calls to Marissa went right to voicemail too, which wasn't unusual when she traveled, but not at a time like this. Not being able to talk to her sister was just making her uneasy.

Hailey's calls to Rick hadn't been returned either, not unusual but that didn't make it any easier. Rick did send her texts with pictures of Emily at camp. At least Emily looks like she's having a blast. Emily was seen smiling into the camera while holding a red archery bow and shooting her suction-cup arrow at the target. In another picture Emily was sitting in a pink tube and laughing with friends in a pool. It made Hailey so happy to see them.

She remembered when she and Marissa were young and used to spend hours and hours in their four-foot above ground pool splashing and swimming with friends. Those were some happy memories. Hailey thought that childhood should definitely be filled with happy memorable moments.

She breathed a sigh of relief knowing Emily was looking so happy, although she missed her and questioned why they had sent her away to camp and not have her stay with her aunt. But that was Rick's choice, he was very controlling. From her perspective, Marissa and Rick's marriage has always been a volatile one. Marissa swore that Rick never laid a hand on her, but in their conversations, there was always an undertone of how controlling he was. Hailey never really liked Rick. He always seemed narcissistic to her. But her sister would leave him and then go back, always saying she was staying for Emily.

Hailey hoped the boat explosion, found by the fire inspectors to be the result of faulty wiring, would knock some sense into Marissa, and she would finally leave him permanently. But she had gone back, and it looked like she already resumed her lifestyle, including spas and travel. Marissa was very unlike Hailey in that way, who preferred her music and her peace.

Hailey went to her top of the refrigerator/ freezer, pulled out a Ravioli Lean Cuisine, and quickly warmed it up in the microwave. Then, she made her way into the living room and settled on her beige plush couch to grade some music papers.

Grabbing the remote off the coffee table, she turned on her TV to find something to watch that she found relaxing and settled on some old Seinfeld episodes. They always gave her a good laugh, and right now a laugh was what she needed. Although, as she worked, her thoughts kept going back to her sis-ter....and admittedly, to Chad.

"Listen," prodded Harding, looking at Chad with a smirk, "you have that googly-eyed look on your face whenever I mention her name."

Chad picked up a Honey BBQ chicken wing and gave Harding a look. He met him blue eyes to brown arching his eyebrows. They were sitting in a sports bar on the Upper West side called Nina's, right across from the campaign office that was scheduled to open next week. It was time to launch the campaign.

Honestly, Chad was getting a little more excited about the whole thing, surprising even himself. He had watched with admiration as his father stepped into the role with ease. Chad would accompany him every time that he ran on the campaign trail. He walked districts with his dad, went with him to political dinners, civic events like parades and fundraisers, and he saw exactly what the life of a candidate was like. Chad was starting to see himself stepping into his dad's shoes, and they were tough shoes to fill. Chad wondered if he was up for the task.

Harding definitely pictured Chad stepping up into his father's former job. Harding admired Chad's work ethic, his family loyalty, and his do-good nature. Chad was always doing pro-bono work, or helping a charity, and would do anything for a friend. Harding saw in Chad the true potential to be an amazing leader, but he did have to remember to make careful choices. His life was defi-nitely going to be a fishbowl.

"Yeah, well...she is connected to that family. So, it's a no go." Chad pushed his hair back and looked at Harding with a sense of frustration. He wished things could be different and that he didn't have to worry about who he would be seen with or associated with knowing the smallest interactions could result in rumors flying and something with a Lynch name could turn into gossip of epic proportions.

Harding assessed him for a moment and conceded, "While I agree campaign wise; I think you need one date with her to get it out of your system. You have been in a dry spell, and it would be good to get those juices flowing again." He raised his eyebrows Groucho Marx style as they went up and down in a comical way.

Chad looked at him and mumbled, "We'll see." He's still hesitant about mixing business with pleasure, besides the fact that anyone connected to the Lynch family could be dangerous.

He redirected Harding, urging him to talk about setting up the campaign office as he pushed his thoughts about gorgeous Hailey to the back burner...for now.

Chapter 10

Rick met his mistress on Tuesdays and Thursdays on a regular basis. He always reserved a suite at the Luxurious Four Stanford hotel, but now he considered adding more days to the mix. Marissa was knocked out; Emily was at camp. He was free in the evenings, but was she? Could she get away? He would just have to keep his law partner slightly busier so he could meet up with his wife. Seems fair, right?

This affair had been going on for a decade, and her husband Trevor was none the wiser. Lana told him she was going to her sessions with her personal trainer, but little did he know that Rick was the man giving his wife a workout.

Rick Lynch got what he wanted. Up until now, he liked beautiful Marissa on his arm and Lana in his bed. But Lana was gorgeous, and the chemistry between them was polarizing. They literally couldn't stay away from each other. Maybe it was time to get rid of Marissa and make Lana his. Now, what to do about Trevor.

Fourteen years earlier:

The dorm room walls were paper thin, and Rick's energy level was out of control after he did a line of cocaine. It was midnight and he was bench pressing and dropping weights in his room. He was blasting heavy metal and the walls literally vibrated from the noise.

"That idiot is going to be up all night again!" blonde haired Lana groaned, turning to her roommate Elisa, her brown hair pulled back in a ponytail. Wearing her pink robe, while sitting cross legged on her bed Elisa typed her English paper on Chaucer. It was due at 8 a.m. She looked up from her laptop and, annoyed, exclaimed, "Someone needs to go shut up Mr. Arrogant."

"I need to get some sleep," Lana complained, pulling her white robe over her long t-shirt that she slept in and sliding her feet into her fuzzy slippers. Lana was a journalism/public relations major and she was due to start her internship at News7 tomorrow. She needed her sleep. She couldn't stand Rick, despite his hotness, he was an arrogant self-centered ass. He needed to think of others in the dorm once in a while. "Be right back," she muttered as she left the room.

"Thanks," Elisa replied and went back to typing. Elisa knew that Lana would take care of it. Lana was a tough cookie and when she was pissed, watch out.

Lana stood outside Rick's dorm room door. She noticed that his whiteboard was covered in messages.

Rick call me ♥ Jen

Rick meet me at the gym at 7

Rick you are a hottie

Lana groaned, who the hell would want to hang out with this guy? Lana's only exchanges with him had been at dorm meetings and he always seemed super cocky. Lana had no time for that at all.

She knocked on his wooden door. No answer, she knocked again and again. She was pissed now and exhausted. "Open up, Rick," she demanded, pounding harder.

After a few more minutes the door opened up and a sweat glistened muscular Rick stood at his door wiping his sweat from his brow with a blue workout towel. Lana felt a reaction which she did not want to feel at the sight of him. He was hot.

Rick smirked when he saw who it was and noticed her reaction.

"Hey pretty lady from next door, come for a little booty call?" Rick leaned against the door and got real close to Lana.

Lana forgot for a moment why she was there, did he just call her pretty? "Um…" She cleared her throat. "It's midnight. Can you turn the music down? We have early classes. You need to stop doing this so late."

Rick stood there grinning. "I will do it only if you come in."

Lana looked at him, crossing her hands over her chest. "Not tonight, Romeo. I need sleep, not problems. Turn it off."

Rick laughed as he watched her storm back to her room and slam the door. He knew he had an effect on her and he loved it. Lana was a former Junior Miss pageant winner and gorgeous, but she wouldn't give him the time of day. He enjoyed irking her and knew the music and the workouts pissed her off. Usually, she and her roommate banged on the walls between them to make him stop, tonight Lana had actually come to his room. He was making progress.

He had an itch to scratch with hot Lana, and he found a way to get to her. The next night and the next Rick played the music and waited for Lana to come back again. A week later she showed up at his door pissed and a little tipsy from a sorority mixer.

"Turn down the freaking music," she demanded, slightly slurring to a grinning Rick glistening from his workout. "Hate you."

Rick took in the situation, Lana's sexy little skirt and halter top along with her inebriated state. "You do, huh?" He looked down on her grinning.

"Yeah, I do. You are arrogant, cocky, self-centered…and oh man…super hot."

Rick took full advantage of the situation and took full advantage of a very willing Lana for months to come. They were like magnets to each other, and the passion was unreal, but they were like oil and water personality wise, always fighting. Lana found him super controlling and upon graduation, ended it without regret. She put Rick out of her mind, or so she thought when she committed fully to Trevor.

She didn't see him again for five years but thought about their sizzling nights often and wished that she didn't. Lana's insides did a flip when memories of their young passion came flooding back to her whenever his name was mentioned, but she didn't let on to Trevor. Trevor knew of her college affair with a person named Rick. But she had never mentioned his last name being Lynch.

Ten years earlier

Brown haired, confident looking Trevor walks into the apartment on a crisp and clear September day eager to share the news with his wife of four years. He had been working for a firm that was essentially burning him out and he desperately needed a change. The field of law was draining on him, and he was exhausted from putting in sixty-hour weeks with very little sense of accomplishment or recognition. They were piling work on him like crazy as the young, novice lawyer.

Trevor had sent out resume after resume and was starting to get interviews. He felt like he was getting close, and finally it happened. "I got a new job! It's a great opportunity at an awesome firm," Trevor announced to Lana as he entered their Brooklyn Brownstone smiling.

"Which one?" Lana inquired, smiling up at him with her blue eyes bright. She can see his excitement and it's contagious. He had gone on many interviews over the past two weeks.

"It's an uptown firm that is on the rise. Lynch, Allen and Coste." He takes off his blue shirt and tie and says, "Let me change and then let's go out to dinner and celebrate."

"I am so proud of you," Lana praises, rushing over to him and giving him a sweet kiss. It wasn't until later that night that it dawned on Lana that the Lynch in Lynch, Allen and Coste was Rick Lynch. She googled it to be sure, and when she saw his picture on the law firm's website, her heart skipped a beat. He looked like sexy Rick, with a more mature face. He was even more handsome now than in college.

She decided against saying anything to Trevor. In her eyes, the past was the past. But the mention of his name and seeing his picture on the website looking as handsome as ever definitely made her heart flutter and memories of dorm room hookups came flooding back. This was dangerous, and too close to home, but Trevor was happy, and at the moment, that is what mattered.

Chapter 11

Present Day…One week later

Hailey's white umbrella didn't keep her dry as the horizontal windblown rain pelted her. She was wearing beige linen pants, gold sandals, and a pink sweater. She felt like a wet rat with all her clothes completely soaked through as she arrived at Chad's office. In this condition she was sure she would repel Chad.

She hadn't stopped thinking about him all week. Admittedly, she had been counting the days until this meeting. With a few minutes to spare before the meeting, she stopped in the ladies' room to try and pull herself together. Luckily, she found an air dryer inside, and she had a brush in her tote bag.

She sat in the bathroom blow-drying her long chestnut hair until it looked presentable. Then, she reapplied her makeup, knowing it was better than nothing. The rest, well, it was what it was. Hailey didn't see herself the way others did. She was the type who could wear anything and look gorgeous. She saw herself as attractive, she acknowledged that, but felt like a disheveled hot mess most of the time.

Hailey believed Marissa could easily keep it together and look stunning all the time. But Hailey honestly felt the most comfortable in jeans and a t-shirt, with her hair pulled up in a ponytail. That had become her uniform of choice when working at the theater with the kids. The amazing kids had become her reason and her motivation for being here.

She started the choir last year and advertised at her school and the local community center. Hailey had arranged for bussing after school, and the children were brought there twice a week to sing their hearts out. She and the children truly looked forward to their practices. Her heart was completely shattered at the idea of losing their venue.

She gathered her things in her beige tote and headed towards Chad's office. Her heart fluttered in her chest as she got closer to his office.

Maria, dressed in a turquoise blouse looked up as Hailey approached and smiled. "Nice to see you again. I will let Chad know that you are here."

Hailey smiled, thanked her, and sat down on the blue waiting room chair. Hailey noticed the assortment of magazines on the waiting room table. She picked up a Newsweek and leafed through it. As her eyes skimmed the pages, she stumbled across an article on theaters in Manhattan that interested her, and she quickly became absorbed in it. Within a few minutes Chad came out. He looked incredibly handsome in his navy suit, red patterned tie, and light blue shirt. Hailey looked up from the magazine and smiled at him. She placed it back on the coffee table and stood up to her full five-feet, ten-inch height.

"Hailey, good to see you again!" he commented, smiling at the confident woman in front of him. "Let's go into the conference room and would you like some coffee?"

"I would love a cup, thank you," she replies, instantly feeling her heart skip a beat at the sight of Chad. He wears his suit well, she notices.

Maria momentarily takes her attention away from ogling Chad. She smiles at Hailey, a knowing look in her eyes. Chad was attractive. Maria was married with three kids, but she appreciated his good looks as well as his kindness. "Milk and sugar?" she asked.

"Yes, thank you," Hailey remarks blushing slightly at being caught.

She followed Chad into the room and sat down in the black leather seat next to him. She's instantly aware they were closer than they were last time. Now she could really see his sparkling blue eyes. He was so good-looking. It was not going to be easy to keep her mind on business.

"Did you make any headway?" she asked him, picking up from where they left off.

"As a matter of fact, I did," Chad claimed, smiling. She's stunning, he thought, absolutely gorgeous. Her beautiful chestnut highlights glistened in the light, her skin was porcelain, and her green eyes were so expressive. He was having trouble focusing on business and fought the urge to grab her hand across the polished wooden conference room table.

"I have met with the project manager from the construction company, and he has agreed to sit down with me along with his team and review their plans."

"Oh, that is great." Hailey's eyes went wide showing her enthusiasm. "That's definitely a huge step. Thank you."

Chad nods in agreement, smiling at her. "But I think we still need to show a need to keep this theater in the community."

"I agree," Hailey declares, nodding. "The kids and I were talking about putting on a fundraising concert to bring a community greenhouse and garden to our center. The kids would tend to it and then they would donate the food to the local soup kitchen."

Chad looks at Hailey thoughtfully, feeling a tug on his heart as he hears the suggestion. She seems like the absolute antithesis of Marissa and her glamor and glitz reputation, although they both share stunning looks, Hailey shows she's beautiful inside and out without even trying. She's so genuine. "That's amazing," he states, smiling at her.

Oh boy! Hailey thinks to herself, lost in thought. I don't know if I can handle just being all business with this man.

Chad's mind wanders back to what Harding said. He needed one date with Hailey to get her out of his system. Chad is not sure how it will go, but he needs to take a shot, he's unable to focus on the work in front of him with her seated so close. "Hailey, what are you doing for dinner tonight?" he asks. Hailey gives him a shy smile and she blushes when she says, "I'm free."

Chapter 12

Marissa stirred restlessly in the bed. She could feel the drugs wearing off and she could finally think. It felt like her first day of clarity in a long time, not realizing it had been over two weeks.

Looking around her room, she saw the clock on her wall that said 9AM. She was wearing a nightgown she wouldn't have typically worn on a hot day; did she pick this out? She desperately wanted a shower. She felt sweaty and her hair was matted. She had no sense of time, no knowledge of anything, other than she was still wearing her eye patch, and she was in her room.

Where was Emily? She longed for her daughter. "Emily," she cries out. "Emily." Usually, Emily would come running in carrying her teddy bear or wheeling in her American Girl doll in her pink stroller. Today she did not come in.

Marissa sat up and looked around the room startled. Everything seemed the same, but somehow different. The sun was streaming through the bay window, the time on the digital clock also said 9:00 a.m., and she could see the steam coming out of the adjoining bathroom. She had no knowledge of what day of the week it was, or for that matter even what month it was. Her memory was a disturbing blur.

Rick opened the door and walked into the room drying his hair, fresh from the shower, with a blue towel wrapped around his waist and his black hair slicked back, glowering at her state of consciousness. He thought his plan through, but too many people were questioning where Marissa was and inquiring about her health. She needed to be seen again for a time, and then he would put his plan into place. He had tapered off the sleeping pills and now she was fully awake and aware. Perfect, all part of his carefully laid out plan.

"Well, hello," he addressed Marissa. "The spa did you good. I'm so glad you are awake." He forced a smile, announcing, "Tomorrow is visiting day at camp, so we need to get you out of bed and go see our beautiful Emily."

Marissa looked at him with glazed and confused eyes. "The spa?" she inquires.

"Yes, dear," Rick remarked with sincerity, giving Marissa one of his sweet smiles. "I can't believe that you spent two weeks recovering. Now you are here, and we get to see Emily."

Marissa looked at him still with narrowed eyes, as confusion settled in. She felt very vulnerable and incredibly frustrated with herself for not remembering anything and yet, as she had done in the past after similar episodes, she believed him. Two weeks?

"Your sister left messages since she was unable to reach you at the spa. Why don't you give her a call and tell her what a lovely time you had and make plans to see her for lunch in the garden this week," he suggested. Then, he handed Marissa her cell phone and left the room. He didn't look back, and Marissa looked after him, still very confused.

Chapter 13

Chad picked up his iPhone when he noticed Harding's number pop up. "Hey, Harding. What's up?" Chad inquired, putting down the file that he was working on. Harding was always a fun, welcome distraction.

"Checking in to see if you resisted the charm of the pretty temptress," Harding retorted, chuckling. "I bet you couldn't resist that one."

"Oh, be quiet," Chad replies, laughing, spinning his office chair towards the window, and taking in the Manhattan view. It was truly spectacular. He watched a pigeon fly by his third story window and land on the building directly across. He took in the view of the pedestrians walking on the streets stopping to window shop. He loved looking out his window and seeing all the city excitement.

"Take your wife out for some fun, maybe a play or go to a museum and leave me alone," he quipped to Harding laughing while he said it.

"No can do," Harding responds, chuckling. "It's way too much fun getting you riled up."

"Yeah, yeah," Chad retorted good-naturedly. "So, aside from prying, what's up?" He spun his chair around again and leafed through a file while Harding spoke.

"Want to meet for a beer and wings at Nina's? We could go over the calendar and maybe shoot some pool?" Harding suggested.

"Can't tonight," Chad declined sheepishly. "I'm going to be busy." His voice changes going down an octave as he says it.

"Oh, you are, are you?" Harding laughs knowing what Chad was up to. "Enjoy that date," Harding prompts, "but not too much."

Chad laughed. "Anyway, let's talk business," he began, changing the conversation to politics as he and Harding went to town planning the launch of the campaign.

Chad knew he needed to start doing some door-to-door canvassing as well as meet and greets with the people in the district. He had gone many times with his dad, and he believes there were some enjoyable aspects to it. The majority of the people were really nice and cared about the community they lived in. Every once in a while, you would come across a nutty individual, but they were few and far between.

Chad learned early on to listen, just listen. He realized that most people just want to be heard. His dad was the master of it. Thad would listen with an earnest look on his face, take mental notes, and then when he got in the car, jot down those notes and make them happen. The people were truly the salt of any community, and a good leader knew this. Chad knew he had big shoes to fill.

His dad called him every few days to talk about the status of the campaign. He wanted to help, but he also wanted Chad to have the pride that he could only feel by knowing he did it himself. Thad knew that although it wasn't in his heart just yet, Chad would grow to be an amazing leader. Chad was still warming up to the idea.

Chad enjoyed his conversations with his dad. He appreciated the recent one.

"Hey, Dad," Chad spoke into the phone, greeting him. "How is Florida?"

"It's amazing here," Thad commented, "sunny and golf weather all this past week."

"Sounds perfect," Chad replied. "Missing politics yet?"

"Oh, I miss the people" Thad began. "I miss the everyday feeling of helping. You will be amazing at it, son, you will feel that feeling of power and know that you have the ability to help. I wish this all for you. You will grow into the role, I promise."

"Thanks, Dad, I am still unsure of it all, but I will try, I promise."

He would try, it was who he was, but in reality, Chad liked doing his pro bono law cases and being on his boat. That's what it came down to, but he knew he couldn't let the family down, and once he was in office, if elected, he could help many who needed it. His ex-girlfriend, Trina used to tell him he was too idealistic, and had a too out-to-save the world mindset. That alone explained why she was an ex.

Trina was very materialistic and, although she's a good person overall, she always wanted more, while Chad was happy with the basics. Grandma Cecelia had insisted that after two years he had to take the next step with Trina. Cecilia felt that Trina, with her blonde good looks, pedigree education, and fine political family would make the perfect political wife for Chad.

"Chad," Cecelia had begun when he had visited her Hampton home for lunch last April. "It's time for you to settle down with Trina." Chad had chucked in response.

"I am serious," Cecelia affirmed in a stern voice. "You have a future to think about." She picked up her tea and took a lady-like sip and gave him a long hard look.

It led Chad to do some serious thinking and he responded with, "Grandma, just enjoy my company and let's not talk about my love life right now." He quickly changed the subject to her garden and temporarily distracted Cecelia. He felt like he dodged a bullet.

Cecelia liked Trina, Chad, on the other hand, got tired of her silver spoon attitude and wanted out. After breaking it off, as he always did with exes, he tried to remain friends. Trina didn't waste any time. She had already moved on and was dating a surgeon. Honestly, Chad wished them well.

Thinking about everything they needed to get done, Chad told Harding he would meet up with him the next day. They ended the call and Chad focused on his upcoming date. He picked out his clothes, khakis, a blue sport shirt and blazer and left them out on the bed while he took a steaming shower. He came out refreshed and applied Drakkar aftershave to his face. He combed and styled his hair, pushing the stray piece that always fell onto his eyes back, and put on his brown loafers.

Chad agreed to meet Hailey at 7PM. She gave him an address where he could pick her up. Then, she informed him that she would be coming straight from work, and for him to dress casually. Chad had laughed at her take charge attitude. He was really looking forward to seeing her.

He liked everything about her, her looks, her smile, her personality, her sense of humanity, and her big heart. Chad was tired of fakes, phonies, and gold diggers. He was looking for authenticity, natural beauty, family oriented, caring and of course, attractive. Hailey seemed to be full of fun, and despite her being associated with the Lynch family, he was looking forward to getting to know her better.

He got into his black Range Rover and drove the five miles down the city streets to his destination. He smiled when he put it into the GPS, realizing she was having him meet her at the theater. He wanted to see it anyway, so this was perfect, business and pleasure rolled into one.

A taxi honked at him, breaking him out of his reverie, and Chad skirted his Range Rover out of the way as it slowed to pick up a pedestrian. He watched as a mom with a stroller and a baby tried to get in. Chad patiently waited for the taxi driver to come out and help. Chad admired chivalry and tried to practice it as much as possible. He was always the one to hold the door open for his dates or help an elderly person to their destination. He sensed that same kind vibe in Hailey and his head was filled with thoughts of her, while his heart beat a little faster in anticipation of their date.

52

He was really looking forward to this evening. They were planning to go for a delicious Italian meal at a beachside restaurant which had a lengthy boardwalk and a beautiful view of the Chesapeake Bay. He was sure Hailey would like it as much as he did.

After twenty minutes, Chad pulled up slowly and saw the warehouse that the theater was housed in needed some repair. It was old and had spots of rust from the obviously leaky pipes. As he glanced at the roof, he acknowledged it has seen better days.

Stepping out of his truck, he admired the metal sculptures outside the theater made by some local artists who have taken up residence in the top floor of the building. As he walked past, he enjoyed the hand painted colorful murals depicting landscape and seascape scenes on the old brick structure. The art added some real charm to the rustic building.

Chad walked through the heavy glass doors, paintings from children lining the hallway instantly captured his attention. He stopped, standing, and staring at one in particular. It was a beautiful sailboat on the glistening bay. That child has some real talent, he thought to himself. He continued looking at some of the others when he heard a sea of voices singing, "This Is Me" from The Greatest Showman. Chad followed the sound to an old auditorium.

With its faded seats and poor lighting, the auditorium looked like it was in desperate need of some serious TLC. But you would never know it from the look on the thirty children's faces, who ranged in age from five to twelve-years-old, as they sang their hearts out with Hailey conducting the group. The little ones stood on the lower risers while the older ones were at the top.

Hailey smiled and nodded her head enthusiastically as she encouraged the group to sing their very best. Her hands were waving to the music as she pointed to the altos and then the sopranos when it was their turn to sing. The children appeared super responsive to her, Hailey has a gentle way about her, and a way of making each and every one of them feel important. "Great job, altos. Keep it up sopranos." The children responded to her and really pelted out the song. It sounded wonderful to Chad's ears.

Chad took a seat and smiled. He enjoyed watching both her and the kids. He could tell how much they loved being there and how much they responded to Hailey. When the song came to an end, all the kids high fived each other and Hailey laughed. She was so beautiful and just so full of joy. Her smile was radiant, and she looked on proudly at her group. Hailey's ponytail bobbed with her movement, making Chad grin. She looked like a pretty young woman happy to be right where she was at the moment.

Chad clapped enthusiastically from where he was standing. Hailey turned around and saw him, briefly feeling like she got the wind knocked out of her sails, their eyes met and held. He stood smiling, dressed in dark blue jeans, a navy-blue t-shirt, and tan sports jacket. He was a wow. She dated wows before. Steven was very attractive but there was an energy about Chad, a good energy that she feels head to toe. To her, it's an incredibly attractive quality Hailey had yet to find before. She was all about yoga, and energy and to her, his energy was like a polarized magnet drawing her in.

Her eyes stayed locked on his and she gave him a wave and smile. "Just a few more minutes," she mouthed before returning her attention to the kids. Hailey's eyes and focus went back to the group, but she felt shaky and filled with nervous excitement knowing he was there. The kids noticed her twinkling eyes and faint blush on her cheeks when she looked at him.

Chad settled into one of the weathered theater seats and enjoyed the rest of practice. When they finished, one of the more outgoing kids, about six or seven years old, stood on the riser raising his hand. He has a missing tooth in the front and he's wearing a Nike blue sweatshirt and jeans and really cool neon sneakers.

"Yes, Josh?" Hailey asked, nodding at him.

"Is that your boyfriend?" he asked in a playful voice. All the kids look shocked but begin to laugh at his confidence and question.

Chad and Hailey both laughed at that and met each other's eyes and smiled. The kids all whispered and giggled. "Miss Everson has a boyfriend!" echoed around the theater.

Chapter 14

Marissa's hairdresser worked his magic on her shoulder length chestnut wavy hair. It was subtly highlighted with gold, and low lighted with a darker tone. Marissa was very picky about her hair and only trusted Felipe to do it. He had been her personal hairdresser for years and they had become friends. She trusted him.

"I am so glad you are here, Felipe. The recovery was awful. Rick sent me to the spa again to recover, and I must have slept the whole time. Pure exhaustion."

In reality, Marissa had zero memory of the spa. It was so much easier for her to pretend that she had memories of these spa moments than spill the painful truth. She only felt comfortable talking to her sister about this. She needed to see her. Hailey was just a calming influence and was extremely reassuring.

This wasn't the first time Marissa's memories were blurred. It always happened during extremely stressful times when she was fighting with Rick. Perhaps she should talk to her doctor about it.

"Well, they certainly didn't fatten you up at the spa," Felipe commented, taking in her thin frame. "We need to get to Serendipity ASAP and fatten you up with a frozen hot chocolate."

Marissa laughed for the first time in weeks, so grateful to be feeling more like herself. Emily and she always loved their Serendipity mother, daughter outings in Manhattan. Serendipity had the best desserts, and she did have to agree with Felipe that the frozen hot chocolate was by far the best.

In a few hours she would be seeing Emily at camp, and she couldn't wait. When she returned home, they needed a Serendipity date. Maybe even Rick would come.

She and Rick were, surprisingly, getting along. She could look the other way on his affair if they didn't fight and he continued to pamper her. She liked their lifestyle and didn't want to give it up, especially now with her memory loss episodes. No use revealing that to anyone, until she saw the doctor.

Rick burst into the room, home from work early after a morning meeting. "Oh, don't we look lovely," he stated, smiling at Marissa's reflection. She did look quite lovely.

Felipe hated Rick and gave him a nod. Marissa, on the other hand, smiled.

"It feels so good to feel like myself," she proclaimed. Staring at her reflection in the mirror, she admired herself as Felipe sprayed her hair and fluffed it.

"Stunning," exclaimed Rick, his eyes appraising her and liking what he sees. "Absolutely stunning." Which is admittedly one of the reasons he kept her around.

———————————

Hailey and Chad sat at the candlelit table by the bay and took in the ambiance. The sun was just starting to set, with the blue of the sky only interrupted by a few fluffy clouds. The bay was calm. They watched as a sailboat and a pontoon boat went by. The children aboard the sailboat waved. Hailey and Chad wave back.

Chad looked across the table at Hailey thinking she looks so pretty in the candlelight. Her hair glistened with red highlights and happiness was shining on her face.

She's relaxed and so happy to be with Chad. She loved that he enjoyed the performance and was able to see the theater. This was such a wonderful evening with an amazing person.

Chad had a moment of sudden awareness as he looked at Hailey in the candlelight with the setting sun behind her making him gasp. She was the wave girl from the beach, the happy beautiful girl he wanted to meet that day when a phone call interrupted.

He laughed aloud at the realization; he's sitting on a date with the stunning woman who was dancing in the waves. She was definitely bringing a beautiful wave of change into his life. She was so unlike the Trina's in his life. To him, she was a woman with a heart, a soul, and a natural beauty inside and out.

"It's so nice being here with you," he whispered, reaching across the table for her hand.

His hand felt nice on hers, and she couldn't deny she felt a spark. A big spark warming her from head to toe.

He definitely felt it too. He smiles at her like it's Christmas Day and he just received the best present. In fact, he feels like he just did. They had a lovely dinner. The conversation flowed and their fettuccine pasta was incredible. It was an amazing, quiet, romantic night with the sound of their conversation, and the gentle waves of the bay. When dinner was over, neither of them wanted the night to end. They had shared wine, cheesecake, and amazing conversation. It was perfect.

"Do you want to take a walk?" Chad prompted, helping Hailey from her seat. Any excuse to touch her right now would do.

Hailey smiled, as she reached for Chad's hand and replied, "I'd love to."

Chapter 15

Rick looks over at the sleeping Marissa next to him in their bed. He is tormented with confusion. Love is combined with the need to have complete control of everything, including her. His feelings often confuse him and especially with Marissa.

His Marissa. She challenged him so much, and he wished she wouldn't do that, yet she is so sweet, so beautiful and a wonderful mother to Emily. One minute he wanted her gone, and the next he was captivated by her spectacular beauty and essence.

Life had always been like that for Rick. He lived and breathed extremes. One minute he would be sitting at his desk quietly working on a case, and almost like a switch going off, he would become restless. He would suddenly decide to run fifteen miles or book a personal trainer for an hour-long session.

One time, at a particularly extreme moment, he booked a sky jumping session, drove to Garson airport a half hour away and sent Marissa and Lana (two separate texts of course) a snap of him jumping from a plane during his lunch hour. From a very young age Rick heard the words bi-polar, ADHD (attention deficit, hyperactivity disorder), and borderline personality disorder from the various therapists his parents took him to. One even added the word Narcissist to his file, unbeknownst to Rick.

Every session with this therapist included Rick speaking of never being wrong and controlling his own world and the world around him. Rick would bully a child, and it would always be the other child's fault. He would physically cause pain to other kids and then say they provoked him. Rick was in and out of six private schools by the time he graduated. He graduated first in his class at his last school, and the administrators congratulated him (while privately, they had a celebration that he was gone).

Rick was ruthless, even as a young boy and always had to be number one. He never liked to lose at anything and would cause a scene whenever he did. The kids on the block hated playing with him for fear of his outrages. He was trouble to almost everyone around him.

His behavior noticeably came under control when he went to college. He made friends, calmed down, and due to being extremely attractive, he had a string of beautiful girlfriends. His parents sighed in relief, believing Rick had gained control of his life, and they settled happily into retirement in Florida. Rick and Marissa saw them a few times a year now.

Rick, in one of his generous moods, bought them a beautiful waterfront home in Tampa. His parents were good people and had always had trouble understanding him. The string of therapists had trouble understanding him, too. Rick stopped going to therapists in college and started to self-medicate.

A tradeoff of Adderall, Xanax and cocaine worked for him. The drugs changed him, but were an expensive, dangerous habit to have. College boy Rick had to resort to some shady work and even some selling to feed the habit. He met some guys who had stuff on him as he moved up the ranks. Those were the men he defended now and kept out of Club Fed.

He didn't like his past getting in the way of his future. He kept a payoff fund for his protection. Anyone who was about to talk either got a visit from his bodyguards along with a warning, or a payoff if need be. Rick was now a powerful man, and few chose to take a chance messing with him.

Climbing out of bed, Rick walked into the bathroom, set up his white line on his handheld mirror, brushed his teeth, showered, shaved, and inhaled his line. This was how he started his morning most days. Marissa doesn't know about his habit, and neither does anyone else. Rick considers it his necessary medication. Although, lately, he's been trying to cut back.

Chapter 16

"This is pure Heaven," Hailey whispered, walking hand in hand with Chad on the quiet wooden boardwalk. "I love summer nights and I love the water." And being with you...oh, being here right now with you.

Chad felt the same way about Hailey. The night was perfect, the dinner was perfect, Hailey was perfect. His chest felt tight, his heart feeling like it was beating a million times a minute. He took the moment to look into her sparkling eyes fixed on him. He gently took her beautiful face in his hands and gave her an unforgettable kiss that lasted for several minutes.

When they came up for air, Chad pulled her into a hug. He felt her shiver, prompting him to take off his sports jacket, and put it around her shoulders.

She looked at him and smiled, her green eyes glittering with happiness. "Thank you," she murmured. Her sister's knight in shining armor was a hero through and through. They stared at each other, completely lost in one another, and unaware of their surroundings.

Jason, a new professional photographer, taking advantage of this celebrity citing, discreetly snapped a few pictures during dinner. Continuing to follow them at a distance on the boardwalk afterwards, he hoped for the shot that would sell.

He smiled to himself, knowing he did his job well. Hailey and Chad kissing would be on tomorrow's front page with the headline, "From One Twin to The Other." This would be Jason's big break!

Chapter 17

Rick was angry. He paced the floor of his library in frustration. Dressed in his gray workout clothes, he had just come back from a five-mile run, but it wasn't enough. He had wanted to see Lana last night. It wasn't their usual night, but he needed her. She had said no making him angry, so angry he felt like tossing the books off the shelf. He was so frustrated, his blood boiling. He desperately needed an energy release.

He still hadn't touched Marissa. He was feeling guilt over the scars remaining on her body from the explosion, and now that they were in a good place, he truly wanted to give her the time she needed to heal.

He couldn't believe that Lana turned him down. Rick was livid. He had sent Trevor out of town on a case and knew Lana was free for him. Her excuse was she had made plans with the girls. Rick told her to change them, but Lana refused.

She would pay next time he saw her; oh, she would pay. The problem was Lana was as cold as he was. She always did things the way she wanted to do, according to her plans, and that bothered Rick. He likes control, and Lana most definitely had her own agenda. Her Achilles heel: her husband and his money. She loved her husband, and she adored the lifestyle he provided for her. Rick was just so magnetic and truly hard for her to resist. He always had been for her.

Rick, out of desperation after not hearing from Lana, called his trainer and arranged for an immediate session. He needed to release this energy some other way before the demons crept back in. He was trying to cut down on the cocaine, but it was nearly impossible. It certainly wasn't an easy habit to break. He knew he needed to stop. There were days lately he didn't like himself and that hadn't happened before. Rick had felt like this when he was kicked out of all the schools. His parents had looked at him with such disappointment, he had felt sorry for hurting them. Rick knew he was a handful but couldn't stop. He didn't know how to stop.

He needed to be optimum today as he was seeing his beautiful eight-year-old daughter at camp, and despite the awful man he could be sometimes, his daughter was his everything. Enchanting Emily was all his wrongs turned right. Despite everything, Rick was an involved father. He attended every school play, parent conference and spent his evenings reading and playing with her. She was his true joy! He couldn't be restless and angry when he saw her. He needed the release before he pounded a wall.

Rick had learned that working out really helped him in college. He had to have a single in the dorm, he knew he would never get along with a roommate. Even though it was pricey, his parents had wholeheartedly agreed to pay the extra and give Rick his own room. Rick kept a bench and weights in there and added a punching bag. He would go to town pounding out his frustrations. He would spend hour after hour lifting weights, running on the treadmill and on his exercise bike.

The boys in the next room often asked Rick, "Do you ever sleep?" They would hear him working out at two, three, or four in the morning. The girls in the room on the other side constantly pounded the walls to try to get him to stop, and that had eventually led to his passion fueled moments with Lana. He blasted his Zeppelin music so loudly while he worked out, that the walls between them vibrated.

The cocaine he inhaled kept his anger under control, but it made him feel like he needed to go from zero to ninety in sixty seconds. True, Rick needed downers to sleep too. He was self-medicating and doing major damage. He didn't care. He was nearly convinced he was invincible. But, right now, he needed to push himself with his trainer doing so many reps with the weights. that he would be near collapse, and it would release that energy enough for him to function. Luckily, the trainer said yes.

Chapter 18

Harding called Chad's cell at 8AM the morning after Chad's date with Hailey. He woke up to the image of Chad and Hailey being featured on the front page of the Sun; they were locked in quite a romantic embrace. Scanning through a few other news sites on his phone, Harding groaned at the fact that many other news outlets had gotten ahold of the story. He needed to get to Chad ASAP.

After the walk on the beach and a lot more kissing, Chad walked Hailey to her car and promised to call her the next day. It was an amazing night with a wonderful girl. Chad slept like he hadn't in weeks, dreaming of his wave girl. The ringing on his phone woke him up, pulling him out of his dreams.

Glancing at his phone, he realized it's Harding. He grimaced and answered, his throat still hoarse from sleep, "Hello?"

"Well, hello, lover boy," Harding remarked, in a different tone than Chad recognized.

He could sense Harding was in a serious mood, immediately prompting Chad to become more awake. "What's up?" he prods, sitting up shirtless in his bed.

"You are on the front page of The Sun making out with Hailey."

"What?" Chad questioned, angrily. "What the hell, Harding? No one was there. We went to Santino's, a half hour away."

"Apparently the photographer was there, and he caught you two crazy kids. Guess the date went well," Harding mumbles, snickering, his sense of humor returning.

"Yeah, it did," Chad agreed, smiling despite this turn of events. "She is incredible."

Harding reminded Chad, "She is connected to Lynch. We will have to navigate this, considering the headline is, 'From One Twin to The Other'."

Chad groaned. "She is nothing like the glitzy Marissa who we see on page six, she is low key and sweet," emphasizing, "nothing."

"I believe you, man," Harding claims, "but we do have a campaign that was just launched. And we need to turn this press into something positive. I will work on it and be in touch. Until then, if you see her again, keep it on the down low until I figure it out. Okay, lover boy?"

Chad mumbled, "Okay," and angrily hung up on Harding. Chad was not happy with this turn of events. He couldn't even go on one of the best dates of his life without having it become a front-page headline.

He rarely fought with Harding, and this honestly angered him. His life was his life. He would see Hailey when and if he wanted, the hell with the press and the campaign.

Chad reached for his phone and quickly sent Hailey a text, hoping he didn't wake her. He wanted to warn her before she saw it on the front page. "Hey, good morning. I had a great time last night… Did you see the Sun?"

Hailey replied immediately with, "I just saw the picture. I want to crawl into a hole."

That was not the reply Chad was hoping for. Now he had a woman wanting to crawl into a hole after a date with him.

"I am not sorry," he wrote. "I had an amazing time, and you are incredible."

There was a moment's pause. He holds his breath as the bubbles begin dancing on the screen. He exhales in relief as she texted back, "So, are you. When can we see each other again?"

Chapter 19

Rick gave his driver the day off. Then he requested that his Range Rover have a full tank and be ready for him. He had the cook pack a picnic lunch the night before filled with all of Emily's favorites including cold fried chicken, homemade potato chips, and chocolate cake. He couldn't wait to see his little girl.

Emily and the nanny stayed in a cottage off the campgrounds and the nanny brought her to the camp each day. It was the perfect summer for their little girl. Away from the city, out in nature, and swimming every day.

It was something Rick dreamed about as a kid as he played with nothing more than his bike and got into constant fights with the kids in the neighborhood. Never once was it his fault.

Rick looked back on it now as an adult and still didn't think he ever did anything wrong. He had that side to him.

Luckily, he was able to channel his Narcissistic side of him into winning trials in the courtroom. If he believed that he, and the client, were always right, and he was a ruthless attorney, he usually won the case.

Rick won more times than not, and the ones he did lose, well, let's just say the guilty party either confessed in the chair, or they didn't show up to court due to a slight accident. Rick turned a blind eye to those cases. They couldn't be won, and, if they could, Rick would have won them.

He was a force. He had brilliance and magnetism, with the jury often mesmerized by him. Women were attracted to his looks, and men wanted to have his machismo. Rick walked into a courtroom like he owned it, and in fact, he did.

That was the business side of Rick. There were many facets to him. The powerful lawyer, the erratically behaved husband, the stallion in the bedroom, and the dad.

Rick liked the role of dad the best. He could hide his other personas whenever he saw Emily. From the moment he held her as a newborn, he swore to never let anybody hurt his precious daughter.

He and Marissa agreed to only one child. One precious princess to spoil, and she captured his heart from the first moment he saw her. He promised to be the best daddy he could be for his precious Emily.

He was dressed casually in jeans and a gray hoodie, and he felt happy, pure happiness at having the day to see his princess. He was so excited to see her after these rough few weeks. He couldn't wait for her to show him around camp and share all the fun things she has been doing.

"Marissa," he yelled. "Are you ready to go see Emily?"

Chapter 20

"Grandma, I'm sorry, I'm not going to discuss my personal life," Chad grumbled. He was upset Cecelia had summoned him to her house after she saw the front page of The Sun. She had no right! "I am a thirty-year-old grown man, and my choices are my own."

"Chad," Cecelia began, giving him a stern look from the wicker chair on the porch, "you have a reputation to upkeep. Think about the campaign, Chad. You need to always put that first."

Chad looked at her with his blue eyes blazing. This was unreal. He had never stood up to his grandmother before, but this was ridiculous. He took a deep breath attempting to get his anger under control.

Was it embarrassing to wind up on the front page? Yes. Did he do anything wrong? No. Although he wanted to, he didn't ask her to come home with him. She's class through and through and he was not about one-night stands. He's a relationship guy and he sensed that about her, too. Why rush? If it's a good thing, a little romance and time are so worth it. She is worth it. He had a date, and it turned romantic. He has absolutely no regrets. None at all. He wasn't about to allow anyone to make him feel badly for this.

It's not his fault the press was there taking an intrusive picture and sharing it with the world. Did he have to wise up? Yes! He was running for office. But he is a single man, and she is a single woman. They are both adults who could make their own choices. Enough of this.

Chad found this all to be unbelievable, he pushed back his hair and sighed heavily. He did nothing wrong and neither did Hailey. "Grandma, I love you, but I think that this conversation is done. Enjoy your tea." Chad leans down, kisses a shocked Cecelia on the cheek and walks out the door without another word.

Cecelia watched him leave, her mouth hanging open for just a second until she regained her composure. After a shocked moment, she straightened her posture, took a deep breath, and reached for her phone dialing Thad. "Thaddeus, we have trouble," she announced the moment he picked up the phone, turning a shade of red.

Chapter 21

Marissa sat beside Rick in their black Range Rover listening to some Country music from a local radio station and staring out the window at the trees and steep rocks. As they got closer to the mountainous area upstate where Emily's camp was located, the roads were beginning to narrow. "Rick, these roads are windy," Marissa remarked, holding tightly to the door handles.

"It's fine," Rick replied with smug confidence, "I've got this."

Rick knew from the GPS there were a few hairpin turns coming up. He couldn't wait, his fingers twitched in anticipation as he held the steering wheel lightly. The bad boy side of Rick longed to ride a Harley through these mountain roads. Maybe that would be good for him, to release some of the anger and energy on an open highway, risking life and limb on those hairpin turns. Exhilarating and dangerous was what Rick loved and craved. He liked to live on the edge.

Rick smiled over at Marissa. She looked like a beautiful young woman with her hair in a simple chestnut braid. Even in jeans and a beige cable knit sweater she looked glamorous. In these moments no one could compare to her.

He's happy they are getting along now. He justified those drugging episodes as a reset for both of them. After each one, Marissa completely forgot why she was mad, believed she had spent the time at the spa, and no longer threatened to leave him.

It all seemed simple to him. He liked having her on his arm and he liked her as the mother of his child. But he also liked having Lana on the side. Why mess with a good thing? If only she would listen to him all the time and wouldn't anger him so much, then there wouldn't be a need for a reset. He didn't like to do it, but she forced him. If only she wouldn't threaten to leave him. Sometimes she just needed a lesson.

He looked over at Marissa and smiled as he watched her look of fear, her eyes going wide and her hands clenching the door handle as he drove fast on those hairpin turns. He was just having a little fun, right?

Meanwhile, unbeknownst to Rick, beautiful Lana was driving a rented Jeep and secretly trailing Rick by three discrete cars, confident he wouldn't notice her. She had a plan, a plan all her own. She wouldn't let anyone get in the way of that.

Chapter 22

Hailey was waiting for Chad at the theater as he walked in. Instantly, he noticed she looked visibly upset. His heart beat a bit faster in his chest at the sight of her. Her eyes appeared red and glassy while her nose looked even redder, but she was still beautiful in Chad's eyes.

He doubled his pace and immediately took her into his arms. She went into them willingly and he held her tight. "I am so sorry, Hailey," he whispered. "I feel awful."

She pressed her face into his chest and smelled his aftershave, feeling safe in his arms. Tilting her head up, she initiated the kiss this time and it was wonderful, helping to ease her worry.

She was mortified that she was on the front page of so many newspapers and being mentioned on TV news. Absolutely mortified. She knew her students' families and her principal would be seeing it. What would they think?

Steve had already seen it and sent her a text, "Moved on, I see." Although it was over with him, she was not one to be that blatant with anything, especially something so new.

Despite being related to Marissa and Rick Lynch, Hailey lived her life low key, not on the front page of a newspaper. Hailey shied away from every media opportunity and stayed in the shadows when she was with Marissa and Rick whenever possible.

Chad pulled away and looked into her green eyes. "Hailey, I am glad you didn't run away from this." He reached up, wiping a tear from her eye. "I can't promise you that it will be easy. You know I will be in the spotlight with the campaign. But I can promise you that if you don't give up on me, what we could potentially be, we can try to keep it on the down low from now on."

Hailey looked at him and smiled. "I may just have an idea." She suddenly got a twinkle in her eye and looked full of mischief as she grabbed his hand and pulled him to the back of the theater.

"Umm, why are we here?" Chad asked, laughing as he took in the rows and rows of costumes.

Hailey grinned, grabbed a cowboy hat, and placed it on his head. It's a good look on him, she thought, making herself laugh.

"I like a cute cowboy," she whispered, pulling him in for a kiss.

He took a pink feather boa and put it lovingly around her neck. "Definitely, you," he proclaimed, laughing as she playfully posed.

"This," Hailey began, "will be our closet. If you want to date me and keep out of the press, we will have some fun with these." She pointed to the costumes, grinning wide. "Get ready to have a little fun."

Chad laughed, thinking she was joking, and quickly realized she wasn't.

Chapter 23

"Rick, please slow down," Marissa pleaded between clenched teeth as Rick navigated the sharp hairpin turns on Highway 28 with a crooked smile on his face.

They were detoured due to construction, and the road seemed to be more treacherous than the original one they were on. Rick had that look in his eye, the same one Marissa feared. It's been happening more and more lately. Between her blackouts and his moments, she was beginning to lose her grip.

"Rick, slow down," she demanded, her fear obvious in the tone of her voice. "Emily…Emily needs us." At the sound of Emily's name, Rick stepped more lightly on the pedal and returned to a normal speed.

Marissa sighed in relief. "Thank you, Rick," she whispered, loosening her grip on the door handle, and wiggling her fingers to regain the circulation. She had been holding on so tight, as if her life depended on it.

Rick loved speed, but she loved calm. During the good times in their relationship, they balanced each other out. During the turbulent times, their differences led to some major friction. Rick turned to Lana during those turbulent times. He was glad he had both women for the roles they served in his life. He wasn't a saint, that's for sure, but a man who knew what he needed.

Lana, still three cars behind, laughed as she took the curves in the road. Had Rick spotted her? Is that why he's speeding up? She doubted it. He would never suspect she would be following him. Rick loved speed, but so did Lana. She matched his car turn for turn.

The two cars sandwiched between Rick and Lana drove more cautious, making it more difficult for her to go quite as fast, she hoped she wouldn't lose them. Lana kept wanting to honk and move them along, but she didn't dare draw attention to her jeep. She needed to be discreet. She didn't want to take a chance that anyone would remember seeing her there.

She tucked her blonde hair into a Yankees baseball cap, and she wore a plain navy t-shirt. Lana usually didn't like to blend in, but this time she needed to. Lana never did anything like this before but being involved with Rick made her do some unpredictable things.

Chapter 24

Chad got in his Range Rover with a duffel bag as he left the theater with a few members of the press hot on his trail. He checked his rear-view mirror and saw two cars stalking him. Chuckling to himself, he decided to play politician.

He pulled into a Donut Delight a mile up the road, and as expected, so did they. He walked inside, and a few minutes later came out with three bags of donuts and three coffees. He walked over to each of their cars one by one and handed the startled photographers a coffee and a bag with the Donut Delight logo on the front.

"Listen," he remarked, "following me today is going to be dull. I took a personal day to do some door-to-door canvassing. You guys will need the coffee to stay awake." Chad knows that canvassing can be long and often tedious work that was a necessary part of the process. They each look at him bewildered but accept the donuts and coffee. Chad stifled his laugh, enjoying catching them by surprise.

He walked away with a wave and a grin, climbed back in his Range Rover, and sits behind the wheel enjoying his donut with a good view of the cars. He notices the photographers from two different gossip papers looking at each other and laughing at what he just did.

While Chad was at Donut Delight distracting the media, Hailey walked out the back door of the theater with her duffle bag. She paused and looked around, grateful not to see any reporters or photographers. Exhaling in relief, she rushed to her Prius and drove home.

She and Chad had plans to meet up later. In the meantime, she has some calls to make and some apologizing to do to her boss and to her students. They all loved Hailey; so, she hoped it would be okay, embarrassing, but okay. Being on the front page of the paper was never part of her agenda. She hated the attention and preferred to be low key. Everything about this was truly awkward.

. . . .

Chad greeted the two campaign volunteers who offered to walk the district with him with a bright smile. "Hello," Chad stated. They were committee members and retired police officers who loved to see their old neighborhood and help a candidate they believed in.

Chad introduced himself to Jeff and Rob, "Hi to you both, I'm Chad. Thank you for being here," he remarked.

"Nice to meet you," replied Jeff, shaking his hand.

Rob grinned and proclaimed, "Happy to be here," as he shakes Chad's hand.

Stepping back, Chad arched his eyebrows, assessing them both as he asked the first question, "Did you see The Sun?" He tilted his head in anticipation of their response.

Both men looked at each other and laughed. "Yeah, we did," commented Jeff, while Rob nodded.

Chad turned a little red at the way Jeff confirmed it and cleared his throat. "It is embarrassing, and not who I am or what I represent. If asked, I am going to acknowledge it and move on. Just an FYI," he declared, his tone serious. Both men accepted that as the final word and let it go with a nod.

Privately, they didn't like that he was associated in any way with a Lynch. He seemed like a good guy and Lynch spelled trouble. Despite it, they were committeemen, dedicated to the party and Chad's dad had been a good leader. From what they had heard about Chad, and knowing his upbringing and politics, they were eager to support him.

Chad, Jeff, and Rob got through the first couple of houses without issue. Chad shook hands, handed out campaign literature and listened, like his father taught him to do. They were in a middle-class neighborhood in the borough of Queens and the houses were neatly kept brick homes with little land in between. Houses stood close together, all townhouse style homes. They easily walked from house to house and up a small stone staircase in front of each.

Chad stepped up to the third house and rang the bell. An older woman wearing a blue house dress and slippers opened the door and peered at Chad. She studied him for a minute, looking him up and down with radar eyes. Her brow furrowed, and she grimaced at him the moment recognition hit. "Hey, you were on front page today messing around with that Lynch twin. Big no to you!" Then she glared at him and slammed the door in his face.

Chad stood frozen, shocked by her reaction, and turned slightly red as he looked down at the ground. "Wow," he commented. "Didn't expect that one."

Jeff and Rob both stand next to him uncomfortably and clear their throats. They feel badly for Chad and this awkward situation. He is a grown man and single. He did nothing wrong by going out with a beautiful single woman. They truly feel sorry for him being treated that way. They had seen it before, candidates literally hated for who they were associated with, something they did which went against public opinion. They liked Chad and needed to steer him away from this.

"Umm, maybe it's best if we hit another neighborhood," Jeff suggested, pushing his Yankees cap further up on his head.

"No," refused Chad vehemently. This was not going to stop him. If he was going to do this job, he had to take the good with the bad. A front-page kiss wasn't going to be the end of him. He was headed towards new beginnings and to show everyone what he was made of. "Let's stay right here and keep going," he insists, striding up to the next house and knocking on the brown door without hesitation.

Chapter 25

Lana parked her brown Jeep Cherokee in a wooded area filled with lush green trees and some older dried-up maples. She gritted her teeth with determination, the crunch of the maple leaves under her feet was a bit too loud for her taste. She walked with trepidation, hoping no one would hear her. She was here for one reason only. Once she accomplished what she set out to do and got what she needed, she would be gone. Besides, Trevor was due back tonight and she wanted to be home for him.

Lana was complicated, she always had been. She loved Trevor, but craved Rick. She had these conflicted feelings ever since she met them and dated both men during her college days . Trevor had money at the time, old money and could give her the world. Rick, well he was pure passion and came with complications. He was way too controlling for Lana, but the sparks she had with him, well they were too hard to ignore. She and Rick recaptured their passion after Trevor joined his firm.

Lana remembered walking into the holiday office party the first December after Trevor had been working there. Trevor had gone off to refill their drinks, white wine for her, a glass of red for himself. Lana was wearing an emerald cocktail gown with her hair pulled up in a chic twist. She smoothed the stray hairs that had escaped out and gently rotated her neck to work out the kinks. Her gold Dior shoes were digging into her feet, she just wanted to go home. Trevor had insisted she come with him that night. She had resisted knowing Rick would be there too. Despite her husband working for him, contact had been avoided, but not tonight. So far, she had managed to avoid him in the crowded hall. Over three-hundred employees and spouses were in attendance.

"You look stunning," a sexy voice whispered in her ear coming up behind her. She knew it was Rick before she even turned around. "You used to tuck your hair just like that in college, and remember when I massaged those kinks right out of your neck? He smiled his sexy smile at her. Lana's body immediately reacted to his closeness, but she did her absolute best to maintain her composure. He noticed her reaction and gave a soft chuckle.

Oh, she remembered alright and felt herself flush. "Good to see you, Rick," she replied, not sure if she meant it. They had parted on not the best of terms. Her eyes did feast on him. He may have aged a bit, a little gray appeared at his temples, but he looked as handsome as ever. He still had a muscular build that was evident even in his navy Italian suit. It fit him like a glove.

"You are as beautiful as ever. I need to see you again." He whispered hastily as he saw Trevor approach with the wine glasses in hand. Rick quickly planned his retreat upon Trevor's return, after a moment of polite small talk leaving Lana flustered.

"Hey, Rick," Trevor remarked, approaching, handing Lana her wine glass. "I see you have met Lana."

"Yes," Rick answered, smiling a fake smile at Trevor, "we had a nice conversation about public relations. I will keep what you said in mind Lana and may call you for our next event. It's been a pleasure meeting you. Both of you enjoy the evening."

Rick walked off and mingled with the crowd without a care in the world, knowing the effect he just had on Lana, although Trevor was none the wiser.

"He is the boss of the firm," Trevor commented after Rick had walked off. "Glad you finally were able to meet him." Lana forced a smile, hiding the fact that she was flustered over the exchange with Rick.

Her eyes continued following Rick, but she turned to her husband and took his hand in hers. "Let's get some food." She needed to distract herself and regain her composure. She led Trevor over to the hors d'oeuvres table and lost sight of Rick for the rest of the evening.

She tried to get him out of her head after that moment, but unfortunately thoughts of him haunted her and she had to see him. Rick's magnetism was pulling her in once again. She was ultimately the one who reached out to him a week later to meet for lunch. Lunch quickly turned into weekly meetings at a penthouse suite. Rick was a dangerous man, a wealthy and magnetic man, a man who Lana craved.

Rick still made Lana weak at the knees and turned her insides upside down. But Rick had a scary side as well. He could be dangerous, and Lana did not want to invest all of herself in him. She satisfied her cravings two nights a week and then went home to Trevor. Her Trevor. She should have felt guilty about having this affair, but she didn't. Her intimacy with him was comfortable and felt like home. Her meetups with Rick were fueled with chemistry and passion. It had always been that way with them. Sparks flew when they were around each other. It didn't matter how much she wished it wasn't that way.

Lana wasn't perfect, she could admit that, but Rick had such a hold on her, such a pull. It wasn't good right now; it just wasn't good, and it needed to change. But he really was magnetic and so hard to resist. After all this time, she finally felt like she had some sort of control over Rick, she was the one who made these evening meet-ups happen. Rick was putty in her hand.

Marissa and Rick got out of their black Range Rover and headed into the camp. The camp was a sprawling spectacle of beauty on fifty acres of land. The river flowed alongside the camp, and one could see happy kids on windsurfers, stand up paddle boards, and in canoes. The sounds of talking, laughter and splashing could be heard as kids swam in a nearby pool.

Lana watched from a distance as she saw Rick and Marissa happily greeting their daughter with hugs and kisses. A young woman stood nearby dressed in a camp shirt and denim shorts, her long blonde hair was tied back in a braid. Lana guessed her to be the nanny. Lana took out her camera and started clicking away. Rick with Emily, Marissa with Emily, the nanny with Emily.

Lana was almost done. She had one more thing she needed to get. With one final glance at the happy family reunion, frowning, she set off to find it. It should be easy to get it now.

Chapter 26

I'll meet you at 7 p.m., at Harding's for the test run. Chad glanced down at his cellphone and smiled. He was getting a little bored at work, while going through his current case files.

Perfect timing, he thought. He texted Hailey back. "Can't wait."

Chad clued Harding into their plan. At first, he had been very angry about it and fought Chad on it, but he finally gave in knowing that this was important to Chad. Chad wanted to see Hailey and he knew the press would always be all over them. They devised a plan to see each other and be discreet about it. It had to work.

Chad couldn't get enough of this woman. She is beautiful, fun, adventurous, and intelligent; everything he always wanted. Looking down, Chad tried to focus on the case in front of him, but it was no use. Once Hailey was in his head, he was a goner.

. . . .

The press was still stationed across from Chad's building which was his reason for meeting Hailey at Harding's. If her plan worked, they would be free to date and not be under the spotlight while getting to know each other. As Chad left his apartment, he saw that the press was hot on his trail. He set out on foot to Harding's place knowing full well the photographers were following his every move. Hiding a smile, he welcomed it this time. It was time to test their plan.

He arrived at Harding's building and greeted the doorman. "Hey, Joe. How are the kids?"

Joe smiled and they chatted for a bit about his two small children before he buzzed Chad up to Harding's place. "Yup, Chelsea is four now," he remarked, "getting ready for pre-k, and Daniel is six and just lost his first tooth."

Chad remarked, "Great ages, bet you sleep well at night running around with them all day."

Joe laughed, "You bet."

Chad walked in, seeing Hailey already there. She had gotten there twenty minutes earlier, wearing her disguise. She had put on a blonde wig, a long glittery scarf, and a headband. She looked 70's chic, complete with bell bottoms and platform shoes. Her white shirt had a peace sign on it caked in fabric glitter. When Joe buzzed her up, he was told she was a possible nanny they were interviewing.

Thankfully, Hailey wasn't trailed by the press but if she had been, they would have never suspected she was Hailey in that get up. Harding grinned when he opened the door and saw Hailey. She looked amusing in her outfit. He held back a laugh but gave her a wink.

"You must be the new nanny," he commented, discreetly winking again at her. He glanced out into the hallway checking to ensure the press hadn't snuck past Joe and gotten in.

"Yes, thanks for the interview," Hailey remarked, winking back.

He led her in and shut the door behind her. Harding had a few years of being a police officer under his belt before he went into law school. He knew the ropes and knew what precautions to take. Once Hailey was safely inside his place, she pulled off the wig.

"Nice to meet you," she commented, her green eyes sparkling. "Thank you for helping us out," she added, smiling at him.

"Nice to meet you too," Harding replied, sizing her up. He was instantly captivated by her beauty, and he could already see that she was very sweet. She seemed very unlike her sister. He quickly found that Hailey was extremely down to earth and not at all aloof. "Well, you did have a solid plan, let's see how it goes. We need Chad focused, but we also need him to be happy."

Hailey smiled shyly at Harding. "I want the chance to get to know him better. He seems wonderful."

Harding smirked at that and quipped, "He's not bad if you like that type." Hailey and Harding laughed at his remark, their nerves easing slightly.

Harding led her in and pointed to the blue leather couch. "Have a seat. Can I get you anything to drink? Lemonade? Iced Tea? Vodka shots?"

Hailey laughed. "Iced tea sounds great. Thank you." Harding went into the kitchen and came out with a glass filled with iced tea.

"Thank you so much," Hailey remarked, accepting the iced tea he offered her and taking a drink. "Beautiful home," Hailey commented from her place on the couch, setting her glass down on a coaster on the glass table in front of her.

"My wife is a master decorator," Harding replied. "She is out playing tennis, or she would be here telling you all about her grand plans to refurnish this place every other day." Harding rolled his eyes and Hailey laughed. Harding was tempted to take advantage of the situation and use his police skills and find out more about the Lynches from Hailey but decided against it for now. His curiosity could be satisfied another time, today was about helping out his brother-in-law. He liked this woman in front of him, and they enjoyed a conversation about Jillian and his children.

Joe buzzed a few minutes later informing him Chad was coming up. Hailey smiled at the news. Harding noticed her look of happiness, and saw the same look on Chad's face when he spotted Hailey on the couch as he walked in. Chad's eyes locked with Hailey's green ones and Harding immediately felt like a third wheel.

"Thanks man," he remarked, patting Harding on the back, and moving past him to embrace Hailey.

Harding cleared his throat after an awkward moment. "Okay, you crazy kids are obviously happy to see each other. So, get the hell out of here and have some fun."

Ten minutes later, a guy dressed in overalls, a baseball cap, and a pretty convincing fake mustache, left the building carrying a garbage bag to the dumpster. Ten minutes afterwards the nanny left, as well. The nanny and the overall guy met up down the road at a burger place.

Meanwhile, the press remained outside Harding's building waiting for Chad to come out. They were sure they could trail and spot him with that Lynch girl. They all needed a good cover shot for their editors. Fortunately for Chad and Hailey, they would be waiting a long time for him to come out.

Chapter 27

"Oh, she has been absolutely no trouble, Mrs. Lynch," Susan, the perky twenty-one-year-old nanny proclaims as she tucks a stray lock of her long brown hair behind her ear. She was a camp counselor for the eight-year-old girls' group during the day and nanny to Emily at night. Camp was definitely a fun place to be. The sprawling acres of land allowed room and space for so many activities. The kids enjoyed kayaking on the river, horseback riding, ziplining, arts and crafts. Susan felt lucky to be there with Emily.

Susan had been the summer nanny for the Lynches for years, and this year they paid her to stay in a cabin off-site of the camp with Emily. While the other girls stayed in a bunk, Emily and Susan had their own place, Lynch style. Susan was paid well and had seen a lot. She thought the Lynches were good parents when they made it a priority, but she had to question what kind of parents sent their eight-year-old to a sleep-a-way camp for eight weeks, visiting her once and calling once a day.

She hadn't even heard from Mrs. Lynch for weeks. She knew she had the accident, but it still didn't seem right. Mr. Lynch called from his office or home each night at 6 p.m. Emily talked every night about missing her parents, and Susan did her best to make up for it. Luckily, Emily was so exhausted from camp she usually fell asleep fast. Susan took that time to either hang out with her boyfriend, Jake on the porch swing outside the cabin, or she was on the phone talking with him all night.

Jake was a counselor on the boys' side. He was a bit of a bad boy and the opposite of Susan's calm demeanor. She believed her parents wouldn't like him. He had dark hair and bright blue eyes that could make her melt, Jake was six-feet, two-inches, with muscles from working out every day. He rode a motorcycle and had tattoos. Susan couldn't get enough of him. She thought he was hot. She knew she had a responsibility to Emily, but after she went to sleep, Susan would sneak in some make out time with Jake.

With Emily's parents visiting, Susan told Jake to stay away from her for the next two days. He smirked and agreed, "Sure." Jake would be hard to stay away from, but Susan wanted to keep this job.

The Lynches were basically paying her tuition at college. She was studying to be a nurse and working for them meant good money if you kept your mouth shut. She had to sign a whole bunch of confidentiality papers when she was hired. It wasn't worth talking about knowing all the fines she would have to pay.

Susan kept her mouth shut, even with Jake.

She didn't only take care of little Emily during the summer, but also after school sometimes. In return, college was paid for. Susan's mom was a single mom and told her that despite Lynch's reputation, this was a deal of a lifetime and reminded her not to blow it. Susan didn't plan to ruin a good thing.

Susan nodded at the Lynches and continued to tell them how amazing Emily has been. In reality, she's a very sweet girl with a slight daredevil side. She had Marissa's beautiful looks with more red in her hair, and Rick's adventurous, sometimes on the edge personality.

The other day at camp she had to be rescued after she randomly decided to jump off the side of a cliff into the lake while the campers were on a hike with the counselors. Dan, a counselor, dove right in and pulled the struggling Emily safely to shore. When asked why she did it, Emily just said she needed an adventure, she was getting bored.

The owner of the camp lectured her and assigned two counselors to shadow her on the next hike. Normally a child would be kicked out for doing something so extreme. But she was Emily Lynch and her father basically funded and supplied the camp. Emily Lynch was not to be touched. She had other mischievous behaviors, part of the reason other campers were glad she and Susan had their own bunk. The last thing they wanted was Emily with them all the time.

Emily was always hiding things and playing tricks on the counselors and other campers. She took the whistle from Tara, a female counselor for the eight-year-olds and filled it with honey from the camp dining hall, she put ketchup in a counselor's shoes, and put whipped cream on the hairbrushes of some of the girls in the cabin. She's always sneaky and finding a way into some sort of mischief. Although it could be funny to some, everyone always feared they would be next.

Emily tried to be pretty good around Susan. She considered her like a big sister since her parents weren't around. She kept the good behavior for Susan and let her 'Rick side' fly around others.

Susan took the Lynches on a tour of the camp while Emily happily held hands with both her mother and father. Emily was smiling ear to ear, enjoying having all her favorite people with her. She loved spending time with Susan this summer, but she really missed her mommy and daddy. Emily showed her parents the river where they went kayaking, and then took them to the place where the ducks were. It was her favorite place at camp.

Unbeknownst to Susan, Jake was off to the side, watching the whole thing and snapping pictures on his phone, even though he was forbidden to do that. All the counselors had been warned they would be immediately fired for disturbing or photographing the Lynches. Jake thought it was pretty cool and snapped away. He thought that a picture of the Lynches may be worth something someday.

Chapter 28

Hailey laughs her head off as Chad's fake mustache starts to droop a little while they eat their burgers. Chad quickly fixes it and laughs, too. To anyone looking, they definitely made a unique couple. She was all blonde and hippie, while he was overalls and country. But they seemed like a happy couple eating a meal and having fun.

Harding texted Chad to let them know the press was still hanging out outside his apartment and had not followed them. The disguises worked. Chad figured they had a couple good hours before he needed to return to the building as the country boy handyman and leave as Chad the politician.

"I have to admit," Chad commented, smiling at Hailey, "this is fun."

She took a bite of her burger and remarked, "I wasn't going to let the press sabotage this before it even started. I want to get to know you more. So far, I really like the man in front of me, a lot."

Chad blushed just a bit then chuckled. "So, you really like Ben the custodian?" He pointed to the name tag on his overalls.

"Yeah, him, too." Hailey leaned across the table and gave Chad a kiss.

Her phone buzzed and she pulled it out to check on it. She had told Chad her dad mentioned he had the flu. Her parents lived all the way in Des Moines, so she hoped it wasn't her mom saying something was wrong. Her parents were in their late seventies and Midwesterners through and through.

Both Hailey and Marissa had gone to NYU and then never left New York. Hailey had finished with her degree in musical theater and teaching, but Marissa never finished. She met and eloped with Rick her sophomore year when she became pregnant with Emily. Rick was older by eight years and swept Marissa off her feet with his power, looks, and fame. Marissa had been featured in an ad for the college, and her modeling career took off after that.

Rick met her at a photoshoot when she was nineteen-years-old while he was there visiting a friend. She moved in with him after five dates and out of the dorm room she shared with Hailey. Their parents were shocked when Marissa quit college and eloped, but they were okay after meeting Rick. He charmed them with his plans to take care of Marissa and the baby, and how he planned to be the doting husband. They had seen him on TV during interviews, saw his charisma, and knew he had money. With a blind eye they trusted him to take care of Marissa. They flew in one or two times a year to visit. Hailey flew home for the holidays, but Marissa hadn't been home in years.

Hailey looked at her phone, seeing a message from Marissa. "Hey, Sis, we are visiting Emily. Here are some pics. Lunch next week?" A bunch of adorable pictures of her niece immediately followed.

Smiling, Hailey turned the phone around to show Chad. "My niece, Emily."

"She is adorable," complimented Chad, smiling. "She looks like her mom."

"Yes, she does," Hailey agrees. "She has Marissa's looks with a little bit of Rick's daredevil thrown in." She grimaces as she says it. Her dislike for Rick seemed a bit obvious.

Hailey's voice took on a bitter tone whenever she mentioned Rick. Chad didn't want to dive into that at the moment. The less he knew about the Lynches the better he would be. Hailey must have needed to vent because she told him the whole story of Marissa meeting Rick, getting caught up in his charm, eloping, and having Emily at twenty-years-old.

"Marissa was so young and so talented," Hailey began. "Rick swept her off her feet, and then she became pregnant within months of meeting him. She gave up everything for Rick." Chad nodded in understanding, listening to her. "But she has a beautiful daughter, and that is the good that came out of their relationship. Emily is a gift. She can keep you on your toes, but I love her spunk."

Hailey's brow furrowed, continuing with, "I had offered to take Emily for the summer so Marissa could heal, but Rick insisted on her going to camp and the nanny going with her. I can never understand sending an eight-year-old away with a nanny for the summer versus letting her stay with an aunt. But that is Rick for you, controlling through and through."

Sighing heavily, she changed the subject. It always ate her up with worry. She couldn't understand her sister and the pull Rick had on her. She looked at Chad and smiled, knowing if this worked out, he would never be that way. He's not that kind of man.

Chapter 29

Rick and Marissa had a wonderful time with Emily. After the tour, they had lunch with her (hot dogs and baked beans cooked over the campfire), played horseshoes and corn-hole games, and stayed until it was dusk. Rick had to hit the road to be home at a decent time to get up early for work the next day knowing he had a trial.

Marissa had tears in her eyes as she said goodbye to her daughter, knowing she wouldn't see her for three more weeks. She promised to Face Time each night; realizing she had not been the best at keeping in touch, a lump formed in her throat as guilt over leaving her baby overwhelms her. Marissa knew she needed to try harder and be there.

The explosion had literally rocked her world, and she had needed to heal. How do you explain to an eight-year-old your memory was coming and going in spurts? Her stomach turned at the thought of disappointing her daughter, but getting out of bed, or eating a protein shake, had been a chore while she healed.

She just hugged her, held her close and remarked, "Mommy will call you each night and see you soon."

She didn't want to leave her, but all the moms in their circle sent their kids to a sleep away camp at her age. Plus, Marissa knew Susan was keeping an eye on her. Here she was safe from their sordid little world, and Marissa needed time to see doctors and figure out what was going on with her. The memory loss really scared her. Was it a brain tumor? She was going to make doctors' appointments the minute she returned home. Hopefully everything would be back to normal by the time Emily arrived home.

She gave Emily one last hug. Then glancing at Susan, she murmured gratefully, "Thank you." She watched as Rick handed Susan an envelope with a generous bonus amount in it and Susan smiled her appreciation.

The couple then climbed in the Range Rover to head home. Marissa began crying as Rick pulled away. He looked at her tenderly. He had really been trying lately. Reaching out, he took her hand and gave it a squeeze.

"It is the right place for her right now," he remarked.

Marissa nodded and became quiet, getting lost in her own thoughts. He could be so tender one minute and so controlling the next. She held on tight to those tender moments because the controlling ones were the ones that made her want to leave. During the rough times he swore he would take Emily away from her and leave her with nothing as no prenup had been signed. During the good times he held her hand and was the loving supporting man she wanted, like right now.

Marissa saw the man she had fallen in love with and put the thoughts of him being with Lana out of her head. If it ever came down to really leaving him, she had the pictures, the files, and the flash drive with all the information to bring him down stashed away. But today wasn't the day to fight.

She squeezed his hand back. She was enjoying this moment and looked lovingly up at the Rick he was right now. She truly wished this was the man she could see every day. She loved this side of him.

Chapter 30

Chad returned to Harding's apartment a few hours later still dressed as Ben the custodian. He walked right past the press and into the building showing the fake ID Harding had made up for him to the guard.

"New guy," he stated, nodding at the night doorman.

"Hey, welcome aboard," he proclaimed, buzzing him into the elevator.

"Thanks." Chad nodded and took the elevator to Harding's and knocked on the door. As Harding pulled the door open, Chad arched his eyebrows in question, saying, "Heard you were having trouble with the hot water."

Harding lets him in, smirking. "Your mustache is a little bent, must have been a good date."

Chad smirked back. "She is incredible."

Harding nodded. "I can see that. She seems so genuine and so unlike her sister's reputation."

They talked for a bit more and Harding agreed to help him out for a bit. "Listen Chad, whatever you need," he commented, "I like seeing you happy, buddy."

Chad smiles in response and pats Harding on the shoulder. "Thanks."

Jillian strides into the room, announcing, "Dad called, apparently grandma got to him."

Chad groaned. "My life, my choices," he states, pushing back his baseball cap. "Listen, I agreed to run, but I am not going to compromise my personal life for a campaign."

Jillian looks at Harding. "Jeez, she must be something special. I have never seen you like this, Chad."

"Like what?" he challenged, feeling defensive. "They are overstepping, just because Hailey is a Lynch relative doesn't make her guilty by association."

Jillian and Harding meet each other's eyes. Harding mouths, "Drop it," to his wife.

She nodded and looked at Chad. He was her brother, and he was obviously hurting. "It's your life, Chad," she added in agreement. "Remember that."

Chad stayed for a few more minutes and changed out of the costume. He left the apartment as Chad put Ben in the duffel bag. He headed back to his apartment shadowed by the press. He turned, waved, and gave them a good candidate smile as he headed into his building.

He texted Hailey when he got into his place. "Ben says goodnight."

Hailey texted right back. "The nanny can't wait to see you again."

Chad went to sleep with a smile, wishing Hailey was here with him now. He was a gentleman, but not a saint and the chemistry between them felt incredible. She had asked him for a little more time before they went to the next level of their relationship. Until then, he would be taking lots of cold showers, but she was worth the wait.

Chapter 31

Marissa made plans for lunch with Hailey at a little tea house they both loved on the upper East side of Manhattan. Marissa left her long chestnut hair down today. She could be herself with her sister. She wore a light summer dress and a pair of sandals, flats in case they did some walking.

She and Hailey tried to see each other when they could, but Rick sometimes put a barrier between them. He liked spur of the moment trips and sent her to the spa often when he felt her anxiety was acting up.

It was funny, Marissa always felt refreshed after the spa trips, but had minimal memory of being there other than the protein shakes and her hair being washed. She guessed she enjoyed them, Rick always said she did.

The one thing that truly bothered her with Rick was his controlling ways. He liked to know her plans from morning to night. Had he always been like that? Yes, to some degree.

The beginning had been amazing. He truly swept her off her feet in a passionate affair. He had been dating Lana all through college, and that ended once he spotted Marissa modeling a bikini for an ad. She and Rick were inseparable after that, their love and passion quickly became all consuming.

Rick had learned to hide his demons from Marissa, showing her his best side. The real Rick didn't show up until after Emily was born. He would hold it together professionally and personally, but then he started to lose it at times. Walls had to be repaired when he punched them in anger, he would go into his phases where he was up all night working out to burn off steam. He would leave the house sometimes at 2 a.m. and come home to change clothes before leaving again for work.

When Marissa questioned him, he would shut her up with four words, "My business, not yours." Shortly after one of these incidents, he would be loving and the wonderful Rick. Despite his flaws, Marissa loved him fiercely, but feared him as well.

Marissa spots Hailey coming in. She looks summery and cool wearing linen pants and a light green t-shirt. Marissa waves her over with her French manicured hand. "Hi, Hailey," she greets her as she approaches.

"Hey, Maris," she stated, taking a seat across from her at the tea house. "Looking good."

Hailey eyes her sister. She looks so thin. She knew Marissa would go through periods of not eating from anxiety and lose weight. She told her sister that sometimes all she could handle were protein shakes. Hailey worried constantly about Marissa, but Marissa was Marissa and wouldn't take suggestions or advice readily. Hailey knew this from experience.

Hailey pushes a stray lock off her face and uses that as an excuse to turn her head so Marissa wouldn't see the concerned expression in her eyes. When she turns back to Marissa, she plasters a smile on her face and continues the conversation.

"Hey! How was the visit with Emily?" Hailey asks her once she sits down on the white wicker restaurant chair.

"She is loving camp," Marissa states, smiling. "I am not used to this sleep away camp idea, but knowing she is with the nanny makes it okay. I mean Rick and I needed the time."

Hailey kept her thoughts to herself and bit the inside of her cheek to keep from expressing her feelings on an eight-year-old at sleep away camp and Marissa and Rick. That was a whole 'nother ball game. She didn't understand why her sister stayed with him. He was good looking and rich, but so controlling and complicated. Marissa knew he wasn't a saint and had talked of leaving him many times, but she always went back.

"Hailey, I feel like something is wrong with me." She paused, looked around the tea house to make sure no one else was listening. "I am having these very weird periods of memory loss. I can't remember going to the spa, although I know I was there. Plus, it's happened before."

Hailey looks at her sister, her eyes wide open and the first thought that comes to her head is stress. Marissa lived in a constant state of stress.

"When did this start?" Hailey questioned, leaning closer over the table, concerned.

"It's been on and off for a while, but more frequently the past few months," Marissa explained, taking a drink of the iced tea she ordered.

The waitress wearing her black apron over her blue uniform stared at them both in shocked recognition, her brown eyes going wide. Hailey and Marissa hear her whisper, "The Lynch lady is here with her sister, wow!"

Hailey smiles and waves at the two waitresses gawking at them, while Marissa glowered. She hated the attention when she was trying to just relax with her sister.

"Can you just bring us our meal please?" she snapped.

The waitress scurried away with an embarrassed look. Her cheeks turned red, obviously upset with Marissa's tone.

"Marissa, you could have been a little nicer," Hailey comments, frowning.

"I can't anymore," Marissa remarks, squeezing some lemon into the tea. Hailey could sense Marissa's stress, and let the comment slide, but she wished her sister wasn't so sharp tongued sometimes. "Will you come with me to the doctor?" She looks intently at her twin, her blue eyes meeting her sister's green ones. "I am scared, Hailey, really scared."

"Of course," Hailey agreed, nodding. "I'll be there."

Marissa breathed a sigh of relief and attempted to change the subject to something happier, "Now, tell me about Chad."

Chapter 32

Chad stopped at his campaign office and saw several volunteers on the phone making some calls and reminding New Yorkers to register to vote. The August heat was fierce prompting the air conditioning to be cranking overtime. The TV mounted upon the wall has the news playing at a low volume drawing attention as needed, but not disturbing the workflow.

Chad wants nothing more than to shed his suit and tie. The meteorologist, Reeve Hanson, was talking about a massive heat wave and temperatures in the 90's for the next seven days. The last thing Chad wanted was to be in the office in this weather.

He longed for a day on his boat and a night with Hailey. He had plans to see Hailey again tomorrow night, or at least someone did. Hailey said they needed to switch up the costumes if they were meeting at each other's places and keep Ben and the hippie girl for when they met at Harding's. Seemed strangely fun.

This was a very different relationship for him, but what the heck, it beat all the women like Trina in his life, and Hailey just made him smile. He was having very strong feelings for her; his heart began beating quicker every time he thought about her. He couldn't get her out of his head.

Chad walked over and thanked the volunteers for coming out to help. He noticed some of them putting labels on the campaign literature featuring his smiling face and reasons why he should be elected. Words like, "Moral, out for the people, and leader," leapt off the page.

Chad would do everything in his power to uphold the standard his dad set in his twelve years of being in office. He's starting to see how honorable a position it was, and he would do the best he could to step up to the plate if he were elected.

He stayed for a few hours, making phone calls, labeling brochures, and truly getting to know the volunteers. Many were retirees who remembered, "the good old days of politics." They saw Chad as refreshing and unjaded. They were all fond of Thad and wanted to be there for his son. Chad treated them all to sandwiches from the local deli. The volunteers smiled, grateful and stayed longer, embracing Chad's energy and morals.

Chad left for home around 4 p.m. He wanted to shave, shower, and be ready for his date with Hailey. He keyed into his apartment and was so grateful for the rush of cold air that greeted him, he breathed a sigh of relief as he shut the door behind him. His AC was a welcome relief from the stifling heat. Chad whipped off his shirt and tie, tossing them on the couch and stood there in his t-shirt and pants, grabbed the remote, and turned the TV on, flipping it to ESPN.

He looked forward to a shower, changing into shorts, and seeing Hailey. They were going to head down to the beach tonight. He hated the thought of having to wear a disguise, but you had to do what you had to do. The press followed him home from headquarters, and he knew they would be there when he left.

Who should he be tonight? Maybe he would wear the wild outfit and match Hailey tit for tat.

He couldn't wait to see her smile and find out how her day was. He was also looking forward to seeing what she would be dressed as. Things were definitely heating up with her. She was everything he wanted and more. Chad knew he had to focus on the campaign and his work, but when a man needed a distraction, he needed a distraction. Hailey was so caring, fun, intelligent and gorgeous.

Grabbing his phone, he texted her, "See you at 7 p.m. at the Beach Hut. I'll be the one wearing the blue hat." He laughed as he hit send. He had the hat from his theater stash, now he had to go through the duffel bag and find the rest of the costume.

Chad stepped into the shower, putting the costume on hold. He lathered up over his muscled body and the stream of water cooled his hot skin. He felt refreshed when he stepped out, wrapped himself in a towel, and walked into his bedroom to change.

"Well, hello there," a sexy feminine voice coming from his bed startled Chad.

Gasping, he almost dropped his towel in shock. He recognized that voice and stiffened. Turning slowly, he looked at the scantily dressed woman laying across his bed. Chad was taken back at the sight of her, and truly angry. His eyes widened, before quickly narrowing. He shouted, "Trina, what the hell?"

Trina smiled seductively and purred, "I've missed you, Chad, come here."

Chad grabbed his boxers and a T-shirt and swiftly threw them on. "Trina, we are done. What the hell are you doing here?"

Trina climbed off the bed and sauntered over to Chad. She's wearing a red negligee which left nothing to the imagination. She put her arms around his neck and purred, "You know you have missed this."

Chad clenched his teeth as he unhinged her arms from around his neck. "You are embarrassing yourself. We are done. Leave, go back to your surgeon and leave the key on the table." He looked at her pointedly. "We are done," he reiterated and turned his back, leaving her in the room to get dressed.

This was so out of character for her, and just plain awkward. Why would she do something like this? It feels like it came from out of nowhere. So much for her being heavily involved with the doctor, what the heck?

He had moved away from Trina and on to Hailey. She needed to move on as well.

Trina came out a few minutes later crying. "I would have made the perfect senator's wife, even your family thinks so." She threw the key and the keychain at him, barely missing his head and stormed out with a smirk.

He didn't like the smirk, it made him feel uneasy. She was up to something, he just needed to figure out what.

Chapter 33

Rick paced back and forth in his apartment. It was Tuesday night and his trial had gone well. He had a TV interview tomorrow to talk about being a trial attorney for a talk show, and he needed to see Lana. She hadn't returned his texts, and their rule was not to call. He stared at his phone. He was giving her an hour and then he was going to call. She was annoying him. Rick clenched his jaw in frustration and pounded his fist on the table. Trevor was acting the same, so he wasn't the issue. Lana was. What the hell was up with her?

The flame from the passion he and Lana had shared couldn't be put out, even after they broke up. They would be incompatible as partners since they were so volatile when together, but their chemistry was undeniable. Almost consistently for ten years, they had carved out two nights a week to satisfy their physical needs, then returned to their significant others.

It worked well for them. They were both emotionless souls who could separate this from their lives. They both had always felt like their coming together those two nights a week were as necessary as eating and breathing. They were like magnets drawn to each other, but in reality, had minimal feelings for each other. Lana was awed by Rick, attracted to him, but she did not like him. Rick thought Lana to be sensuous, gorgeous, but he did not respect any woman who cheated on their husband.

Yet, two nights a week for the last decade, they met at the hotel in their suite, had their hour of intense passion and went their separate ways. It worked. Why was Lana changing the game? Why the hell was she changing the game?

Rick wanted to pound his fist into the wall but went to his punching bag instead. He then turned to his weights and finally the bike. It helped to curb his anger a bit, but not enough. Finally, after forty-five minutes a text came through from Lana. "I can't tonight, not feeling well."

Rick looked at the phone, unsure of what to believe, but that could be plausible as a flu was going around. He glared at the phone and cold-heartedly wrote, "Make next week happen," and pushed send.

He showered, found Marissa, and planned a romantic dinner with her. He had an Italian place in mind he had wanted to check out for a while on the Upper West side. He couldn't have Lana, so Marissa would do.

Chapter 34

Chad could not get over Trina being in his bed and pulling that stunt. When they had broken up, they had amicably parted ways, both realizing that it wasn't meant to be. She moved on to a surgeon and now he had started dating Hailey. He didn't get what had gotten into her and made her do something so extreme. It wasn't flattering, it was disturbing.

Immediately, he called the locksmith, changed the locks, and spoke to the doorman about keeping her out. He was going to tell Hailey what happened. He wasn't the type to keep secrets from one relationship to another. He wanted to see where this would go with Hailey, and it was best to not have secrets. They had been together over a month now, and he could definitely see them going the long haul.

Chad walked out of his building as himself. The press seemed to be buzzing around him more than usual.

"Is it true that you are back with Trina? We just saw her leave the building. Why was she so upset?"

Another reporter jumped in. "Does Hailey know about Trina?"

Chad was taken back but stopped in his tracks to give them a quote. "My personal life is just that, personal. I care about the community and my job right now is to focus on the people. I am heading over to my brother-in-law's place to work on my campaign. If you'll excuse me, I am late. Thank you for your time."

He walked the six blocks to Harding and Jillian's with the press trailing him. Joe the doorman stood at the entrance, and he commented, "You can't catch a break," as he buzzed him up to Harding's place.

Chad arrived at the apartment and filled Harding in. "She did what?" Harding questioned, his tone shocked as he ran his fingers through his hair. "We are talking about conservative Trina? The true lady Trina?"

True Lady Trina was what the press had dubbed her years ago. Trina came from an old money; a high-profile family who had been in the press for years just for being wealthy. Trina was always profiled for being the lady through her years of boarding school and European trips. She did everything right while her petulant younger sister was climbing out windows to run off with an assortment of shady guys throughout high school. The press loved the extremes in one family. Trina was True Lady Trina, and her sister was Midnight Meghan.

"Yup," Chad confirmed, nodding. "Red negligee and all. I have no idea what got into her." He paced the room, his anxiety growing. "It's all about Hailey for me, Harding. Trina and I have been done for months and not so much as a text or phone call since we broke up. We were both done."

Jillian stepped out of the playroom after hearing her brother's voice. She had caught most of the conversation. Grimacing, she announced, "I know what got into Trina tonight. She had tea with grandma yesterday. Grandma Cecelia is at it again."

Chapter 35

Rick brought Marissa to the set the next day. He never did that before, but last night had been so romantic and passionate, just like how they were in the beginning. His anger over Lana had dissipated as he realized he and his wife could enjoy the evening. Their private chef came over and whipped them up a dinner of filet mignon, twice baked potatoes, and asparagus. They had taken a quiet walk and settled on the rooftop of their penthouse apartment to look at the stars. The night ended with some passionate love making.

Ever since their visit to see Emily, he and Marissa had been doing well. The volatility had faded with their time alone. So, Rick, still in the moment, brought Marissa to the set.

Marissa marveled at the pictures on the wall of all the celebrities who had been interviewed there. Rick's picture hung next to the others as he was a frequent guest on the show. True, Rick was considered to be a ruthless and brilliant trial attorney. His feared and daunting reputation followed him everywhere, but the people remained fascinated by him, and the ratings always went up when he was on the show.

The production assistant led Marissa to the green room to watch her husband do the interview. The green room was tastefully decorated with leather couches, a coffee maker which was brewing fresh coffee on a small table off to the side, and a big screen TV. A tray of fresh fruit and assorted pastries sat in the center of the coffee table.

Marissa settled in on one of the brown leather couches excitedly watching the process. She listened as the anchors chatted about their line up and saw a glimpse of Rick being wired with the microphones. They were going to go on shortly.

The door to the green room opened and Marissa recognized the man coming into the room as Reeve Hanson, meteorologist. She smiled warmly at him.

"Mrs. Lynch," he commented, smiling back at her. "Sorry to bother you, but the coffee maker decided to die today in our breakroom, and I need my fix."

Marissa nodded and said, "Good morning! Reeve smiled at her and waved. "Please tell me it will be a sunny day."

Marissa takes in his classic handsome looks and broad smile. He seems like a nice guy, and she had heard he was a new dad.

"How's the baby?" she asks, smiling at him, her turquoise eyes bright.

Reeve, being a proud dad, pulled out his phone, showing Marissa his son, Niles. He kept Marissa occupied for a few minutes with pictures. "He is adorable," Marissa remarked. "It's such a fun age, right?"

"Oh, it is," Reeve commented, showing her a picture of his son in a blue swing at the park. Niles can be seen smiling a huge smile as Reeves' pretty, brunette wife stood behind him pushing the swing.

"Your wife is very pretty," Marissa added, smiling.

"Thank you," Reeve replied. Suddenly, Marissa became distracted by the TV monitor. "Nice talking to you, Marissa," Reeve added, noticing her distraction.

Marissa smiled and waved. "Thank you, you too." She spun back towards the monitor as he discreetly slipped out of the room. She turned her attention to Rick's interview. Marissa was sorry Reeve left, he seemed like a nice guy and she enjoyed talking to him. She hoped he cherishes the time with the baby, they grow up so quickly.

Rick was charismatic on camera. Marissa watched with pride as he debated with another legal expert about whether a statement is hearsay or not in a trial. The other legal expert continued questioning Rick's strategic approach to his questioning witnesses. Rick pushed bringing up the importance of cross examining a witness on something you know is not true.

"You have to back it up," Rick insisted. "It just can't come out of the blue."

He began citing examples of cases when this occurred, and the other legal expert soon backed down. It turned ugly at one point when the other expert accused Rick of being deceitful and getting dregs of society off the hook. But Rick never wavered, and despite there being some truth to his accusations, Rick turned the other legal expert into on-air mincemeat.

The beautiful talk show host used all her powers of persuasion to calm the two guests down, but she had her work cut out for her. "And that is why we bring you both sides of the story. See you next week on Both Sides of the Coin. This is Tara Holiday saying, 'make it a good day.'"

"Cut," yells the director.

Followed by the assistant director calling out, "That's a wrap!" Tara looked at both her guests, thanked them, and hurried off the stage. She had enough of the two male egos sitting in front of her and just wanted a cup of coffee.

Rick eventually found his way to the green room and to Marissa who gave him a half smile. She hoped his ruthless attitude on camera did not carry over into a day which was supposed to be fun for them. They had plans to go for lunch and a museum after the show.

Luckily, Rick was jovial and on a high. He knew he would be invited back after that one. Audiences love that stuff.

"What did you think?" he asked her, taking off his tie and loosening his collar buttons.

"I think that you are a force," stated Marissa, looking at him with both awe and fear.

He smiled with a cold look that reached his eyes. For a moment he turned into the other Rick, the one she feared. He took her hand in his, gave it a squeeze, and stated, "Don't you forget it."

She never could and never would. She always felt her stomach churn when Rick reacted this way. She hated his possessiveness. Her eyes went downcast for a moment, and she looked back at Rick in disdain. Off to the side, Reeve Hanson observed the whole thing and felt chills down his spine enhanced by seeing the look on Rick's face along with Marissa's look of fear.

Chapter 36

Chad left Harding's apartment in a wig with dreadlocks, a blue baseball cap, baggy shorts, and a shirt that said, Hang Loose. He looked like a reggae loving surfer dude. He walked right past the doorman and the press without anyone looking at him twice. He gave the hang loose sign to a young guy walking his dog and the guy gave it back to him.

Chad had to admit he loved the costume thing. Harding and Jillian had cracked up, but they too admitted it was a clever way to date Hailey and keep this aspect of his privacy, at least for now. Chad borrowed Harding's truck to drive the forty minutes to the beach.

He pretended to be on the phone when he walked by the press earlier and was overheard saying to the person on the other end that he would be spending the night at Jillian and Harding's. The photographers overheard him, sighed, and left their watch. They knew they weren't going to get the "big picture" tonight. They even wondered if Chad was still seeing Hailey. They hadn't been spotted together since their first date, while Trina was seen coming out of his apartment crying.

Chad got in the truck and texted Hailey, "I'm on my way."

She replied, "Can't wait."

They booked a beachside hotel room under the name, Ben Watkins. It would be their first overnight together. He was so happy. Their relationship had escalated to intimate more rapidly than either of them anticipated, but it feels right. They were falling in love. He was glad to finally spend the night and not have to scramble out of her apartment at midnight to get to Harding's to change back into his suit. It was truly exhausting being different people, but a man has to do what he has to do. Hailey was so worth it.

Chad parked the truck and walked onto the beach. It was a nice night and he smelled suntan lotion and salt water. He fixed his dreads and baseball cap, took a seat on the bench by the concession stand they agreed to meet at, and waited for Hailey. She said she would be wearing a pink hat.

Within minutes Chad's eyes locked with Hailey who ironically was dressed in a wig of blonde dreadlocks, a bright pink wide brimmed hat, and wearing a tie dye sundress and espadrille sandals. They both burst out laughing when they saw each other. Chad brought her in for a kiss and they held onto each other for a bit. Hailey was the first to break away.

"Great minds think alike," she said laughing.

"I could get into this look," Chad mumbled, giving her the hang loose sign.

She laughed again. They did get a few looks when they entered the Beach Hut, but the crowd there had a few and appeared to only be interested in their drinks and appetizers. It seemed the crowd didn't care who was there. The Friday night crowd looked at the dreadlock couple and thought they looked chill and went back to their business of hanging out on a Friday night. Work was done for the week; they didn't seem to have a care in the world.

Ironically, a reggae band was being featured that night, so most of the crowd had come down to hear them play. Chad and Hailey fit right in. The hostess seated them close to the stage. They smiled in appreciation looking forward to their night together, and the fact they were staying over at the motel down the road.

"So, about Trina," Hailey began, sipping her iced tea when it was placed before her. "Do you see this as the end?"

Chad called Hailey soon after he asked Trina to leave after that stunt. He didn't want any secrets between them.

"Listen, we weren't in love. It was good for a time, and then it ran its course. This," he said, pointing to them both "is love. This," he took her hand, claiming, "is the real deal."

Hailey smiled at him and held his right hand. "I love you, too," she said to him, smiling. "I know what you mean. After a while the spark burned out for Steve and I."

Chad nodded. "I don't care how long we have to wear get-ups and be low key, I just want it to feel like this."

They looked deeply into each other's eyes. Dreadlocks kept falling into their faces, but they didn't care. The senatorial candidate and the sister-in-law of the bad-boy attorney were having a great time together and falling in love like it was meant to be.

As they were enjoying their meal, the reggae band started playing. They had some really good sound, and Chad and Hailey were talking softly, loud enough to be heard over the music, eating their crab cakes, and listening to the music.

"Yaa, man," the singer in the band called out, "we need a drummer up here. Someone out there with some rhythm needs to come on up and join us." He scanned the audience and spotted dreadlock Chad deciding to focus right on him. "Yaa, man." He jumped off the stage and sauntered on over with the mic to Chad. "What's up?"

Chad's eyes widened, looking like a deer caught in the headlights when the spotlight went on him.

Great, he thought. My cover is blown.

In reality, the audience was checking out the guy in the dreads and the Hang Loose T-shirt, not Chad.

"Go on up, man!" the crowd shouted all around them. "Get up there."

The singer with the microphone laughed. "They want you, man. Come on up and let's get drumming."

Chad looked at Hailey who shrugged her shoulders and laughed. Chad, aka Reggie, the name he told the band, went up on stage. He was suddenly really grateful for the drum lessons he took when he was eleven-years-old. They put him in front of the reggae bass drum and taught him a basic rhythm. Reggie caught right on and with dreads flying got into the music. The audience went wild.

"Reggie, Reggie," they chanted as he took off on his own beat doing his own thing.

It felt incredibly freeing, and Chad loved every minute of it. He finished the song with the band, receiving a standing ovation, and took a bow before returning to the table to a grinning Hailey.

She laughed when he sat down. "Guess who is performing with my chorus at their next concert."

Chad grinned. "Anytime. I hope to be around for many concerts...Yaa, man."

Chapter 37

Rick and Marissa strolled arm and arm through Central Park. It had been a nice day. After leaving the studio, they headed for a light lunch at Elegant Eatery. As usual, they received many looks and one older woman even approached Rick for his autograph, which he signed with a smile. Rick liked to be recognized. With recognition came a sense of power. And he loved power.

"This is nice," Marissa stated, looking up at Rick.

They made a striking couple, he in his dark suit, and she in an electric blue sundress which brought out her turquoise eyes. One couldn't help looking and admiring them.

Rick, as always, was discretely shadowed by his bodyguards when out in public. He asked them to blend and not be noticed, but he knew they were there. He generally had one on Emily, too, when she walked with her nanny to and from school. Although, he didn't have one for her at camp, knowing she was safe so far away on camp property.

"This is nice," Rick agreed, and he genuinely felt that way.

The talk show had gone well. His cell was buzzing with the press wanting follow-ups on the tidbits he revealed on the show. Rick knew how to keep his name in the press, and what he said would definitely cause a stir. He liked it that way. Then, he had a nice lunch with Marissa, enjoying a glass of wine and delicious filet mignon and roasted potatoes.

During lunch, Lana had texted, "I need to talk to you." He was ready for her to grovel, but he put her on mute and gave his attention to his wife.

"Rick," Marissa whispered, looking up at him "do you remember when we took a carriage ride when we were dating?"

Rick smiled down at her. "Of course, I do. It was the day I proposed. You had just found out you were pregnant with Emily, and it was such a happy moment."

She smiled back at him. He and she had the same thought at the same time. Why couldn't it always be like this? Rick looked at Marissa and lovingly summoned a horse and carriage. He whistled loudly enough for the driver to bring over a beautiful white stallion attached to a polished wood carriage. He signaled the bodyguards to let them know what he was going to do, and they nodded in acknowledgement. They would travel by foot and shadow the slow-moving carriage.

Marissa hopped in with Rick's help. Then, looking towards the driver, he tipped him handsomely and mentioned, "Take us around twice." He put Lana and the press out of his mind, and remained the good Rick, the one Marissa had fallen in love with.

That night, Marissa and Rick had an amazing night of passion. It was an unforgettable night for them both. Rick almost didn't even want to see Lana anymore...almost.

Chapter 38

Hailey woke up in Chad's arms after an incredibly romantic night. She is so in love with him and could see them going the distance. She cuddled next to him on the white satin sheets and pulled the beige comforter around her tighter. She felt safe and warm in his arms. Her heart fluttered when he turned to her with a sweet smile on his lips.

"Good morning," Chad whispered to her in a deep sexy voice. He had been awake for a few minutes already and was just enjoying watching her sleep.

She was beautiful, like an angel. He didn't want this to end, or for her to leave his arms. They still had the morning together, and then Chad had to leave to do some meet and greets and street fairs. It was time to rev up the campaign.

Hailey had to be at the theater at 1 p.m. to play the piano for the kids' play practice. "Play practice today at 1, but can we get together later?" she inquired, her green eyes staring into his blue ones.

He leaned in to kiss her then and whispered, "Can't wait."

"Me either," she whispered, kissing him back. They planned to spend a little time together here in the room and then venture out in their dreads to breakfast. Hailey turned to Chad, admiring him with a bright smile, and their talking ceased for a while as their passion took over.

Later, they ventured out to the boardwalk and stood side by side mumbling phrases such as, "Yaa, man," and "Hang loose." Hailey took a few selfies and they set off hand in hand to brunch. They made a striking couple despite their costumes.

A few random people recognized Reggie from the night before and complimented him on his, "Sick beat," on the drums.

Chad gave them the hang loose sign and uttered, "Thanks, man." He was enjoying this.

Hailey turned to him and put her arms around his neck and pulled him in for a kiss. "I don't want this to end," she whispered, looking into his eyes.

"It doesn't have to," Chad declares, looking down on her. "I'm not going anywhere."

Just then Chad's cell phone buzzed and ruined the moment. He saw Harding's name flash on the screen and knew he needed to answer. Talk about ruining a romantic moment.

"What's up?" he asked grumpily. "I was planning to be there in an hour." Pausing, he replied, "Yes, she's still here." Chad smiled at Hailey. "No, we didn't turn on the news. We have been a bit busy." Chad laughed and grabbed Hailey playfully around the waist. She laughed and leaned into him.

He suddenly stopped, his smile falling and his hands dropping to his sides as he utters, "She did what? I'll be right there." He hung up from Harding, his face a little white and commented, "Trina is out for revenge."

"Oh no," Hailey replied, her face marred with concern. "What is she capable of?"

"The problem is, I don't know," replied Chad looking flustered. His eyes locked with Hailey's. "I need to find out."

The romantic mood was quickly broken as they went back to the seaside hotel and packed up their things. Chad roughly threw his clothes into the suitcase and Hailey, sensing his mood, gave him his space. When they were done, he called for car service. Closing the door of the hotel room as they left, Chad put his arms around Hailey and whispered, "Promise me that you will trust in us. I won't let Trina ruin me or what we have."

In response, Hailey kissed him. Pulling back, she insisted, "She won't." They walked off hand in hand and headed back to the city.

Chapter 39

Rick desperately needed to see Lana, he just needed to. It had been over two arduous weeks and it had never been that long. He didn't love her, sometimes he didn't even like her, but he needed her. She was like air to him. He needed it to breathe. He believed he needed Lana to be the complete version of himself. She was like the drugs he used to self-medicate and regulate. The two hours a week of being with her fueled him.

Lana was his intellectual equal as well. Their physical actions satisfied that need, yet their verbal sparring satisfied another need. Lana was the female version of him. She could debate politics, current events, and finances. He missed that. He just needed to see her.

It was Tuesday night and she agreed to meet him in the suite at the hotel. Marissa was taking a tennis lesson and he told her he was doing the usual, working out with his trainer. She gave him a look when he left, one he hadn't seen before. She stared at him intensely, her blue eyes blazing. He turned away from her stare and went back to packing his gym bag. "What's with the look?" he inquired.

"Just going to miss you," Marissa stated.

"I need a good workout," Rick answered. "Then I will be home and we can do something." Marissa nodded, still looking forlorn.

They had been doing well together. It has been a romantic, calm two weeks and he had fallen in love again with his wife. She was behaving, she wasn't questioning his actions. She was just being the sweet girl he had been captivated by when she was nineteen-years-old. This all was wonderful to Rick, yet he still had to see Lana.

Rick got there ahead of Lana. He got to the hotel, entered the elevator, and pushed the button to the penthouse. A hand appeared and pushed the door open just as it was about to close. The man stepped inside, and Rick stiffened as his eyes met Trevor's, his partner.

Trevor looked a bit flustered when he saw Rick in the elevator and then quickly regained his composure. "Hey," he mumbled to Rick, "you and Marissa staying here, too?"

Rick clenched his fist and tried to keep calm. "You're staying here?" he asked Trevor, debating what button to push and what floor to get off on, even though he had already pushed the buttons for the penthouse.

He was not prepared to have the husband of his mistress at the same hotel he was in. What was going on? What was Lana up to? Did Lana even know he was here? Trevor and Rick were never at a loss for words with each other and filled the awkwardness with talk of sports and current events. Neither went into detail on why they were there.

Trevor pushed the 18th floor and Rick the 20th. It was not his real destination, but he didn't want Trevor to push the button for the penthouse in case this wasn't Lana's doing. They were climbing 14...15...16...17... and suddenly the elevator came to a jerking stop. The lights flickered wildly. Rick and Trevor were tossed around a bit and suddenly all went dark as the elevator screeched to a halt. They were stuck. Trevor's eyes went wide with shock, and he reached over to steady Rick, who momentarily lost his balance. They both looked at each other with stunned expressions as the elevator settled to its stop.

Chapter 40

Chad was fuming. His blue eyes darkened at the thought of what she could do, as his jaw clenched in extreme frustration. Word was out that Trina was going on The Chat to talk about him and his campaign. They hadn't parted on good terms and apparently, she was really angry about the rejection and that he had a hot date with Hailey. The press loved Trina. This couldn't be good for him. Word also got back to him that his grandmother was going to phone in adding fuel to the fire that was already raging inside of him.

When he called his grandmother, she claimed, "Oh, Chadwick, we are doing what is best to ensure your candidacy."

Chad once again began fuming. He asked Harding to speak to her and stop her. He would deal with Trina. Chad tried to call her, but she didn't answer and blocked his text messages. He figured if he had a conversation with her, she would be reasonable. She was always very level-headed when they were in a relationship. He had to get to her before she went on the air. He knew she would regret it later if she said something to ruin him.

Chad arrived at the station and stepped into the elevator to go to the fourth floor. Standing in front of him when he got in the elevator, he saw the meteorologist, Reeve. He greeted Chad with a friendly, "Hello."

Chad nodded his hello, intent on stopping Trina and focused on what he wanted to say. While Reeve stood off to the side checking his text messages. The elevator began to move and then suddenly with a jerking motion it stopped, the lights flickered and went black. The elevator was stuck. Chad and Reeve were left in the dark and startled.

"What the heck?" Chad grumbled.

Reeve looked at him in the dim light from the one bulb working in the elevator. "Hopefully it'll just be a minute."

"Yeah," murmured Chad, eyeing the elevator phone. He picked it up and after about ten rings, the guard on the fourth floor picked it up. "We're stuck in the elevator."

"We know," the guard affirmed. "You two and five people in the one next to you, I see you all on the backup camera on my phone. It's a blackout. Hopefully you are up and running in a few."

His shoulders sagging, Chad mumbled, "Thanks." Then, he glanced at Reeve as he hung up, informing him, "Blackout."

"Wonderful," grumbled Reeve, sighing. He was due on the air in ten minutes.

Chapter 41

The camp where Emily was with Susan also went dark. The kids were all screaming. It was pure chaos. The counselors quickly took out flash-lights and tried to make it fun for the kids. They tried playing games and had them make shadow puppets on the wall.

Emily and Susan were already back in their own cabin for the day and Emily began showing her petulant side.

"I don't like the dark, and I am missing my shows," she whined.

"No one likes the dark," comments Susan. "Let's have fun with flashlights." She tried to entertain Emily and it worked for a bit, but then she became bored.

Jake texted, "Boys going insane. It's my night off, too. Wanna meet?"

Susan texted back, "If she goes to sleep. She doesn't like this and she's nervous."

She wanted to see Jake so badly. She was so torn with being infatuated with the hot guy and her responsibilities. She always reasoned if Emily was asleep, she was fine, and Susan was entitled to a little free time. Tonight, though, she felt obligated to Emily.

A thought suddenly popped into her head. Her mother rented a cabin for a week down the road with her sleazy boyfriend. They just arrived and Susan had seen them briefly earlier.

She hated him at first sight. He was a greasy looking guy, typical type her mother went for, and the type that made her own stomach churn. They met when he came into the diner where her mother worked as a waitress. Her mom always had horrible taste in men, but she was a good woman and good with kids.

Susan really wanted to see Jake. Who better to watch Emily than her mom? She sent her mom a text, "Mom, power is out here, can we come over? Emily is miserable."

Her mom replied immediately, "Sure and we have a generator."

Done deal! She would get her time in with her hot man and Emily could watch her shows. Seemed like a perfect plan.

Oh, Jake, she thought, tonight may be your lucky night.

Chapter 42

Marissa stood in the darkness of her Park Avenue Manhattan penthouse apartment. The candles she had lit gave an eerie glow and her cell phone service was spotty at best. She texted Rick, "Are you ok at the gym? Coming home?"

She wanted him here with her. She hadn't had a memory loss episode in a bit, but the post-traumatic stress from the boat accident made her more skittish than usual. She sent a text to Hailey, "Doing ok? I don't like this."

Her text rolled around and didn't seem to send. Marissa tried again and the same thing happened. She tried to text Rick again and the same thing happened with him. Was cell service down? Could this get any worse? Stuck without power and no cell service. This gave her a very eerie feeling. Her stomach began churning and she felt incredibly queasy.

She tried to call Susan from the house phone to check on Emily, forgetting that it wouldn't work without the power. She hung up the phone in frustration. Was the camp affected? She didn't know. It's two hours away, but she didn't know how far the blackout went. It's not like she could turn on the news or even the internet to check. She wanted to hear her daughter's voice, her husband's voice. This whole thing was freaking her out! Her heart started to race.

. . . .

Emily happily got in Susan's blue 2017 Camry. She was miserable without her Nick at Night shows. Susan said her mom had something called a generator which would let her watch TV, so she was excited to go. Susan had her bring her purple sleeping bag, a change of clothes, and her teddy bear. This felt like an adventure and Emily, like her dad, loved adventures.

Susan tried to send texts to Rick and Marissa letting them know she was taking Emily to her mom's, but the texts wouldn't go through. She would try them again later. They had been checking in and Face Timing a lot more since their visit, Emily was so much happier since they had visited, and was excitedly due to go home next week. She had a lot of fun at camp and made some new friends, but she missed her mom and dad.

Susan's thoughts drifted to hot Jake. She wondered if she would still see him after the summer was over. She hoped so, but for now she would focus on tonight. He was picking her up at her mom's and they were going to a party with a big campfire down on the beach. The counselors all met at that same spot many times over the summer, and they always had a fun time.

She couldn't wait. She was so glad her mom was there to help. Jake was picking her up at their cabin so her mother could meet him. Susan asked him to borrow a car tonight and not ride his motorcycle, hoping for a good first impression. She still really liked to get her mom's approval.

Susan pulled up the driveway and saw her mom standing outside taking in the fresh mountain air. Her mom looked older than her forty-six years, life hadn't been easy for her working as a waitress for ten-hour shifts for extra money and raising Susan alone. But she did it. She always made sure Susan went to the library each week, played after school sports, and arranged carpools to get her rides to school plays and dances not wanting her to miss out. Sherry did what she could. Susan was her pride, her joy, and her priority.

She was so proud her daughter was going to be a nurse and that she worked as a nanny for the Lynch girl. This was it, her ticket to education, and a way out of the life she had led. She wanted better for Susan. Susan answered an ad seeking a nanny and the Lynch's had hired her after a reference check.

Trust had been built up over the years that she had watched Emily. The Lynch's adore Susan's gentle ways with their daughter and Susan enjoys her time with Emily. Susan watched Emily after school when Mrs. Lynch went out to her social events and on the many nights out that Rick and Marissa had. Sherry was always happy when Susan was over there nannying. She knew where she was, and that she was earning money towards her bright future and education.

Sherry was a good woman, but Susan knew her mother's downfall were the men she picked. They were lazy underachievers like her father had been. She picked guys similar to what she knew. They never lasted long. She never had one live with her until now.

Susan had her own rental room in a house with friends during the school year and Sherry was lonely. She met Jeff at the diner when he came in for a sandwich and the rest was history. He treated her okay, but he was lazy, and recently lost his job working for a contractor. The work had dried up and he called out a lot, so he was the first one gone. Jeff settled right in to collecting unemployment, sitting around the house all day, and barely doing anything. Sherry would come home to dishes in the sink, laundry not being done and questioned what the hell she was thinking? Then she remembered her mother's lonely end and kept him around.

He gave her companionship. She was tired of being alone, so she let him stay at her place. She hoped Jeff would find a job soon. He just seems to be sitting around drinking beer all day and talking about a way to score easy money. She hated that talk, and told him to look for another job, while she worked her ten-hour shifts. At least she came home to someone, and she wasn't alone anymore. But was it worth it?

Sherry hugged her daughter when she came out of the car and greeted Emily with a warm, "Hello." She adored children. Emily responded to her warmth and followed her into the cabin. Sherry had cookies and milk waiting for her and the TV was already set up. Emily walked in and settled right down on the carpet with her sleeping bag. Sherry turned on her Nick at Night shows and Emily was in Heaven.

Jeff was snoring away on the weathered plaid couch wearing a plaid flannel and jeans but woke up from the noise. He nodded to both Susan and Emily and got up to get a beer. He couldn't be bothered with some kid and his girlfriend's daughter was a nasty thing to him, so he didn't bother.

Loser, Susan thought when she saw him get up. She cringed at the thought of him. Total Loser. He looked greasy and sloppy and had an attitude when they met.

Jeff knew Susan was a counselor and watching some kid, but he had no idea who the kid was related to until he heard the words from Susan's mouth that she had tried to contact the kid's parents, Rick, and Marissa Lynch. Hearing those names, Jeff sat up a little straighter, instantly wide awake as he saw dollar signs dance before his eyes.

"Mom," Susan began, "I tried to contact the Lynches to tell them that Emily was here, but cell service is out. I couldn't reach either Marissa or Rick."

Susan and Sherry didn't see Jeff's reaction, or they would have known he was up to no good. Jeff sat up and looked from Susan to little Emily and his mind began reeling with the possibilities of making some money off those rich Lynch's. Everyone, even lazy Jeff knew who the Lynches were.

Chapter 43

The elevator was getting hot. Chad and Reeve had removed their suit jackets, shirts, and ties at this point. They had spoken to the guard on the phone a few times and he said they were working to get the backup generators up and running. The guard said the entire east coast was in a blackout. Cell service was down. Reeve and Chad had given up trying and were just talking to pass the time.

Chad now thought of Reeve as a down home country boy who raced cars at the Roadhemge Raceway on the weekends. He had a fourteen-month-old and his wife was expecting another baby in a few months. Chad liked him and they talked about Reeve helping him out on his campaign. He asked Chad why he was there.

"The campaign is just getting underway," Chad began, sitting on the brown carpeted floor of the hot elevator. "It's definitely a lot of work but rewarding to meet the people and hear the issues."

"I bet," Reeve added. "Lots of legwork and meet and greets." Reeve continued "Are you here for an interview?"

Chad looked at Reeve, assessing him. He had loosened his collar and was sitting back on the other side of the elevator resting against the wall. Reeve seemed like a good guy and Chad needed to vent to someone.

"Honestly," he began, furrowing his brow, "I need to stop my ex, Trina from saying something about me that she will regret later. I guess it wasn't as clean a breakup as I thought."

Reeve sighs heavily and mumbles, "Watch out for a woman scorned. Listen, she is a press favorite. You better calm her before she makes waves. When we get out of here, I'll take you right up."

"Thank you," Chad replies gratefully. "I would sincerely appreciate that."

As they were getting more comfortable with each other Reeve brought up Hailey, asking, "Still seeing her?"

Chad nonchalantly shrugged, admitting, "A few times. Just, you know, getting out of the thing with Trina and not in a rush. If you know what I mean, dating around." He didn't want to give too much away just yet.

Reeve nodded. "Her sister was here the other day when Rick was on, gorgeous woman, but she just seemed unhappy. I picked up that vibe, anyway. Rick seemed controlling. Something a little off there."

Reeve had been genuinely concerned about Marissa and had found her email. Reaching out, he sent her a baby pic of his son telling her it was nice meeting her and he hoped she and Rick had a good time on the show. On the bottom of the email was his signature and contact info.

He told his wife he had picked up some weird vibes between Rick and Marissa and thought maybe she needed a friend. Reeve did this a lot. He was just a good ol' boy and tried to be a friend to all. He genuinely wanted to help.

Chad nodded. "Yeah, I agree." He recalled the press conference. Something was definitely off between the Lynches.

Chapter 44

Rick began losing it in the elevator. He needed a fix of his drug concoction, and he had nothing on him. It's now been hours in this hot elevator. He had expected his hour or so with Lana and then to be back home to his stuff. He never expected to be trapped in an elevator with his mistress's husband. Talk about hell. He and Trevor had talked business, politics, and skirted around why they were both at the same hotel or where their wives were.

Trevor noticed Rick getting agitated but thought maybe he was claustrophobic. Nobody suspected that the almighty Rick used drugs.

"Hey, you okay?" Trevor prods, noticing Rick starting to sweat and get fidgety. "They said they are getting the generators working."

Rick knew this. He had been the one who called down to the guard on the phone. Trevor was starting to get on his nerves now. "Yeah, not fast enough," he mutters, clenching and unclenching his hands.

He pulled out his cell, glancing at the screen and grimacing, still no service. It only agitated him more.

"Here," Trevor murmured suddenly, afraid Rick would lose it. He pulled something out of the brown bag that he had beside him.

Why hadn't Rick noticed the bag before? It was a bottle of Cabernet Sauvignon. Rick gratefully took the bottle, used his keyring to uncork it and took a big, long swig. The wine went down just the right way at just the right time cooling his temper.

Trevor handed him some crackers, too. What the hell was he doing with all of this?

Trevor read his thoughts and shyly explains, "This is not for Lana." Trevor meets Rick's eyes, looks uncomfortable and turns away.

Rick inhaled and took another swig of wine, processing this. While he was playing around with Lana, Trevor was playing around, too. Interesting. The one thing he knew was Marissa wasn't playing around.

He either slipped her a sleeping pill when he went to see Lana, or he had his guards follow her. He never had them with him on his Lana nights. Marissa did nothing but see her sister or did the mom thing with Emily. He wouldn't stand for cheating. Him doing it, there was a need, but her, disgusting. He looked at Trevor who was suddenly very uncomfortable and loosening his collar buttons.

"You're screwing around on Lana?" Rick probed, giving Trevor his cold look.

Ironically, he felt defensive. Lana could be with him, but Trevor being with someone else? It could definitely mess up the equation.

"It's new," Trevor mumbled, sounding nervous.

"I suggest you make it old," Rick insisted. The very last thing he needed was Trevor in this hotel where he had the suite where he met Lana.

Trevor nodded. He knew Rick was right. He had seen Tracy two times for quick lunches, and this was going to be their first night together. He found her on the internet, a website for married men looking for women.

Lana was detached lately, and he just had an itch for something. This was out of character for him. Maybe it was the Fates telling him to go home. When this elevator opened, he was heading down the stairs and going straight home.

"Yeah, you're right," conceded Trevor nervously. "Can we keep this between us?"

Rick looked at him with his eyes cold and giving Trevor a direct stare. The fool, he thought. "Consider it done."

Just then the elevator started to move after three hours of hell.

Chapter 45

Chad followed Reeve up the back stairs to the fifth floor. That's where the talk show Trina was appearing on was filmed. Reeve claimed they were definitely going to be way behind schedule with the blackout. Chad hoped he was right as he sprinted up the last flight of steps.

Reeve used his pass to scan Chad in. "The show is filmed over there," Reeve advised, pointing to the studio on the left. "I need to get in there and get on the air." He pointed to the studio to the right.

Chad looked where Reeve was gesturing. and nodded in acknowledgement. "Okay, thanks so much."

"Listen, Chad." Reeve commented, shaking Chad's hand. "If I had to be stranded in an elevator, glad it was with a country music loving racing fan."

Chad chuckled. "Me too. Quite a story to tell your kids someday."

Reeve chuckled, "You got my vote. Call me to help with your campaign."

"Thanks," Chad answered, and they quickly exchanged numbers. Chad liked Reeve and definitely would be in touch. "I'll talk to you soon," he mumbled, holding up his phone before pocketing it as he steps towards the studio to find Trina.

Chad spotted Trina sitting in the makeup chair when he walked into the bright studio. He heard her saying, "That was a long three hours. At least I was here and not stuck in the elevator like those poor people."

The makeup girl nodded, agreeing with her.

"I was one of them stuck," Chad announced, surprising Trina, and startling the makeup girl who dropped her brush.

"What are you doing here?" Trina asked Chad coldly. Her blue eyes drilled into him.

He stood his ground, begging, "Don't do this, Trina, don't bring me down because we aren't us anymore. We can be friends."

Trina looked at him, gulping hard. "You embarrassed me," she accused, looking contrite. "You broke up with me, and then appeared on the front page making out with that Lynch sister. Do you know how embarrassing that was for me? Do you? I loved you, Chad. I only agreed to end it because I thought you needed a break, but I thought we would go back to us."

Chad really looked at her, seeing the hurt in her eyes. His heart clenched and he truly felt sorry for her.

"Trina, I am sorry," he uttered. "I am truly sorry, but it's not what I want anymore. I care deeply for you, but I'm not in love with you."

Trina looked at him and started to cry. The makeup artist looked angry, her eyes narrowed, and she pursed her lips. She paused what she was doing and gave them both a nasty look. Her work was ruined.

Trina looked at Chad and commented, "The truth hurts." But she walked over and gave him a hug.

He really was a good guy and despite everything, she couldn't bring him down. Trina went on the show and despite the commentator's attempts to find out about her breakup with Chad and continuing to try to dig up skeletons in Chad's closet, Trina successfully dodged his questions.

"Listen," she began, "we may not be together anymore, but I am not going to trash a good man for you to get your ratings up. If you would like to speak about my charity work, then we can continue this interview."

Steve, the host, appeared sheepish and backtracked, "Of course, Trina, of course." Then he steered his line of questioning to her work on helping special needs children in the arts.

Trina smiled, satisfied, and gave Chad, standing discreetly off camera, a small smile. Reeve, who was watching from the other studio, smiled, and felt relief for Chad knowing everything had worked out.

Hailey, watching from home, felt badly for Trina. But she was impressed by the way Trina navigated the personal questions. Chad managed to get a text out to Hailey right as the show was about to air. He left out the part of being stranded in the elevator, but he would fill her in on that later.

Chapter 46

The elevator started to move, and it wasn't soon enough for Rick. He was agitated and needed to get the hell out of there. Trevor still looked a bit green around the gills about getting caught, while Rick was slightly amused by the irony of the whole situation.

"Get the hell out of here and go home," Rick urges Trevor as the doors begin to open.

Trevor nodded. Rick burst out when the elevator stopped on the fifth floor and gasped as he took his first breath of fresh air.

Trevor mumbled, "See you," and took off down the stairs.

Rick sat on the bench by the elevator with his head between his knees. He felt like a train wreck and needed his fix. He would deal with Lana later.

When he pulled himself together, he went up to the penthouse suite. He would shower, change into his workout clothes that he kept in the room, and return home to Marissa.

A text had come through from Lana, informing him, "I returned home when the blackout happened."

He wondered what she would say if she knew about Trevor. He would tuck that little nugget of information away and use it if needed. Right now, he was desperate for his fix. He had to get home. Rick was in an agitated state and that wasn't good, it wasn't good at all.

He stepped outside the hotel and thought of calling his driver to get him there, but he always walked the six blocks after his time with Lana and had him pick him up at the gym. He might as well do that tonight, too. He texted him to get him from there. "Kevin, pick me up at the corner of Columbus and 7th Street in 20 minutes."

Kevin replied back, "Certainly, Sir."

The city seemed restless after the blackout. He could feel a crackling energy. People were talking about it like crazy. The city was generally an electrified place, full of excitement but throw in an East Coast blackout, and it's bound to get people revved up.

The signs in Times Square were just coming back to life, and what remained dark for three hours was now super bright. Rick saw a few shielding their eyes. He blinked a bit adjusting to the light, too.

"Hey, need something, man?" a guy wearing cutoffs and carrying a backpack asked Rick, noticing his edginess.

Dealers can spot users. Rick was normally not one to buy street drugs, his were always imported and picked up at his pharmacist, but he was a bit desperate after the elevator incident.

"What do you got?" he asked the dealer.

"Whatever you need," answered the guy smirking at him. He motioned Rick to follow him into a dimly lit alley.

Normally, Rick would know better than to do this. Usually, he would have better sense. But at this moment, he was desperate Rick; the Rick who's about to lose it and followed the guy blindly.

He woke up an hour later, slightly beat up and bruised with his wallet missing. He was found by his driver who traced his phone. The stench from the alley was overwhelming, a mix of urine and garbage. Rick was sprawled out in a pile of recyclables, the plastic bottles digging into his back. He felt pain there and pain in his side. He felt this kind of pain a few times before after his middle school and high school fights. He winces, confident this immense pain was from his ribs.

Rick stumbled to his feet, and Kevin looked at him pointedly after helping him up. "Mr. Lynch, I really think that you need to go to the hospital."

Rick shook his head, refusing, "No."

"Mr. Lynch, please, at least let's get you to a walk in," he begged. Kevin furrowed his brow as his jaw clenched with concern.

Rick grumbled, "Alright." Then he finally allowed Kevin to put his arm around his shoulder and help him to the Town Car.

Rick slumped down in the leather seat on the ride, grimacing in pain. Kevin kept looking back in the rearview. His brown eyes met Rick Lynch's blue eyes a couple of times and Rick would look away groaning from the pain. Kevin drove as fast as he could navigating taxis, pedestrians, and traffic lights. When he arrived at the clinic, he helped Rick in through a side entrance. He had called ahead and thankfully, they had a room ready for Rick.

The doctor pulled his white coat and stethoscope over his khakis and blue button down as he walked into Rick's room to assess him. He had a technician take some x-rays and reviewed his findings. Shortly after, it was determined that Rick had two busted ribs and some bad bruises, but he would be okay.

"You are a lucky man, Mr. Lynch," Kevin proclaimed helping Rick back into the car after the checkup. "Let's get you home." Rick was nauseous the whole way home, but he held it together for the ten-minute drive, taking in huge gulps of air and deep breathing.

Kevin wanted to help Rick into his apartment when he pulled up in front of his building. But Rick insisted that he drop him off. "I can do it myself. Thank you, Kevin," Rick announced getting out of the car and grimacing from the pain and his taped-up ribs. He limped into the building. He was tired, beat up, done in, but he was Rick Lynch and insisted on going it alone up to his apartment. Kevin raced over to him when he saw him grimace. "I've got this," Rick reiterated, wincing "go home. Thanks."

Hesitant, Kevin looked after him concerned, but Rick was the boss, and Kevin's job was to do what Rick Lynch wanted. After Rick walked inside, Kevin sighed and drove away shaking his head. He would check on his boss tomorrow. Right now, he wanted to get home to his wife, Maria and his new baby, Bryce.

Rick took the elevator up, and keyed into his five-bedroom penthouse apartment, battered and bruised. He ran right into his bathroom, despite his pain, determined to get his fix and hopefully avoid Marissa.

Marissa heard the door open and watched wide eyed as Rick darted into the bathroom. He was hard to miss and looked disheveled, his shirt was untucked, his jeans dirty and ripped, and his hair was in disarray.

"Rick, are you okay?" Marissa asked just outside the bathroom door, her voice laced with concern.

"Fine," Rick retorted in a tired voice. "Go to bed, now."

"Rick, what happened?" Marissa prompted, "tell me."

"Go to bed, Marissa. I am sore, but fine. Let me take a shower." He exclaimed in a belligerent voice. "Just leave me alone."

Marissa sighed with frustration and worry and went back to her room knowing she wouldn't get anywhere with him tonight. This was how Rick was, sometimes he could be so cold.

Rick, meanwhile, rummaged through the medicine cabinets and swallowed his secret stash of pills hidden behind the Benadryl and Tylenol bottles. Thankfully, he had enough to get him through the night.

Chapter 47

Chad was hot on the campaign trail the next day. The blackout had stirred something in him. He did not like the way it was dealt with. Many buildings were still without power, and many businesses had disruptions in services due to not having backup generators. The lack of power led to the loss of refrigeration and spoiled food in many homes and restaurants that did not have generators. The high-rise apartments remained without air conditioners and the occupants in them were miserable. Chad was worried about the elderly, people who relied on power for their oxygen tanks, pregnant women and just the citizens in general.

Chad wanted to improve the emergency preparedness of the community and had some fresh ideas. The political candidate in him was further ignited when he saw the homeless on the streets. He felt a tug at his heart when he saw a family walking by, and he knew instantly they had spent the night on the street. The young kids looked dirty.

Chad approached them and spoke to them about their situation. They told him there was no room at the shelter, and they had been living in tents under a train trestle.

A young father came up to Chad, recognizing him from the news, with his young toddler on his shoulders. The dad looked tired. "Listen" he began, talking to Chad, "I lost my job and my apartment. I need to get my kid to some place safe and get something to eat."

Chad quickly dialed social services and had them set for the night in minutes, along with a scheduled meeting with the social worker the next day. As he disconnected the call, Chad took out $100 from his wallet and handed the shocked father the bills. The man looked at Chad with immense gratitude as they parted. "Thank you" he replied looking back as Chad walked away, "we appreciate you".

Chad turned around and smiled at the man and urged, "You'll help the next guy who needs it. That's what it is all about."

Chad truly realized this was why his dad did what he had done for three terms. Maybe, just maybe, he could be the one to make a difference.

Chad set out for his campaign headquarters, more determined than ever. He called his dad on his way and admitted, "I can see why you loved the job."

His dad on the other end of the line, smiles to himself. He knew that once ignited, Chad would be on fire.

Chapter 48

The power was still out upstate. Marissa kept trying to call and check on Emily to no avail. She was nervous but knew from the news reports the power was still out and she trusted that she was in good hands with Susan. Marissa continuously tried to calm herself.

When Rick arrived home full of bruises and a story about having been trapped in an elevator after running into Trevor, going for a drink at the Four Seasons bar, then heading to the gym and getting mugged, she was beyond upset.

It could have been so much worse for Rick. She told him he needed his bodyguards more than he used them. He generally only had them for public events.

Rick nodded in agreement. "You may be right," he conceded, icing his ribs.

Marissa looked at him with concern. He seemed strangely different...calmer. Rick was on an assortment of pain killers, and they seemed to have a very mellowing effect on him.

The police called him with some news. They found his wallet dumped in an alley by Rockefeller Center, his cash was missing but everything else appeared to be in there. An officer dropped it off a few hours later.

Rick rested, while Marissa played nurse. Things were good there. Rick was the Rick she loved, and all was well.

. . . .

The old generator continued cranking away. Emily wound up falling asleep in Susan's mom's cabin. Sherry loved having a little girl around and told Susan to have a fun night with the other counselors and pick her up in the morning. Susan, eager to have a full night with Jake, didn't turn down the offer. She knew Emily would be well taken care of by Sherry.

Sherry had met Jake, looked him up and down with her radar eyes and although he seemed rough around the edges and a bit of a bad boy, he made her Susan happy, and she would deal with it. Sherry wasn't one to speak about picking out a good man. Jeff, her current one, was lazy but there, and in Sherry's eyes, that was good enough.

Sherry had been raised by a single mom and all her life she had seen a parade of men come and go, in and out of her mother's life. Eventually, her mom died alone without ever finding her true love. Sherry unfortunately was following the same pattern. Men stayed for a year or so, wound up showing their true colors and eventually wronged her in some way. She hoped Jeff turned out to be different.

"Let the kid stay for a few days," he suggested, coming out of the bedroom in a t-shirt and jeans. His two-day growth and beer belly were prominent, as he tried to hide his cold eyes with a smile. "I like having little kids around again." Those words warmed Sherry's heart and she walked over and hugged him.

Jeff had divorced his kids' mother and was in fact a true deadbeat. Unbeknownst to Sherry, he owed $80,000 in unpaid child support. He believed this little Emily Lynch might just be his meal ticket. He didn't want her going too far.

"Oh, Jeff, thank you. You know how I miss Susan. I am going to bake some cookies with Emily when she wakes up." Sherry is so excited to have a child to care for again, even temporarily. She lights up like a Christmas tree and rummages through the cabinets searching for the ingredients for chocolate chip cookies.

Jeff pastes a smile on his face thinking, Bake all the cookies you want. Her daddy will be shelling out some cookies to me to get his little girl back.

Chapter 49

Hailey was over at Chad's place sitting on his beige couch. She managed to sneak in the back door of the apartment building. She had a brown wig ready to go and a pair of overalls on hand in case she had to change into a disguise in the car, but she didn't have to do that. The press had gotten bored with the Chad and Hailey thing. They hadn't spotted them together in a while, and Trina was nothing but complimentary about Chad on the talk show. The media thought their story had gotten pretty dull.

The Lynches were now the hot topic. Rick Lynch had been pretty beat up and the press lapped it up. The guy that metaphorically beat up others had been taken down. Although his deep bruises and broken ribs were luckily healing, he was still in tremendous pain and sleeping a lot.

Marissa called Hailey. "Rick is unfortunately down for the count," she informed her. "Will you go with me to pick up Emily from camp? Our driver will take us."

"Absolutely," Hailey replied instantly, excited at the idea of being asked to pick up Emily. She couldn't wait to see her. Hailey agreed and Marissa informed her, they would be heading up to camp tomorrow to get her. Hailey was excited! She loved taking her precocious niece places and she didn't see her nearly enough. There was still a bit of summer ahead, she was eager to take Emily to see Aladdin on Broadway and to the Museum of Natural History. Having her niece home would be so much fun. Hailey was so happy that Marissa reached out to her.

"I hope that the power is back on by the time we go" Marissa expressed to Hailey. "I've been trying to reach Susan, the nanny and haven't been able to, but we had arranged for pickup tomorrow."

"Power is probably out up there too," Hailey stated. "I heard it was the whole coast. What time do you want me ready?"

"Is 9 okay?" Marissa asked.

"Perfect," replied Hailey, "looking forward to seeing her."

"So am I," Marissa answers in a wispy voice. "I miss her so much. See you tomorrow sis, and thanks."

"Get some sleep and bye," Hailey replies, ending the call.

Hailey still couldn't understand Marissa and Rick's way of raising their daughter, but it was not for her to say. When Hailey had a child, and she could truly dream of having one with Chad, she was never letting that child go.

Chad came out of the bedroom. He had a long day of campaigning and just wanted a night in with Hailey. That sounded perfect to her, too.

She now had a drawer and kept clothes over at his place, and she had a shelf for her makeup and bath oils. Chad wanted her there for more than a night, and they briefly discussed it, but both agreed not to officially move in together until after the election. They both felt like this relationship could go the distance.

Chad ordered some groceries and he and Hailey were going to cook dinner together.

"Okay, buddy, let's get cracking," she jokingly ordered, pulling out the lemons, the chicken, the pasta, and the Alfredo sauce.

They were making a lemon chicken dish with Alfredo pasta and asparagus. She handed Chad the lemons and a knife. He started slicing them up with finesse.

"The boy has skills," Hailey joked.

Chad laughed as lemon squirted upward. "It was all the summers of having a chef in the house at Grandma's. He loved to teach Jillian and I his tricks of the trade."

Hailey loved hearing his childhood stories and just loved him in general. Chad loved the water and spoke of his days at camp learning to sail, and his days on the crew team in college. "Greatest times" he remarked reminiscing.

In addition to his campaigning, Chad was still working tirelessly to save the theater and had made tremendous headway. He had met with the construction company attorneys numerous times and they were making progress towards a compromise. Harding Construction was just waiting on the final plans to be approved. Essentially, the town had offered more land to the east of the factory in exchange for leaving the theater untouched. Harding's engineers agreed. They just needed the final approval.

Hailey had been thrilled and incredibly appreciative. She lived and breathed those kids and the theater. She couldn't wait to hold the fundraiser performance to raise money for the greenhouse.

Chad loved that about Hailey. He loved her down to her earthiness and sincerity. She and Marissa looked alike but were so different. Hailey said Marissa always had a little prima Donna nature to her. Marissa would be playing dress up, pretending she was royalty when they were little, while Hailey would be gardening with their mom and digging in the dirt.

They both shared a love of music. Marissa had been an excellent flutist and Hailey did her singing and theater performances. Marissa was concert level when she gave everything up when she met Rick. Hailey still hoped she would try to get some of herself back a little now that things seemed to be going better with Rick, and Emily was getting older.

Marissa hadn't brought up the memory loss and health issues in weeks, and so Hailey assumed things were okay. Marissa seemed happier and that gave Hailey some peace. She never quite understood Marissa's allegiance to Rick, but when things were going well, Marissa was happy. When their relationship was not going well, it was often volatile, and Marissa was left upset. Rick seemed like a complicated man, and Hailey was glad to have a man like Chad in her life.

She turned and smiled at him. "I love this, I love us." She walked over and threw her arms around him.

He embraced her. "Since dinner is cooking," he said with a wink, "let's get cooking."

She cracked up and led him into the bedroom.

Chapter 50

Jeff woke up and searched his girlfriend's phone while she was sleeping. He smirked when he found what he wanted. Rick and Marissa's phone numbers. Susan had left her mom their numbers in case of emergency.

Susan was picking up Emily each morning and bringing her to camp, dropping her back at her mom's and going out with the counselors and Jake. She had tried to text the Lynches, but service was still out. They were due to come back tomorrow to get Emily, so tonight was her last night there.

Emily and Sherry already had such a bond. Sherry had been teaching Emily how to cook various dishes, and Emily really had a knack for it. She loved being with Sherry and begged Susan to let her stay. Jeff just kept to himself, watching his sports, and plotting his financial future. Little Emily was his meal ticket. He liked Sherry well enough. She was a good woman. But he liked money more. So much more.

Jeff had a burner phone. He always had something that couldn't be traced on him for his little here and there side jobs. Jeff had never been in trouble by the law but walked the fine line. He put the numbers in the phone, and left Sherry a note about heading out for a bit.

He left quietly trying not to not wake Emily and Sherry as he went out with his truck at 4 a.m. to search for Wi-Fi and cell service. The Lynches would be shelling out some big-time dough soon. Jeff had child support to pay off and he wanted to disappear to Mexico and live the good life on the beach. He deserved it right?

Jeff drove twenty miles in the darkness of winding mountain roads. He found the spot he wanted and knew would have cell service. It was the little town of Spudunk, a little nothing place no one would think twice about. Jeff had gone there often as a kid to see his grandfather. His parents were drunks and his only happy childhood memories were of visiting his grandfather in Spudunk. He died when Jeff was ten, and life went to pot for him after that. All he knew was drinking, yelling, and beatings.

Life plain sucked for Jeff, always. His ex quickly became tired of him, he knew Sherry would, too. This plan would get him some dough and the life he deserved. So, without further thought, he used his burner phone and texted both Marissa and Rick Lynch, "If you want to see little Emily alive, bring two million in cash to 188 Spudunk Lane. Drop it in the well and don't call the police. You have until 8 p.m. tomorrow." The text was attached to a pic of a sleeping Emily. Jeff hit send.

Satisfied, he drove back to the cabin to get the next part of the plan in place. Jeff came home to find Sherry awake and Emily watching cartoons. He walked in the door and said, "So, I just saw Susan on the back of Jake's bike, and they are heading to Greenwich to elope. Can you believe that one? I tried to stop them, but they took off."

Sherry looked like she was going to burst into tears. Her face instantly turned red, and she began trembling. She exclaimed, "Oh no, she can't do this!" She reached for her phone to text her, and realized they were still out of service. "We have got to stop them, Jeff. She can't mess up her life like I did."

Jeff smirked when she turned around. I knew it would work, he thought to himself. Aloud he stammered, "Then, let's go."

Without an ounce of thought, Sherry had Emily get dressed and ushered her into the truck for Jeff to make the eight-hour drive to Greenwich to stop her daughter from eloping.

Susan came by the cabin two hours later to pick Emily up for camp and found the cabin empty. She had no cell service and no way to reach them. She didn't panic. Emily was with her mom, her wonderful mom. Maybe they had gone to get groceries. The truck was gone. The Lynches were due up by evening and she needed to get everything packed and ready. She hoped her mom and her sleazy boyfriend were back soon.

. . . .

Rick Lynch received the text at the same time Marissa did. She was in the kitchen going over the menu for the week with the chef via Skype. He came a few times a week to prepare their meals, and with Emily coming home, he wanted to have her favorites ready.

"Yes," Marissa was saying to Chef Enrique, "she loves your chili dogs and your Mac and cheese with the breadcrumbs. Oh, and your chocolate cake. She adores that."

Chef Enrique was an older, pleasant man and he enjoyed cooking for celebrity families. "Of course, Mrs. Lynch," he said with sincerity. "I will prepare those for her homecoming."

Marissa was about to thank him when she looked down at the phone and saw the text from Jeff. She screamed, "No! Rick!" She ran into the other room, her heart pounding in fear, leaving Chef Enrique puzzled. He was used to the weirdness of celebrity families, waited a few moments, and disconnected with a sigh.

Rick was startled from his drug induced sleep. The pain was still a seven on a scale of 1-10, even with the painkillers. The perp had bruised his ribs, his pancreas, and his face had taken a beating. The police said he fought back; they could see the signs of it. You bet your ass Rick fought back, he had no memory of it, but he knew he did. Rick Lynch wasn't a wimp, a guy who needed a fix, yes, but no wimp. He swore to himself the drugs were gone after he healed.

His desperation and beating were a rude awakening. He was even thinking about telling Lana it was over. They hadn't seen each other in weeks, and although he missed the raw affair with her, he did not miss her. Marissa was a treasure, and he was really starting to see it again. The time with her this summer, focusing on just the two of them, had been good for them. Rick was going to be a changed man when he healed.

Right now, he was in a hell of a lot of pain. His nurse was due in a few hours. In the meantime, he took a pill next to the bedside and swallowed it, praying it would numb the raw agonizing pain.

He reached for his phone after a few minutes to check his dozens of ignored messages from the press, colleagues, the few friends he had who weren't after his money and saw Jeff's text at the same time Marissa came running in, his heart dropping. He looked at her and said through clenched teeth, "My men will be on it." Rick angrily dialed his security team, filled them in, and they were dispensed.

Marissa, crying and trying to help Rick up, didn't know what to do. Her Emily was kidnapped. She should have never let her go away. What kind of mother was she? Her Emily. While Rick called the rest of his people, Marissa texted the only friend she felt she had right now that she could trust... Reeve. After that, she would call her sister.

Reeve answered her right back with, "What can I do to help?"

Marissa's reply was instant, "Get us up there as fast as you can." She knew from their texting and friendly conversations that Reeve was a race car driver in addition to working for the news station. He told her he had five race cars and could navigate a mountain road with his eyes closed. Marissa needed him.

Reeve always helped a friend. He handed the baby to his wife, explained the scenario, got in his race car, and headed to pick up Marissa Lynch.

He arrived in minutes, and with a brief explanation to the now semi drugged out Rick, she hopped in the car with Reeve, determined to make record time to save her daughter.

Marissa called Hailey who was with Chad, and they, too, got in Chad's Range

Rover and hit the road.

Meanwhile, Rick, despite his writhing pain and drugged state, made a few phone calls and was on a helicopter within an hour. This was his daughter, and he would stop at nothing to get her back. This is when defending shady characters paid off. They didn't tolerate anyone touching a child. That broke the code, which is why they knew it was an outsider and not one of them who had done this. They were in it with Rick to find this child and the perp who did this to Emily.

Now to keep this out of the press, which was his next obstacle. He did what was against his code and called Lana. She picked up on the second ring.

"Why are you calling here?" she asked sternly into the phone.

"Emily has been taken," was all he said.

"Oh, no, I am on it," she responded, and hung up. Lana was well connected with the press, and she would diffuse it. She soon texted him, "Done." Lana told Trevor, and they, too, were on the road to get up to the camp and help.

Everything went to the wayside when it came to finding a child. Their relationship issues could wait. A child was missing. Lana put the address into GPS, and they were on their way. She didn't tell him she had been to the camp before. That was information to share on another day. They all had to talk, soon, real soon.

Chapter 51

J eff drove with a purpose. He wanted to get Emily to his fishing cabin and away from the camp. He needed her and Sherry out of the way.

He would drive, collect his money, give Sherry the keys to his beat-up truck, let her bring Emily back to camp none the wiser, and Jeff would be long gone with the two million. Hell, he could buy a fleet of trucks. He didn't need his 2010 beat up Ford pickup anymore.

He was going to tell Sherry he needed to get to his kids over a toothache or something stupid and just leave her. She was a good woman, but money was money. He would leave her a little something and the truck. To him, that seemed fair.

Jeff stopped at a rest stop. He let Emily and Sherry out to use the bathroom and buy some snacks. Sherry was flipping out over Susan eloping and wanted to get on the road as soon as possible.

While they were gone, he pushed a button and switched his license plate. The license plate flipper had served him well many times and would certainly come in handy now.

Sherry and Emily came quickly out of the rest stop. Emily was holding a drink, a burger, and fries, totally oblivious to the fact Jeff was kidnapping her.

Meanwhile, Marissa was feeling her heart pound, her stomach was doing flips and Reeve was doing his best to both calm her and navigate the mountain roads at top speed. He drove his race car as if he were driving the Indy 500. Twists and turns were taken easily as he navigated the hairpin turns like the pro he was. Reeve remained a focused man. He had some Luke Bryan tunes playing and hummed along on the calm parts of the highway.

Marissa would have been amused had she not been panicking. Cell service was still out, and she had no idea where Chad and Hailey were, or how Rick was doing at home. She just knew she had to reach the camp and find Emily.

Susan's nerves began swirling in a frenzy now. She started texting her mother like crazy. They hadn't returned to the cabin, and it had been hours. She didn't know what to do. She left a note in the cabin, hopped in the car, and went to find Jake. He would know what to do.

While Susan was leaving a note, Lana navigated the road the way she did the last time she drove it. she remembered the curvy and winding road from the last time she had gone to the camp to spy on Rick and Marissa and get what she needed there. Trevor sat beside her. He had been very loving and affectionate since the night he'd been trapped in the elevator. They loved each other with all their hearts, but Trevor was usually not super affectionate. Neither was Lana, which is why she was so emotionally removed from her affair with Rick. It was strictly physical and had always been. Now, she needed things to be different. Things were about to change, but first they needed to find Emily.

Chad and Hailey were driving at a safer speed and trailed behind the pack by about twenty minutes. Hailey was scared for Emily and felt guilty over not being there for her. Maybe she should have pushed harder when Rick insisted Emily go to camp with the nanny. Then, maybe she would be here with her and safe from this terrifying experience.

Rick was in agony, gripping his stomach, but he didn't care. He needed to rescue Emily. His men were working on finding her. They had their leads. It wouldn't be long now until they found her. They were communicating with Rick through the radio on the helicopter. When they found her, there would be hell to pay for all involved.

Chapter 52

Let's check out the cabin," suggested Jake. He was a bit suspicious of Jeff and he's sure he was behind Sherry and Emily being gone but didn't want to say anything to Susan and increase her worry.

Jake was in love with Susan. It surprised him, but he didn't want this to just be a summer romance. The rough around the edges boy had fallen for the girl next door. He wanted to go the long haul with her and hoped she felt the same way about him.

When she came to him and told him Emily and Sherry were gone and so was Jeff's truck, he knew Jeff was up to something. That type always had an agenda. His dad had been that type, left him and his mom when he was nine and wound up in jail by the time Jake was twelve.

Jake helped his mom and raised his little brother, who won a scholarship to camp. That's how Jake became a counselor and met Susan. Jake knew guys like sleazy Jeff would jump on any opportunity. Jake had to help Susan find them. He was sure there would be a clue in the cabin. Jake easily pried open the door with a piece of plywood and broke in.

Susan ran into the cabin and started looking around frantically. "What do we look for?" she questioned, panicking.

"Something that tells us where they may have gone," mumbled Jake, pushing papers around. He found what he was looking for within minutes. It was an indented piece of paper that had been under a piece of paper that had been written on. "Get me the crayon." He motioned toward a blue crayon Emily had been using on her coloring book.

Susan handed it to Jake and watched him rub it sideways over the indented paper, words soon coming into view. It said, "Greenwich Hotel." Jake had his answer.

"Let's go," he urged.

"Go where?" inquired Susan, as she quickly followed him out of the cabin and hopped back into his truck.

"To find Emily and your mom."

They took off, leaving a trail of gravel and dust and headed toward Greenwich. Rick's men were a few minutes behind Susan and Jake. The three bodyguards with prior military background searched the cabin and were soon on the trail of Susan and Jake, unsure of their involvement, but certain they were somehow connected. They radioed Rick in the helicopter. They quickly gave him the description and plate for Jake's truck.

Rick told the pilot the direction to go in, and off they went. He was going to find this criminal if it was the last thing he did.

Marissa and Reeve were the first to arrive at the camp and ran right to Emily and Susan's cabin. No one was there, but they found the door unlocked. Marissa went in and started crying when she saw Emily's things. She took her teddy bear and held it close to her chest. Suddenly, she felt nauseous and ran to the bathroom.

Reeve heard her retching and felt badly. Was it motion sickness from the speed of the car? As he listened to Marissa, he felt sure it was something else, after all he's the father of a fourteen-month-old, and he also had a wife who was expecting.

He knocked on the bathroom door and inquired, "Marissa are you okay?"

Marissa groaned, "No," dragging out the word.

Reeve asks her in a concerned voice, "Marissa, are you pregnant?"

Marissa cried harder. She was so sick with worry over Emily and sick to her stomach now. But could this be more than her fear? Could she be? She threw up a few more times, rinsed her mouth with mouthwash that she found in her bag and opened the door to Reeve. "I really don't know if I am," she admitted and burst into tears.

Lana felt similar to Marissa, she was feeling green around the gills. She made Trevor pull over twice on the ride up to the camp. She had to go to the bathroom so badly and felt nauseous. Trevor was worried about her. "Do you want to turn back? We can help them from home, too."

Lana shook her head. "No." She needed to find Emily. Afterall, she was possibly going to be the half-sister of the baby Lana was pregnant with. "I need a bathroom." Trevor turned off the highway and rushed to get queasy Lana to a truck stop as quickly as he could.

While Lana stopped for the restroom, Chad got a flat. He ran over a nail or something sharp in the road and heard the tire deflate with a swift swoosh. He managed to keep control of the car and pull it off the mountain road onto the narrow gravel and grass side.

"Oh no," muttered Hailey nervously, as Chad carefully brought the car to a stop.

He was grateful it happened on a flatter part of the road versus if they had been on the curvy part of the mountain. That would not have led to the same safe results. Chad silently thanked Mr. Stern, his Driver's Ed instructor who taught him how to do an emergency stop. Sighing, he reached over and hugged a shaken Hailey.

"We are okay," he murmured, comforting her. "I will change it."

Chad climbed out of the Range Rover as traffic whizzed by, opened his trunk, and unscrewed the spare tire from its holder. He saw the jack and went to work on the tire. Within minutes he had it changed, and he breathed a sigh of relief.

Hailey nervously watched from the side of the road, afraid for Chad's safety. Chad was able to remove the deflated tire, hurl it in the trunk and replace it with the spare. They were soon on the road again and both relieved until they heard the same sound again a few moments later. The passenger side tire apparently also had a nail in it. Down it went, and off to the side of the road Hailey and Chad drove once again.

Hailey was near tears and Chad couldn't believe his luck. What now?

Chapter 53

Sherry nervously kept trying her cellphone to see if she could get a signal to reach Susan. Jeff had thought ahead and removed her SIM card in case service came back on. He didn't want her screwing up his plan. He was a few hours away from being a millionaire, nothing was getting in his way. Emily was napping in the back of the car and Jeff was singing along to the radio, acting like he didn't have a care in the world.

In reality, he was being hunted. The security team that worked for Rick had radioed him they were looking for a 2010 black Ford truck with plate number THI-7586. Rick was in agonizing pain at this point, but he told the copter pilot what to look for just before he passed out. The pilot had been instructed what to do if this happened, and as per Rick's firm instructions, kept flying the copter and searching for Emily. Within minutes he spotted a truck fitting the description, but it had a totally different plate number, so the pilot dismissed it and continued the search in another direction.

With the helicopter rerouting, Jake and Susan were probably the closest to Jeff at this point. Jake was shrewd and unfortunately had witnessed too many unsavory sorts at work during his childhood. Jake may have strayed here and there as a young teen, dabbling in drinking and vaping. But he had straightened himself out and would continue on that path to keep Susan.

He tried thinking the way Jeff would think and drove on some side roads and off the main highway. Eventually, Jeff would have to stop for gas, or a bathroom for Emily and Sherry. Jake was going to try to think like a criminal.

He began laughing to himself. His pathetic excuse of a dad would be so proud he was using the skills he passed on. Jake wished he had a father who played ball with him and coached his little league team. Instead, he had one who taught him to pick locks and defend himself on the street.

He looked over at Susan and promised her in his head to be a little league coach and role model if they ever had a kid. Right now, Emily was in Susan's mind, her kid, and Jake had to help her save her and her mom. Jake hit the gas and floored it.

When Marissa was done throwing up, she was back in the car with Reeve.

Pregnant. The thought went through her head. She tried to remember how she felt when she was pregnant with Emily, but it was a blur.

She had been twenty years old, and Rick swept her off her feet. It was all a romantic blur. Pregnant, that would explain her blackouts and forgetfulness. It all made sense. But what kind of mother would she be? She let her poor daughter be kidnapped. Marissa started to cry again.

Reeve focused on driving the car at top speed on the mountain roads, fueled by her tears, he drove even faster. He had to find this child, he had to.

Lana and Trevor wanted to help, but they kept driving and stopping. Trevor was getting worried about Lana. She was nauseous and needed him to pull over numerous times. She said maybe it was food poisoning, or something she ate. He wanted to turn around and go home.

She insisted she needed to help. Lana was like that. She was all about a cause, and Rick had explicitly asked her to keep it out of the media. The only way to do it was to be physically there in case they showed up. Lana was a powerful force in her own way, and no one messed with her.

Rick came to in the helicopter and groggily asked the pilot, "Did you find her yet?"

"No, sir, I haven't," he answered regrettably to a semi coherent Rick.

The pain felt intense now and the pilot didn't like how Rick looked, but Rick insisted he keep searching as he floated in and out of consciousness. That's his daughter out there.

While everyone was desperately searching for her, Emily sat in the truck, still oblivious to her situation. She had to go to the bathroom after drinking the big cup of juice. She was squirming, and Sherry was getting agitated that Jeff wouldn't stop.

"She has to go," she emphasized to Jeff.

He sighed heavily. They were in a pretty populated area, and he didn't want them to be recognized.

"Five minutes," he commanded. "The next rest stop is cleaner." And less crowded.

Sherry sighed, Emily squirmed, and Jeff kept driving.

Like Emily, Chad and Hailey were feeling pretty desperate. They were on a mountain road, had another flat without another spare, and no cell service. They made the decision to leave the truck with the flashers on and walk off the main road to see if they could find help.

Luckily the weather was decent, and they had water. Weather could change in a heartbeat on a mountainside. One minute could be sunny, the next dark clouds could appear over the mountain top and result in torrential downpours. It was hit or miss. Right now, they were okay.

Chad used the sun as a guide and headed West. "I am thinking, in about two miles we should be near a town."

Hailey nodded. She was so worried about felt desperate, wanting to find help. Chad and Hailey walked for about a half hour with no one passing them on the hot, dirt road.

"This has to lead somewhere," Chad suggested. He was getting tired, and the mountain heat was becoming intense.

They were chugging water but were down to only two bottles left. They walked for about another fifteen frustrating minutes when they saw a bus coming towards them. Hailey and Chad started waving. The purple bus pulled to a stop. It had the sign, "Horthorne Gospel Choir" on the side and it was filled with about twenty people who were staring at Hillary and Chad.

The bus driver slowed. He was a big, burly man with a gravelly voice. "Well, hello there," he uttered to Hailey and Chad. "You two, okay?"

"Sir," Chad said, grateful he stopped. "Our truck has two flats from some nails. Where can we get help?"

Cries of, "Oh, dear!" and, "Have mercy!" were heard throughout the bus.

"Nothing around here for miles," the driver said, shaking his head. "Climb aboard, we're heading to a choir competition, and we can bring you to safety."

Hailey nodded and smiled in relief as she joined Chad as they climbed into the purple bus headed to parts unknown. But it sure beat the heat and manure smell they had been enduring for the last hour.

"Thank you," they both said, and settled in with waves and nods at the occupants who chanted, "Praise the Lord," and "Let's keep them safe." Hailey smiled at Chad, and he laughed. Nothing else one could do in this situation.

While Chad and Hailey had been forced to slow down, Jake was going too fast. Susan urged him to slow down. He didn't listen. They went around a bend at eighty miles per hour and although Jake tried to gain control of the wheel, he was too late. Susan screamed, and that was the last sound Jake heard before he blacked out. Susan was knocked unconscious as the car projected into the air and landed on its driver's side up against a guardrail. Jake and Susan were pinned inside.

Chapter 54

J eff finally stopped at a rest stop. Emily ran out of the car with Sherry trailing behind her. Emily really had to go. Sherry felt badly for her and couldn't understand why Jeff wouldn't stop.

She sure could pick them. Why couldn't she find a decent guy who doesn't think of himself first? She never had. Maybe she'd go for some counseling when she got home. Maybe it was time.

First, she needed to stop Susan from making the same mistake she made. Susan was young with a bright future. She didn't need to be tied down at twenty-one years old. She was going to be a nurse. She needed to finish her education and get a job, get on her feet. Sherry couldn't let her elope with a guy she just met this summer.

Sherry helped Emily reach the sink to wash her hands and ushered her back in the truck. They needed to get on the way and stop her, stop her before it was too late.

"Let's go, Jeff," Sherry said, urging him to start the truck. "We have to stop them."

Jeff laughed on the inside, but said to Sherry, "I'm on it." His plan was working out perfectly.

"Oh, we found the glory! We found the glory," sang the choir as the bus driver grinned in the rear-view mirror and danced along in his seat as he drove. A chorus of Amens followed.

Hailey murmured to Chad, "This would be amazing if I wasn't so worried. I would be leading this choir."

Chad held her hand. "I bet you would. I am starting to get some bars on my phone. Hopefully we get some cell service soon."

Reeve was now the closest to Jeff without even knowing it. He passed the accident two miles back but didn't recognize the car and saw an ambulance heading that way. He secretly wished the people well, knowing it looked pretty bad as he kept driving.

Marissa was quietly weeping next to him. Reeve felt bad and kept driving in search of Emily. Marissa looked down at her phone, which had been dead until now and heard a ping. A message came through showing a picture of Emily looking miserable and crying.

"You better have the money, or you will see Emily cry." Marissa wailed even louder when she saw it, and Reeve, being Reeve, drove faster. He blasted some Clint Black and slammed on the gas.

Rick didn't see the message or the picture that was texted of Emily, while everything in him was throbbing. The helicopter pilot radioed ahead that he was bringing Rick back to get him to the hospital. The pilot knew he was The Rick Lynch but would not take responsibility for Rick dying in the air. He had already passed out three times. He circled back and landed on the roof of Snyder Hospital. The staff was waiting for him, loaded him on a gurney, and secured him.

Rick was completely out at that point and had no idea what was going on. He briefly regained consciousness and just mumbled his daughter's name, "Emily," before he passed out again.

While Rick was struggling, Lana and Trevor were just taking it slowly at this point. Lana was nauseous, very, very nauseous. Trevor felt bad for his wife. He truly loved her and never ever should have thought about cheating on her. Good thing Rick had talked some sense into him.

Lana clung to the side of the car, with the open window trying not to lose her cookies. She prayed the baby she was carrying was Trevor's but knew it definitely could be Rick's increasing her anxiety and nausea.

"We have service," Hailey announced as her phone came to life and a zillion text messages began pinging as they loaded.

"Awesome," said Chad, who quickly checked his phone. "She hasn't been found yet." He squeezed Hailey's hand. "But she will be."

Hailey teared up and squeezed his hand back. Chad's heart swelled in his chest with love for her. They had to find this child. He quickly got on the phone and made a few calls. Rick had insisted they keep the police out of it, that he had his security team working on it, but Chad trusted Harding and his FBI background and gave him a call.

"So, you are on a gospel bus searching for a missing kid with Hailey. Your Range Rover is on the side of 180, and you walked for an hour by a cow farm. Typical day for you."

Chad had to chuckle at that one. Harding said he would be discrete, make his inquiries, get the car taken care of, and call him back. He would arrange for transportation for them in the next town up which was twenty miles away.

Chad asked the gospel driver if he could let them off there. "Listen, would you mind doing us a favor and dropping us off in Grover Creek? I have a friend setting me up with a car there. Thank you so very much."

He eagerly agreed, "Surely, Sir."

Chad expressed his appreciation, "We can't thank you enough for helping us."

Chad filled Hailey in, and she turned to the gospel choir, filled them in, and thanked them.

They all answered by saying, "Hallelujah" and burst into song. Hailey and Chad couldn't help themselves as they laughed and joined in.

Chapter 55

Sherry heard Jeff's phone ping and looked at hers. She couldn't get it on. She noticed it didn't say the cell carrier anymore, instead, it kept saying no SIM card. Something was wrong with it.

"Jeff, I need your phone to check on Susan, mine isn't working."

"I just checked," Jeff insisted in a nasty tone. "Nothing."

"Can I see the phone?" Sherry asked in an angrier tone. "Just let me use it."

Jeff was nervous about getting caught and snapped, "Shut up and let me drive! Forget about the damn phone. Let me get to Greenwich."

Sherry chewed on her bottom lip in frustration, angry and sick of the men in her life starting out nice and then always turning. She needed some counseling after this, she had to figure out why she kept going for the same horrible type.

"We are done after this," Sherry snapped.

Jeff shrugged. He didn't care, he was twenty minutes away from dumping her anyway and getting his money.

Little Emily reached into her backpack. She was given an emergency phone from her mom and dad along with a charger. She was afraid of Jeff and kept it hidden. She would give it to Sherry when they went to the bathroom again.

Jeff pulled into Greenwich a half hour later and stopped at his old fishing cabin just outside of town. Sherry again asked him for his phone, but he refused.

"I checked," he snapped, "there is nothing from them. Let's use the bathroom and get to the chapel to stop them."

Sherry sighed and followed him into the dusty unused cabin. Emily followed them in, coughing from the dust. All the cabin furniture was covered in white sheets and the floor was caked with dirt. It looked as if no one had been there for many months.

"I need to use the bathroom, but I am scared," she whined. "Sherry, please come with me."

Jeff nodded and pointed to the bathroom. Sherry brought her in and tried to clean it up the best she could for Emily to use it. "Don't touch anything," Sherry instructed Emily. "I did the best that I could cleaning it up."

"Thank you, Sherry" Emily answered and did what she had to do. After

Emily was done, she turned to Sherry and whispered, "He is being mean. I have a cellphone in my backpack. Use that to find Susan."

Sherry smiled at her and hugged her. "Thank you, honey."

When they came out of the bathroom, Jeff was outside. Sherry took the phone out of the backpack and frowned, seeing it was dead. She needed to charge it, but away from Jeff. She didn't trust him right now. She had the feeling he was keeping something from her. Did he have another girlfriend? Was he hiding the phone to keep her from seeing it? Who knows, but she needed to talk some sense into her daughter. Jeff came back in, and Sherry quickly hid the phone.

"Listen," he began, "you stay here. The chapel is closed until tomorrow at 9 a.m. They can't do anything anyway. I will go to town, get some food, and then we can go looking. This place needs some cleaning. You do that," he advised and turned. Without looking back, he slammed the door and was gone.

Little did Sherry and Emily know; he was really gone. Jeff left the truck, walked the two miles into town, went to the only garage in town, and picked up the truck he had stored there. It was his grandfather's and still ran like a charm. It would get the job done and get him his two million.

Chapter 56

Hailey finally reached Marissa, she was hysterically crying and gasping for air from the anxiety of it all, she had her head between her knees trying to stop the nausea and keep the panic that was setting in at bay. Marissa sat up, clenching her stomach. Her mascara was smeared, and she looked broken, the same way she felt. It was just reported to her that Rick was in the hospital unconscious. She didn't know what to do.

Reeve had pulled over on the side of the road to let Marissa talk. Her daughter had been kidnapped and her husband was unconscious in the hospital. He felt badly for this poor woman. He looked at her with compassion and concern, his eyes welling up a little at the pain she was going through. Remaining silent, he listened to Hailey's exchange with Marissa.

"Go to Rick," Hailey urged. "We will go after Emily and Rick's security people are on it. Go there and we will call you."

Marissa was shaken up, but she listened to her sister, not able to think for herself. "Take me to the hospital, please," she asked Reeve, not realizing they were maybe fifteen minutes from Emily.

"Absolutely," Reeve answered, patting her hand in support. Reeve was happy to help. He revved up the car, took it over the grassy median, and headed back on the journey to Gracey Hospital.

The same hospital admitted Susan and Jake. They were lucky to be alive. Both were unconscious with multiple injuries, but they were alive, and they would both make it. The hospital searched their phones for emergency numbers and left both Susan and Jake's parents messages. Neither one heard the messages.

The press got wind of the story and even Lana couldn't stop them from coming out in droves. Word was Rick Lynch was in a helicopter after he was assaulted and robbed the other day, and he's now in the hospital unconscious. No one knew why or what happened, but it would make great news.

While Rick was in the hospital, his security detail was surrounding the area that would be the drop off, they would get the guy real soon. They sat poised, hidden on the property with their weapons ready. Nobody messed with Rick Lynch or his family.

While Marissa went to the hospital to check on Rick, Hailey and Chad arrived at Gleason town. They were dropped off by the gospel choir who wished them well and insisted on a picture with their new friends. They had no idea that Hailey and Chad were the famous Hailey and Chad. They only knew they made some new friends and they found it inspirational.

Hailey and Chad posed with them for one picture in front of the bus and Chad handed them $200 as a donation to the choir and a thank you for the ride. They sang, "Hallelujah" and climbed back on the bus, leaving Hailey and Chad in front of the garage Harding told them to go to. He arranged a loaner car for them from someone who knew someone. Harding always seemed to know someone. Harding was Mr. Social, and everyone knew he was, and he seemed to know most people.

Like Harding, Lana knew people, but this time she wouldn't be able to help. Lana and Trevor turned to go home. Lana just wasn't feeling well, and they got word the press got wind of it. Now there was nothing even she could do at this point to stop it. Trevor drove the two hours home and tucked Lana into bed.

Hours later, Jeff hadn't returned to the cabin. Sherry used Emily's phone to try Susan, but she didn't answer, so she left a frantic message. Then, she tried Jeff who didn't answer, and she left him a message. "Susan, this is Mom. Please, honey, don't do anything just yet, let's talk about it. Please, Susan don't make the mistakes that I did, you need your education. Call me, please." Her voice trailed off in tears. Emily listened and walked over and hugged Sherry around the waist. Sherry hugged her back, holding her tight. "Thank you honey."

Unbeknownst to her, Jeff had tossed his phone and was only using the two burner phones he bought. So, he didn't hear Sherry's message calling him a cold-hearted loser. If he had, he wouldn't have cared. He was about to score big time, and no one was getting in his way. He certainly didn't want anyone tracing him. When neither Jeff nor Susan answered, she gathered Emily up and asked her to please go in the truck so they could look for Susan. She got in and realized Jeff had the keys. Sherry put her head down on the steering wheel and cried.

Emily put her hand on Sherry's in comfort and stated, "It will be okay."

Sherry's heart squeezed and she forced herself to smile as she gazed adoringly at little Emily. Children were so innocent. She decided right then and there, after all this was over, that she was done with men and would become a foster mother. Raising children made her happy, while the men she picked in her life made her miserable. She knew her Susan would be proud of her and approve.

Sherry picked her head up, and with a new strength proclaimed, "Let's get out of here." She took Emily's hand and led her into town. Sherry thought then that she should call Emily's parents to let them know she was okay and dialed Rick Lynch's number. "Mr. Lynch, this is Sherry, Susan's mom. I just wanted you to know that Emily is fine and with me. We took her in after the blackout 'cause we had a generator. You can reach us on Emily's cell."

Emily shouted, "Hi, Daddy! I learned how to make cookies," into the phone.

She and Sherry hung up and walked hand and hand into town to find a ride back home. She was resigned to Susan getting married. There would be no stopping a young girl who had made up her mind. Let her make the mistake and get out of it young rather than make it when she was old like Sherry thought herself to be.

Sherry would bring Emily home to her parents, and then go right to social services and fill out the paperwork to become a foster mom. She had a plan and needed a fresh start.

While Sherry was making some positive plans, Hailey and Chad's picture went viral. This could have been a true negative letting the cat out of the bag that they were together. Unbeknownst to them, the Grady Gospel Choir was known internationally and had a huge following. They posted a picture of Chad's Range Rover on the side of the mountain and how they had made new friends. The post praised the Lord for putting them in the right spot to do the rescue. The picture of a smiling Hailey and Chad with the twenty-five-member choir dressed in their robes went viral and the press got wind of it. This was their lucky day, both a Rick Lynch story and a Hailey and Chad story on the same day. What could be better?

They soon found out as Marissa and Reeve pulled up right in front of the hospital where the press stood waiting. This felt like their luckiest day ever. Marissa Lynch stepped out of the race car, pulled off the helmet, looking green around the gills, and threw up. The press snapped it all, including Reeve helping her making their eyes go wide. Was that meteorologist Reeve Hanson driving the car and handing a tissue to Marissa Lynch? What?! The press went wild. Trifecta in one day. This was incredible.

Chapter 57

Jeff approached the drop off point in Spudunk and looked around. It seemed like the quiet little sleepy place it always had been. Nothing suspicious at all. Jeff parked the old Toyota truck and went to the well to retrieve the money he was sure Rick Lynch had given him to get his precious daughter back. He had left the truck with Sherry but taken the keys. By the time anyone discovered that little Emily was with Sherry, he would be long gone.

He forgot to leave her the $100 he said he would. Oh well, not his problem anymore. He would live the good life in Mexico and find himself a senorita. Jeff had a plan.

What he didn't plan for was Rick's people being there with guns. Jeff wasn't the sharpest tool in the shed and didn't account for the fact that Rick was a powerful force, and believed Jeff had his daughter. Jeff thought he could pick up the cash and go. Twelve guns were pointed in his face, and he was forced to the ground by the military trained security team. It was over for Jeff.

While Jeff was being detained, Marissa checked on Rick, hoping Emily and Rick would be okay.

Reeve asked, "Will you be okay if I leave you here?" He looked at her with caring and concern.

"I'll be okay. Go home to your family. Thank you for your help." Her eyes met his and they teared up with gratitude.

He saluted her as he pulled away. He said he would be there if she needed him. He had become a good friend, but he had to go home right now and be with his wife and baby, while Marissa needed to know Rick was okay and then return to the search for Emily. She had to admit it felt good to have a friend. A friend that wanted nothing from her, only gave. Reeve was one in a million. And she's so glad to have met him.

Marissa walked past the paparazzi and into the hospital. She watched as an ambulance pulled in carrying a young woman and a man. They looked pretty beat up and both had their necks stabilized. Marissa recognized the girl and screamed, "Susan...no!" and then fainted.

Seeing Susan on a gurney bloodied and immobile was too much for her. Within minutes a team surrounded her, having recognized her right away.

"Mrs. Lynch, Mrs. Lynch wake up, can you hear us?"

Marissa woke up in a hospital bed with an IV stuck in her arm and memories of the explosion in her fogged-out brain.

"Mrs. Lynch, you fainted after screaming 'Susan'. Do you know that girl? We have been trying to reach her family."

Marissa shook off the dizziness and said, "She was our nanny, and our Emily is missing."

"Do you know how we can reach her family?" Doctor Pearson inquired looking pointedly at Marissa. "We need to get in touch."

"I don't, but I can try to find out. Is she okay?" Marissa asked near tears.

The doctor and nurse looked at each other. They were afraid to tell Marissa more bad news, Rick was just brought in for emergency surgery. His spleen had ruptured, and they weren't sure if he would make it.

Deciding to wait, they stated, "Okay, we will find your daughter. We'll keep you overnight for observation. You know you are expecting, right? About eight weeks along. The baby is fine, but you are dehydrated. We did find evidence of sleeping pills in your system. Stay off them for the safety of the baby."

With that the doctor turned away, gave the nurse a look and whispered, "Save the news about the husband until he is out of surgery, and we know one way or another. She is under too much stress and the news could put her health and her baby's health at risk. Alert the police about the daughter."

Things were definitely interesting with the Lynches around.

Hailey received Marissa's text letting her know she arrived at the hospital when she first got there. As Chad turned on the radio of the rental car, she heard all the news reports coming in. "We are waiting for word on Rick Lynch's condition. It is unknown at this point whether he is conscious, last reports were that he was taken into the OR upon arrival at County General. We will update you as we know more."

The reality was that Rick was in surgery, Marissa had fainted, the nanny was wheeled in on a stretcher, and Emily was missing. It was all too much. Hailey's head began spinning trying to process it all, and she became uncharacteristically snappy.

"Can't you go around that car?" she prodded Chad.

He tried to make her happy, understanding her stress, but unfortunately everyone was bringing their child home on the same day from camp. It was bumper to bumper traffic and the GPS was showing it not letting up for twenty minutes. He was afraid to tell Hailey and wanted to find a way to fix it. Taking a deep breath, he did something he never thought he would do, he dialed Grandmother Cecilia, briefly filled her in, and asked for a favor.

Cecelia thought about it from two angles before she made her decision. Would the Lynch girl be an asset now? Would this help Chad's political career? Undecided on both and hearing the dire need in her grandson's voice, she did something very uncharacteristic for her, and went with her heart. The helicopter Cecilia sent landed right on the side of the highway on a flat, gravely area.

Chad managed to pull the rental car onto the side of the highway. He and Hailey got out of the rental, made their way through the strong wind created by the propellers, and into the copter.

The people still sitting in traffic took out their phones and filmed the whole thing. Chad, once again, would go viral. He could care less. Let it be known that he was with Hailey, let it be known that he was in love. He would make a damn good senator and having Hailey by his side would make him a better man.

The helicopter pilot had been told to bring them right to the hospital, but Chad felt that he needed to do one more search.

"Do me a favor Butch," Chad asked the pilot, "do one more circle around the area and see if you can spot her, please."

The pilot obliged. "Of course, Chad," he replied and pulled back on the controls and circled back over the area giving it a final look.

Chapter 58

Jeff was talking, actually squealing, now that the security team had him lassoed and hogtied.

"Where is the girl?" Sven, the head of security, asked Jeff, yanking the ropes tighter.

"Damn it!" cried Jeff. "That hurts."

"It will hurt a hell of a lot worse if you don't speak," Sven threatened, yanking his head back.

"Greenwich, she's in Greenwich," he screamed. "I left her with Sherry."

A little more pull on the ropes and some more screams from Jeff resulted in the answers they needed, and Sherry's identity. They also got out of him that Sherry had no idea what he was up to. That they would see for themselves. They had been instructed by Rick not to kill whoever the perp was, to turn him over to the cops, and Rick would serve his own justice later. Rick wanted the chance to see whoever dared mess with his family and look them in the eye.

Unfortunately, Rick layed on the operating table floating between life and death. They put Jeff in the back of their truck and headed for Greenwich. They would dump Jeff in jail once they safely got to Emily.

The helicopter landed on the rooftop of the hospital with so much fanfare, one would think it was royalty arriving. It was turning to dusk now, and the flood lights lit up the sky just as the moon was settling into its spot. The blades came to a slow, sputtering stop. Chad thanked the pilot, grabbed Hailey's hand, and led her out of the copter.

The social worker stood just inside the door waiting, and she filled Hailey in on what was going on with Rick and Marissa and asked about Emily. "Did they find her?" she inquired, holding tightly onto her clipboard, looking concerned. "Any word yet?"

"No, not yet," Hailey replied sadly, "nothing yet."

The social worker frowned and went on. "Mr. Lynch is very weak and just came out of surgery. He is in ICU." Hailey nodded, tearing up. "Mrs. Lynch is in a room quite upset, I just left her. We are giving her limited information right now for fear of jeopardizing her pregnancy."

Hailey's eyes went wide at the word pregnancy, but she tried not to look surprised. Unfortunately, you never quite knew who to trust in their world and who would go to the press. "Thank you for the information," Hailey replied gratefully and gave the social worker a half smile. There was just too much for Hailey to process right now, Emily was missing, Rick just came out of surgery... Marissa was pregnant.'

The social worker began, "I have one more question. The nanny for Emily was brought in here hurt, and we are trying to reach her parents. Would you happen to have any information on how to reach them?"

Hailey took this information in. "No, I don't, but we can try to find out." Hailey looked at Chad and said, "Can we please get Harding on it?"

"Of course," Chad replied wiping a tear from Hailey's face with his hand after thanking the social worker.

He dialed Harding and filled him in on everything happening and what he needed from him. Harding promised his contacts would do a search.

"Thanks, Harding," Chad states.

"This situation is a mess," Harding replied. "I'll do what I can, Chad. My thoughts and prayers are with everyone. Keep in touch." Harding hung up and Chad pocketed his phone.

He walked back to Hailey and gave her a hug. She hugged him back. "This is unreal," she whispered in his ear. "I feel so helpless." They walked together towards the room they were told Rick was in. As they got closer there noticed a lot of chaos.

Alarms went off screeching over the hospital PA system. "Code Blue," was announced and doctors and nurses with carts and medical equipment went running into Rick's room. He was coding.

Rick crashed badly. The code team went in to stabilize him. Chad and Hailey stood right outside the door and saw the whole thing. They watched as the experienced team used the paddles, announcing, "Three, two, one...clear," a few times and were finally able to bring him back.

Marissa had been in the room across the hall and came out during the code. She instantly fell into hysterics. Hailey, reaching for her, held her up. The doctors made her leave as she tried to get inside the room, but their priority was saving Rick. "Rick...no," she cried over and over again.

Hailey tried her best to soothe her sister. "It will be okay," she whispered, rubbing Marissa's back and hanging on tight.

Once Rick was stabilized, Marissa was informed that Rick was critical, and his bloodwork showed high levels of cocaine and Xanax in his system. If he survived, he would need to detox. The medical staff would keep this confidential of course, but they now knew what made Rick Lynch tick.

While this was going on, Emily, nearly bounced with every step, so excited knowing she would be seeing her parents soon when they picked her up. She held Sherry's hand as they walked through town in search of a ride back. Sherry just bought Emily some snacks and they headed toward Todd's garage to see if he had a loaner car. There was definitely not a car rental place in this sleepy town. Emily was singing and Sherry smiled, enjoying her youthful exuberance when all of a sudden, they were surrounded by ten cars with sirens blaring.

"Step away from the child, lady, and drop to your knees with your hands up."

Sherry looked shaken, her brown eyes went wide, and she appeared very pale, but did as she was told. Emily was frightened and pleaded, "Don't hurt Sherry!" and began to cry.

Amanda, six feet tall and austere looking in her blazer and brown pants, walked over to her as one of Rick's security team members. "Hi, are you Emily?"

Emily nodded between tears.

"I work for your daddy," she informed her and reached out her hand.

Sherry nodded between tears and prodded, "Go with her, Emily, you will be fine."

The officer gave Sherry a nod knowing she most likely wasn't involved, but they had to be sure and go through protocol. Amanda guided Emily away from Sherry to the security car. They had to bring her to the same hospital as her parents. With Emily safe in the car, Sherry was led away for questioning. Nothing mattered to the security team except knowing Emily was safe.

Amanda lifted her radio and happily announced, "Little Red is away from the wolf."

The officers all cheered!

Hailey was the first to see her when they brought her to the hospital. She was holding Amanda's hand and a stuffed bunny that had been given to her to help calm her down over Sherry being taken away.

"Emily!" she screamed, running over, and hugging her. "You are okay!"

Emily hugged Hailey back and Amanda watched with a smile. She loved happy endings.

Chad walked over. "Did you catch the perp?" he asked in a whisper, as

Hailey listened to Emily's stories of Sherry and how she taught her how to cook pasta and bake cookies.

"I love Sherry," Emily whispered.

Hailey's eyebrows draw down in confusion, wondering how Sherry got mixed up in this. "Who is Sherry?" she inquired trying to piece the whole thing together.

"She is my babysitter Susan's mommy," Emily explained. "She was so nice to me. Her boyfriend was always cranky, though." Emily rolled her eyes on that one.

Chad put it all together. "So, Sherry watched you? And where was Susan?" he asked, bending down so he was eye to eye with Emily.

"She was there, but then we lost power and her mom had a gen something that made the cabin light up."

"A generator?" clarified Chad.

"Yes, that's it," Emily confirmed, laughing. "You are so smart! Yes, it let me watch my cartoons."

Hailey and Chad laughed. They were just grateful she was okay. Hailey held her hand and went with her for the required exam, and then asked permission to bring her up to Marissa.

Marissa was doing ok and had gotten word that Emily was safe, unharmed, and with Hailey. She burst into tears at the news, her whole body sagging with relief. Emily was safe. Now, she just needed an update on Rick. No one had told her anything else about him yet.

Chad realized he had to somehow find out Sherry's involvement and get word to her about her daughter and boyfriend. Chad was able to find out Amanda's information and he left a message. "Amanda, can you please give me a call back to provide us with some information and clarification?"

Amanda quickly called Chad back and told him Sherry was cleared of any knowledge or wrongdoing. Jeff had admitted he acted alone, and they were able to trace and verify Sherry's voicemails to Rick's phone. Sherry was being driven by the police to the hospital, hysterical over the news that Susan was hurt.

They told Marissa more about Rick and his condition after she was reunited with Emily. He was stable for the moment but critical. Marissa was devastated, but the nurses reassured her that they were doing everything in their power to keep him alive. They said that the doctor would come by in a few minutes to update her.

Marissa hugged Emily tightly after hearing the news from the doctor. She cherished the gift of having Emily returned safely so much right now. The reunion had been so wonderful for mother and daughter. "Mommy," Emily shouted running into Marissa's arms when she spotted her in the hospital.

She truly had no idea what occurred, which Marissa was incredibly grateful for. "Oh, baby," Marissa cried, pulling Emily into a warm embrace. "I am so glad that you are okay."

"Okay?" Emily asked. "Oh, you mean the blackout. It was fun for a while playing with flashlights, and then Sherry and I baked cookies in the gas stove." Emily excitedly rambled on to her mother, oblivious to the possible danger that she had been in.

"Oh, Sweetie," Marissa replied, pulling her back and assessing her in the only way a mother could. She looked clean, pretty, and happy. Marissa hugged her again and looked at Hailey. "Emily, daddy is resting in the hospital, he has a little injury. He needs his rest. Aunt Hailey will take you back to the hotel and you can see daddy tomorrow. He will be so happy to see you."

"Daddy is hurt?" Emily asked her eyes wide.

"He will be fine, honey. I need to stay here, please go with Aunt Hailey." Marissa was tearing up and looked away.

Hailey met Marissa's eyes and mouthed, "I've got her," and distracted Emily by bringing her to the candy machine to pick out a chocolate bar. Within a few minutes, Hailey waved to Marissa, who blew a kiss to Emily, and Hailey brought her back to the hotel.

With Emily gone, Marissa went into Rick's room. Seeing him lying there hooked up to the machines truly devastated her.

A few minutes later the doctor came into the room, his surgical mask under his chin and his stethoscope around his neck. "Mrs. Lynch, I need to be up front with you," Dr. Rengle began. "Your husband suffered massive internal bleeding and loss of blood. He's in critical condition right now. The next forty-eight hours will tell us about his recovery. He will be monitored by our nursing staff 24/7."

Marissa started to cry. "Will he be, okay?" she stammered.

"We will know more in the next day or so what the status of his recovery could be. He has the best care." The doctor left shortly after, wiping his brow, and saying a silent prayer that Rick was strong enough to make it.

If he did survive, he would need to detox from all the drugs he's on. But that could wait until they knew if he would live.

Chapter 59

Two months later

Marissa became stronger than she ever imagined. She just had her hair done and felt good. She wore a leather brown belted jacket over her tan skirt, pink silk blouse, and nude heels. It's cooler in New York now. The weather had gone from Indian summer to autumn chill. The days have started getting shorter while nights fall earlier and darker.

Marissa rode up the elevator on her way to visit Rick at the hospital. They had called to tell her Rick began stirring and finally coming out of his coma. It's been a rough two months. Marissa dealt with parenting Emily, media attention, and a hidden pregnancy. She didn't want to reveal the hidden pregnancy just yet. Rick had remained in a coma for the last eight weeks. He had been medevacked to NYU hospital and had been receiving the best care.

Doctors seemed hopeful he would survive, but they weren't sure how he would be when he woke up. They warned Marissa to be prepared. Marissa was prepared alright. She learned quite a bit in two months. She had pictures, documents, and witnesses. Oh, Marissa was prepared. The two months of being on her own made her question so many things. Learning of Rick's drug use was shocking, but it definitely explained a lot of his actions. Marissa was a mixed bag of emotions. She felt anger, pity, concern...love. Her anger had been the dominant emotion these past two months. The lies, the deceit, the affair all played on her mind.

Then she saw Rick. She had been to the hospital many days during his recovery, and he had always been unconscious and hooked up to tubes and machines. She could compartmentalize her anger and feel badly for the poor man in a coma hooked up to machines. Now he was awake and staring at her.

"Hello," he said in a raspy voice when she entered the room. He looked thin and tired in his hospital gown.

Machines had been breathing for him for weeks and had taken their toll on his vocal cords.

"Rick," Marissa began in a cautious voice. She felt a mixed bag of emotions at seeing him awake.

Rick had a blank look on his face. His eyes met Marissa's but seemed different. She couldn't quite put her finger on it. Maybe it was him coming out of the coma, maybe he needed a moment.

But then, he stared at her for a moment, a long moment, before asking, "Who is Rick?" He didn't remember a thing.

Marissa stood there for a moment, her blue eyes went wide, and she replied, "Rick...are you being serious right now?" When he looked back at her blankly, she hit the button for the nurse.

While Marissa was paging the nurse, Lana snuck in a visit to the hospital. Trevor now knew that she was pregnant, and he was thrilled. Several years ago, the doctors informed him he would have a difficult time conceiving a child due to an issue he suffered as a teen. Lana was focused on her Public Relations career and fine with being an aunt or godmother and not a parent herself. Now, she and Trevor were about to become parents. Lana and Trevor were stronger than ever. In her mind, this baby was Trevor's, even if it may be a part of Rick, too. She wasn't completely sure and didn't feel the need to find out just yet, especially when there's still a chance it might never be necessary.

Lana was just starting to show, so she could still disguise it with her clothing. Lana took a deep breath, surprised at her nervousness of seeing him again after all this time. She was pregnant, this was her long-time lover. She felt so out of sorts seeing him, very unlike the confident woman that she was.

Bracing herself, she opened the door slowly to Rick's room. He was wearing sweats and he had just gotten done with a session with his physical therapist the nurse outside revealed as she pointed out Rick's room. After two months of being in a coma, Rick's body needed some strengthening. The doctors scheduled him to be moved to a rehabilitation facility in the next few days. His progress pleased them, and they were hopeful his memory would come back.

He suffered two traumas in a row, and the doctors were convinced his memory loss was a result of his drug withdrawals combined with the attack, stress of his daughter's kidnapping and the high altitude of the helicopter. Rick was in fact lucky to be alive. They planned on working with him on a therapeutic drug protocol once they had a grasp on why Rick did what he did to his body.

"Hello," Rick mumbled to the pretty woman who entered his room. The woman seemed somewhat familiar to him, but he didn't know her.

"Hi, Rick, you're looking well," remarked Lana. She noticed a blank look in his eyes when she spoke. Lana sensed the difference in him and wondered if she was imagining it.

"Do I know you? I'm sorry," he apologized. "They told me I lost my memory, and it will hopefully come back. I think I know you, but I don't know your name. I am sorry."

Lana could sense his frustration. "We are good friends," she simply stated. Biting the inside of her cheek, she tried holding in her shock, this was not what she expected at all. She was planning on checking on him, telling him it was over for good, and go home to Trevor. Instead, she was looking at a Rick she didn't know; a man who looked like her Rick but was a completely different person.

Rick looked at her with relief, his tense body relaxing and a smile reaching his eyes. "Oh, it is good to know I have friends. I was starting to wonder. Thank you for coming in. The guards let you in?"

Lana knew the family had hired twenty-four-hour guards and no one was allowed visitation. The nurse had told her when she had to show her credentials to get in. Lana's public relations pass gave her access to patients' rooms. She snuck in with her credentials, she had access to the floors on the hospital for press and public relations purposes. She used them to get past the guards and sneak in to see Rick.

"I just came to say hello and see if you needed anything," she claimed.

"I am okay," he replied. "Thank you. I asked my wife to bring me a vanilla shake and a burger later, but other than that I'm good. I apologize, I am not very good at conversations right now. It's just such a challenge when you try to remember things. I need to go back to bed now." He walked with a slight limp back to the hospital bed, grimaced at the pain he felt, but managed to smile at her, and settle in.

"Good seeing you, Rick," she stated, and left feeling incredibly sad for him. Lana walked out of the room sighing. As she stepped outside, the door closed, and she slumped against the wall for a moment in total disbelief. When she regained her composure, she turned and left, but not before looking back thoughtfully at his room. For just one moment she was nostalgic for the old Rick and what was but feeling the baby's slight kick brought her back to reality and to the moment.

He really had no sense of who he was. She hoped his memory returned. Rick was a force and if anyone could come back from this, it would be him. She rubbed her stomach as she left the room, truly hoping the baby she's carrying was Trevor's.

Chapter 60

Jake cleared the dishes from the table since Susan and Sherry cooked the lasagna. They turned into a nice little family. Jake and Susan recovered. Susan's journey was a little bit more difficult than Jake's. She needed two surgeries on her left leg that had been shattered in the accident. Although she still wore a boot, she's doing okay.

Jake moved into the spare bedroom in Sherry's house. Like Susan, Sherry saw the goodness in him and the love he had for her daughter. She made them promise to get their education first before marrying. Thankfully, they both agreed.

Jake loved how Sherry was playing mother to him. He never had anyone who cared before. Jake felt so happy to have that family feel. It was foreign to him and incredibly wonderful. He wore a bright smile around Sherry. His rough around the edges persona quickly faded with Sherry's tender loving care.

Sherry's name had been cleared, and she received a recommendation from Hailey and Chad to become a foster mother. She started the training, and she's going to therapy at the same time to understand her bad choices in men. She decided on fixing herself for the sake of the next child in her life. They would need her. Susan was thrilled for her mom and supported her any way she could. Sherry also enjoyed helping Hailey at the theater and Chad on the campaign. She's grateful for the good friends she made and liked being there for them, the way they were for her.

While Sherry, Jake and Susan worked on their family unit, Chad was doing some work on the campaign. "We need to walk two more districts today, speak at the civic association at 1 p.m. and dinner with the committeemen at 5 p.m." Jillian stated, going over the day's schedule with her brother.

Despite the crazy publicity from the Lynch kidnapping attempt and the revelation that he's definitely a couple with Hailey, he was doing okay in the polls. The press had gone wild over the Lynch connection, but Chad had been forthright and as honest as he could be. Yes, he's serious about his run for office. Yes, he could give the job his attention if he won. No, he was not connected to the Lynches other than dating Hailey and being a good guy who helps. No, he was not having an affair with Marissa and dating Hailey, too. He was honestly disgusted by some of the questions and swiftly diffused them. He talked about his run for office, changed the subject as often as he could, and left the rest up to their imagination.

Which may or may not have been a good thing. He would find out in six weeks on election night. For now, he was campaigning as often as he could, incredibly grateful and impressed by all the tireless volunteers.

"Sounds good," he commented to Jillian with a tired half smile.

"How are you holding up?" she asked.

"I am good," he replied, pushing back his hair. "I really want to do this."

Jillian smiled and nodded. "You needed to realize you could do this, and not hear it from Grandma and Dad."

Chad nodded in agreement.

"Oh," Jillian added with a teasing smile, "I like Hailey, too, she is a keeper."

Chad laughed, loving her comment. "Yes, she is. Yes, she is." He smiled at the thought of Hailey. What that woman did to him.

They were pretty much living together at this point, going between their two places. They talked of scaling down to one of them when both their leases were up in the spring, but for now this worked. They just loved being together. She had her theater groups and chorus rehearsals, while he had his work and campaigning. They met at one place or the other, cooked dinner, or brought it in. The romance felt wonderful and to both of them, it felt like home.

The real test would be this weekend as Cecilia invited the two of them to lunch, and Hailey would be meeting her for the first time. Of course, Cecilia sent them the helicopter to get to the hospital during the Emily crisis, and Hailey called and thanked her afterwards. That had gone well, and now the invitation to lunch. Cecilia had always been politically motivated. Chad feared she was plotting something, but he would try to give her the benefit of the doubt. Chad loved his grandmother, but did he trust her? Nope!

Chad's iPhone buzzed. He looked down and saw a text from Hailey. "Rick is out of the coma but has no memory of anything. They are going to bring Emily over to see if he recognizes her. I hope that is the right decision. What if he doesn't recognize his own child?"

Chad processed the whole thing. His face was one of shock. How could this even be? Rick Lynch without a memory? Wow! Chad hoped it was temporary, but at least he's out of the coma and alive. Everyone wondered.

Marissa had been a mess for a while, and Hailey stayed with her. Then Marissa learned things about Rick that made her angry, and she sought therapy to get through it all. Marissa seemed stronger, different after everything she's gone through. Chad really liked this Marissa he had gotten to know. She had a strength about her and she's a smart, focused woman.

Hailey still seemed very different from her sister, but Marissa had a good side she now shows. She was a product of an abusive relationship and Marissa as well as her daughter became quite close with Reeve and his family. Emily liked playing with their fourteen-month-old son, Nolan.

Marissa did what she could to help Reeve the way he helped her. With her influence, he had been promoted to host a science, nature show. It was Reeve's dream, and it had come true. Reeve often spent time coming down and volunteering at Chad's campaign office. He insisted on only listening to country music when he was there and was a hit with the ladies.

"Dad may not remember you," Marissa cautiously advised Emily, who looked sad, her face crinkled in a frown. She really missed her daddy so much! "He had a bad injury. But we are hoping that seeing you will help him to remember."

Marissa consulted with her counselor and Emily's counselor to see if this was the right thing to do. Both had spoken to Emily, and she wanted to see her dad. Emily's counselor planned a telehealth session with her immediately after the visit to make sure she was okay. Emily also asked to call Sherry, as they remained close. Marissa had been hesitant of the relationship at first, but soon realized what a good woman Sherry was and allowed her to come over each week and visit Emily. They mostly baked together, and it seemed to be a therapeutic thing for them both.

Marissa had come far in the two months since she hadn't been under Rick's control and his apparent drugging of her and himself. She found Adderall, cocaine, Xanax, and the sleeping pills that were found during her blood test all over the place in Rick's private bathroom and closets. Marissa was so hurt and angry. Tears flowed down her face, and she clenched her jaw tightly. She threw everything away and cried herself to sleep at his betrayal and hidden lies. She sought lawyers, and prepared to say goodbye, but she was pregnant again. Pregnant with his child. A child conceived with love when things were going well.

She owed it to herself and the baby to wait. Wait until this man had his memory back, wait until she could confront him about Lana and the drugs, wait until she could have her peace. As angry as she was, she couldn't abandon him now. She needed to help the man she loved to function again and be okay. Then and only then, when he was in a good place would she confront him.

Wide-eyed, Emily entered the hospital room. Marissa held her hand, and she gripped it tighter. Marissa let go of Emily's hand because her hand began to tremble from nervousness. She didn't want to let on how anxious she was to either Emily or Rick. Rick looked up when they walked in. He was still exhausted; his physical therapist was working him hard to regain use of his muscles.

"Hi," he said to Marissa and the little girl holding her hand. She was a pretty little thing.

"Hi, Rick," Marissa began. "How are you doing today?"

Rick smiled and replied cautiously, "Feels good to be alive."

The doctors told him how lucky he was to be here. They explained the amnesia was most likely temporary. They told him a little bit about his identity and that he was a lawyer, married to Marissa, and they had a child. He assumed the child with Marissa was his daughter, but he didn't recognize her at all. Rick was confused by this and upset that he didn't know her. He squeezed his eyes shut for a moment, forcing himself to have a recollection of her, but none came.

Emily shyly looked at him, biting her lip and exclaimed, "Daddy, I've missed you so much." She ran to him and hugged him.

Rick was caught off guard but hugged the poor child. He wished he could remember her. She did seem familiar. Her hair color, bright auburn, was striking and he could almost recall it, but he didn't know anything about her. She jumped into his arms and hugged him tight. He must have been close to her.

"Aww. Thank you," he whispered, hugging her back.

"Do you remember me, Daddy?" she asked with big curious blue eyes.

Rick's heart began to race, and his blood pressure machines started beeping. Emily swiftly jumped off the bed.

Marissa's eyes widened in fear. "Maybe we need to go now," Marissa murmured, cautiously, taking Emily's nervous hand in hers.

Rick settled back on the bed and the beeping stopped. "I am glad you came, Emily. I am glad to see you." The girl meant something to him. Rick sensed it. He hoped he could remember more about her. "Will you both come back soon?" he asked, looking shyly at them. Rick was slightly red faced and his eyes wouldn't meet theirs. He was nervous about their response back to him.

Marissa nodded and Emily agreed, "Yes." They both waved goodbye and left. Rick's face lit up like a Christmas tree. Their visit had made his day.

Chapter 61

A month later

Lana sat and had coffee with Marissa in a small cafe on the upper East Side called Our Cup of Tea. They were seated at a small glass table in a private corner. Marissa wore her hair up in a high ponytail and sunglasses. Somehow, she had managed to evade any attention. Usually, she was recognized wherever he went.

"I'm glad we have reached this place after everything that has happened," Marissa began, taking a sip of her decaf coffee. It was her one cup a day treat for herself since finding out she was pregnant again. She and Lana had navigated a lot in the past few months, coming to terms with the affair and Rick's memory loss.

"You are quite a woman, Marissa," Lana commented, looking across the table at Marissa, meeting her eyes and smiling. They were friends now; Lana had come to Marissa on her own and told her everything.

"I know already," Marissa replied, looking stoically at Lana. "I've known for a long time." The anger Marissa felt over Lana and Rick dissipated with therapy and time. Lana kept checking on Marissa daily, and at first it was a thorn in her side, and she felt nothing but anger. After a time, loneliness and fear took over, and Lana became someone to lean on. She knew Rick as well as Marissa did, sometimes she thought maybe more. Marissa finally had the guts to ask her the question she feared the most. "Is the baby Rick's?"

Lana claimed, "It is Trevor's." She looked Marissa square in the eyes as she said it. Lana wouldn't let any other thought enter her head now that her marriage was back on track.

Trevor and Lana were in marriage counseling together. They both acknowledged a rift, and when Lana started to tell him about someone else, he stopped her by saying, "Let the past stay there, our future is this child."

He questioned, his voice quiet, "Is it over?" in front of the counselor.

"It is." She's going to be a mother and Trevor a father. The baby deserved them both vested in its future. With hard work, things started looking good for them.

Marissa sipped her tea and looked at Lana. A lot changed in the months since Rick's accident. Marissa, being Rick's wife, knew a ton about entertaining. She had worked with chefs, party planners, and musicians. While Lana knew everything there was to know about public relations and marketing. It was still hard for both of them to believe they were business partners.

After their tense beginning, Lana and Marissa realized they had more in common than sleeping with the enemy. They were both bright women who shared a common vision. Marissa felt like a bird set free from Rick's control. She shared with Lana that she suspected him of drugging her.

"I wouldn't put it past him," Lana acknowledged. "He hid his drug use from both of us. It was probably his way of dealing with everything, pills, and a line."

Lana and Marissa decided to fill their void created by Rick and channel it into a little side business. They sent a few emails, found a few clients, and had been an instant hit. L&M corporate events were booked solid for the next three months. They even had to hire some staff. They did everything from business lunches to large events. Lana already had a name for herself, but Marissa was creating one for the first time. She discussed the next event with Lana, a lunch for twenty at Gleason Corp. and looked at her cell.

"Can we touch base later?" she asked Lana. "The doctor wants to meet with me at 2 p.m. over Rick's memory."

"Sure," Lana agreed, nodding, sensing Marissa's sadness.

Rick hadn't regained his memory yet, but he was getting to know her in a new way which was intriguing. Marissa had been asked to bring wedding pictures and anything she could think of that could help trigger Rick's memory. Every time she went to the rehab facility, she brought something different.

Today she was bringing their engagement photo. It's a twenty-year-old Marissa with her chestnut hair flowing down her back, a slight baby bump and Rick at twenty-seven years old looking like he stepped out of a modeling magazine. He and Marissa made a stunning couple. The photographer even commented they both should be models. Marissa was wearing a lilac bathing suit and Rick was in his turquoise swim trunks, the photographer had caught them in a romantic pose staring into each other's eyes.

Marissa hoped this happy photo would open a door. She wanted Rick's memory back more than anything. She liked this new, gentler Rick, but she wanted the old Rick back, too. She would love old Rick to have new Rick's gentleness. She hoped when his memory came back, a piece of this Rick stayed with him. Marissa said her goodbyes to Lana and headed to Skyline Rehab to meet with the doctor and Rick.

Rick sat inside Skyline Rehab, feeling excited for the first time in months. He had a memory, and he couldn't wait to see Marissa and have it validated. His physical body was getting stronger. He was allowed to ride an exercise bike now and use some light weights. He was starting to feel like a man again and not like a patient. He read every day, law articles, current event magazines and just some mindless magazines on finance and business.

They were still keeping him from using the computer and internet unattended which bothered him. Apparently, there's a lot on him on the net and the doctor said he didn't want to overload Rick. He wanted his memory to come back organically. The fact Rick had a memory was a wonderful sign. He was off all drugs at the moment, but it took work and detoxification. Rick was most definitely a closet addict, and the doctors formed a team to get him off and healing.

When he returned to full memory, they would put him on a medically prescribed regimen. The doctors had many conversations with this new Rick, and he understood the old Rick had a serious problem. They brought nutritionists in to see him, and psychiatrists had done evaluations. The old Rick was a brilliant force to be reckoned with fueled by drugs. The new man could still be a force, but he would be forced to slow down and not self-medicate. It would be a process.

First, they needed to work on getting his memory back. He seemed to be confident this particular memory could be validated. If so, he was opening the door for his subconscious to heal. It's a great sign.

Rick heard the door open and saw Marissa walk in. She looked stunningly beautiful, and he felt the wind get truly knocked out of him every time he saw her.

"Hi, Rick," she remarked, waving, and entering the room.

Sometimes she would hold his hand, but there hasn't been more than that. Marissa explained she needed to get to know him again, and he needed to get to know her. She wanted to take things very slowly.

He asked her once if he was a good husband.

She hesitated when answering, remembering his proposal in the park, being with her when Emily was born, the way he treated her the first five years, and then she remembered the affair, the mental abuse, the control, her heart clenching and beating faster in her chest. She thought of her next words carefully. "When you were good, you were amazing. When you weren't, it was difficult." Her eyes locked onto his, and her whole demeanor changed. Her shoulders tensed and her jaw locked as she thought about the anguish he put her through over the years.

He saw the hurt in her eyes when she admitted it. He wanted to hug her, but he barely knew her and didn't want to startle her. He hoped his news would bring her back to a good place.

"Marissa, I had a memory," he remarked, excitedly. "I know it was one."

Marissa smiled and sat down, waiting for him to go on.

"Our first date was at a place called Antonio's. You wore a red silk dress, and we talked about traveling to Rome."

Marissa looked at him wide eyed, gasping and burst out crying. His first real memory back after five months was of their date. She reached for his hand and caressed it, holding it in her own. The memories warmed her heart.

"Yes, Rick, and the next weekend you flew me to Rome on a private jet. Oh, Rick, your memory is returning." She hugged him then. Rick was startled but moved by her affection. He wiped a tear from his own eye and held her close, breathing in the fresh scent of her hair.

She hoped this would be the return of him coming back. On the other hand, she feared the return of the old Rick knowing what she knew now.

"It's a wonderful start," she whispered, knowing how important this moment was to him. "Wonderful."

Chapter 62

"Welcome to my home," Cecelia proclaimed, smiling at Hailey. Cecelia was wearing a pink button-down cardigan, blue skirt, white crisp linen shirt and her trademark pearls. She looked elegant in her attire sitting on her chair on the porch with her crocheting.

Hailey and Chad had driven from the city out to the Hamptons on that early fall Sunday. The leaves were rapidly changing, and the air was definitely crisp. Chad had a ton of campaign work to do, but he promised his grandmother she could meet Hailey.

"So nice to meet you." Hailey smiled back at Cecelia. Cecelia studied her for a moment, her head tilting to the right, and pursing her pink lipstick covered lips. She must have liked what she saw because Hailey's smile was returned, reaching Cecelia's eyes, lighting up her whole face.

Hailey looked gorgeous in her long turquoise skirt, tall brown leather boots, and beige sweater. She wore her hair down and to him she looked like a wholesome girl next door. She made Chad stop and pick up flowers for Cecelia and a chocolate frosted cake from the bakery. As they arrived, she went over and handed both to the regal Cecelia.

"Thank you," Cecelia commented, smiling. She called for Ingrid, the housekeeper, who came out of the kitchen.

Without a word and a glimmer of a smile, Ingrid took both from Cecelia. She winked at Chad and went back into the kitchen. Ingrid had worked for Cecelia for over fifteen years and knew the real her. She was up to something, and Ingrid wanted to eavesdrop and find out what it was.

"I am so glad to see you two. You are quite the striking couple," Cecelia comments. "I think you are more beautiful than your sister."

Hailey exclaims, "Oh, no! I thank you for the compliment, but Marissa is gorgeous. I am happy being me." She blushes at her words.

Cecelia looked at her with sincerity and a sweet smile on her face. "You may not have the flash and dash, but you are sincere and that, my dear, is a much more attractive trait. She points one pink manicured finger at Hailey. You keep being you."

Hailey smiled turning a deeper shade of red as she murmured, "Thank you."

Chad sat back a little more relaxed. This seemed to be going well. Cecelia was animated for her and smiling the whole time. Her posture relaxed as well.

Ingrid came out with tea and finger sandwiches. They all enjoyed the meal. Then Cecelia turned to Chad and insisted, "After you are sworn in, we need to plan your wedding. It should be here in spring on the main lawn. Now, set a date."

Hailey looked at Chad with wide eyes, Chad looked at Hailey with a smile tugging at his lips, and they both burst out laughing.

"I guess you like her," Chad replied, grinning.

"Chadwick," Cecelia warned in her stern tone, giving him a pointed look, "you would be a horse's behind to let her slip away."

Ingrid, truly eavesdropping on the other side of the door, fell into the room. The door fell open when she leaned against it laughing so hard. Everyone, even Cecelia, burst out laughing at the sight.

Chad and Hailey left hand in hand. Hailey glanced up at him, noticing he seemed to be lost in a daze. Hailey squeezed his hand asking, "What are you thinking?"

He smiled and remarked, "I'm glad it went well."

Hailey didn't know he liked the idea of the wedding on the lawn in the spring. He'd been waiting for the election to be over to move forward with them as a couple. But now that Cecelia had planted the idea in his head, he wanted to get her a ring. Chad leaned over and kissed her. He couldn't wait to surprise her.

Chapter 63

Rick began having more and more memories. He had memories of Emily's birth and her first words. His heart leaps, ecstatic at remembering his child. He was remembering his child! He remembered her first pink bike with the basket on the front and her learning to pedal, he remembered her swim lessons at the private school pool. Smiling, he remembered the first time she read The Cat in The Hat. Rick was so emotional over this, he felt so much love for Emily, all-encompassing love. This was such a breakthrough and Rick felt extremely grateful to have this tidbit of memory return about Emily.

The doctors were thrilled with his progress and encouraged Marissa to come by more often. Although she did, she remained guarded and cautious. She was still concealing her pregnancy from Rick. She had been warned it may be too much for him to handle just yet. Marissa always wore a jacket or something that would hide her middle.

They were keeping Emily away at this point. She had been freaked out at seeing her daddy like this. She called him on the phone or waved to him on FaceTime, but it was controlled and only for short spurts. Emily certainly missed her daddy and was always busy drawing pictures for his room.

"How are you doing today?" the doctor asked him on his rounds.

"I think better, honestly. I remember more and more each day and I have been keeping a journal like you advised. The problem is, I am not sure I like the me I'm learning about."

Dr. Stern, the psychologist, looked at him and replied, "You can still be the man you want to be, Rick. This is really your chance at a clean slate. You can't change the past, but you can change the future."

Rick nodded in acknowledgement, looking down at his hands nervously.

"I think it's time for you to have a visit home."

Rick smiled. He had seen pictures of his majestic home and some of the pictures gave him a feeling of being familiar. He was scared, but ready to see his home. "I need to try a visit," Rick acknowledged. "Hopefully it helps bring back my memory."

The doctor nodded in affirmation. "Great. I will call Marissa."

Chapter 64

Chad had been doing some heavy-duty campaigning as the election approached. It was down to the wire, and his opponent was starting to come on strong. His latest trash campaign had Chad being patted on the back by his dad while being wheeled in a stroller. The ad claimed, "Born and raised to take over for Dad." Another campaign had him walking hand in hand with Hailey and stating, "Too in love to worry about real world problems." It was getting nasty and it disgusted Chad.

He had amazing ideas to help the community stay safer, help the homeless population, make lunches free for school children, and provide more theater and after school programs for children. Chad also wanted to do more for seniors. He would have Cecelia be on that committee. She would get those seniors involved in all sorts of programs for civic associations.

Chad wanted this job, but he wanted it ethically, based on who he was and all that he could do for the people and the community. Chad didn't believe in having a slanderous campaign and refused to stoop to that level. Jillian and Harding got him out there in the community, he attended store openings and library programs. The most fun he had was appearing on Reeve's show called, "Reevelation." His show focused on environmental aspects of the area, nature preserves, and animal rescues.

Reeve was an instant hit and had quite a following as a meteorologist. Now, his fans seemed excited to see him branch out. Marissa may have been the one who helped him make his dream come true, but he's the one who's making it a success.

Chad went on the episode focusing on preservation and recycling. Reeve had him on to talk about his plans and prospective policies of restoring a historic lake in the area that had been unfortunately polluted. Lake Ronsona was a historic lake formed by a glacier, and the subject of many stories and legends. Cecelia often spoke of how it had once been a resort. But tragically, it was now unswimmable, and mainly uninhabitable for fish and other wildlife.

Reeve focused on Chad's plans for restoration and the ratings flew off the charts. Reeve had Chad's opponent, Todd Lansing, on the other day to be a fair journalist, and he brought up none of this. The press had loved the idea of the restoration of the lake and had featured a story in a positive light on Chad. "Changing the environment Chad" became his press nickname. Chad didn't mind that one bit.

Chapter 65

Hailey went with Marissa to pick Rick up for his weekend out of the Rehab center. The doctor felt it would be good for Rick to try to be home. Rick's memory may have a breakthrough being back in his own environment. It had been over five months at this point.

Marissa also knew she wouldn't be able to hide the pregnancy anymore. She was nervous about the big reveal and everyone's reaction, especially Rick's.

It's time for a conversation. Did she still love Rick? Yes. It's definitely a yes. She's also falling in love with the new Rick. This man was a softer, less intense version of the old Rick. Marissa still had a lot of anger over his affair with Lana, and knowing he drugged her at times. It was insane. She probably would have thrown the old Rick out, money and all, but this new Rick was worth giving a shot to. Afterall, she was carrying his baby.

"Welcome home," Hailey proclaimed to Rick, opening the car door when the driver pulled up to the majestic home.

"I live here?" Rick questioned, giving a wolf whistle. "Nice place." He arched his eyebrows and looked so surprised, his eyes went wide at the enormity of the home. It was a brick structured building with white siding located in the suburbs of Manhattan in Westchester. The home had six bedrooms and five bathrooms, and it was situated on ten sprawling acres of land and bordered a river. They had to drive up a driveway that went uphill for 300 yards. The house was spectacular.

Marissa and Hailey both laughed. Hailey had to agree with Marissa, this new Rick was sweet and humble. It was like having all the great traits of Rick all the time.

"Yes." Marissa states. "One thing you always did was work hard. You are quite a successful lawyer and legal commentator on talk shows."

Rick had heard that before. He squeezed his eyes shut trying to pull a memory from the computer in his mind, but none came at that moment. He pursed his lips in frustration, but then let it go as he looked around the beautiful home. He did have memories of work; they were coming a lot. He had been reading constantly in rehab and requested law books. He felt confident once his memory came back fully, he could return to work. He shared that with Marissa. So odd he remembered trials, but not his house. Rick sighed and looked at the wall clenching and unclenching his hands in frustration.

Marissa took his hand. "Remember, the doctor said to take it slow. Memories may start to come back, and if it feels like it's too much, we can go back."

She watched as Rick smiled at her and squeezed her hand. "I want to do this."

Hailey thought it was time for her to leave. Marissa asked the driver to take her back to Chad's place. Rick and Marissa needed this time alone. Marissa thanked Hailey and the driver and brought Rick up the steps to their home.

Marissa punched in the code for the door lock and led Rick in.

"Wow," he mumbled under his breath, taking in the magnitude of the house.

Rick looked at the gold banisters and marble staircase. He took in the expensive art, carefully matted, and framed. He walked over to a portrait of him, Emily, and Marissa when Emily was around four. Her auburn hair was up in a high ponytail, and she wore a purple dress and tights. She was clutching a teddy bear in the picture.

"Marissa," Rick began excitedly, "I remember that bear and that picture. I remember."

Marissa smiled and enlightened him, "Yes, your parents sent it to Emily. It's still her favorite."

Rick smiled and excitedly started moving around the room. He was trying to bring back more memories. He started moving a bit frantically and Marissa stepped towards him reaching out. "Stop, Rick. It's okay." He took her hand and held it in his own as she continued, "The doctor said not to force it. Let's go have some lunch. Emily will be home soon from the park."

At the mention of Emily's name, Rick's lips tugged up in a grin. He was remembering more and more about his daughter, and it made him smile.

Rick followed Marissa out to the enclosed garden area. There was a beautiful table and wicker chairs in there, with the whole room filled with exotic flowering plants.

The house, resting on the ten acres of property and bordering the river had a view from the room that was spectacular. Rick once again could not fathom the amount of money he must have to afford this place. He had no idea of the amount of blood sweat and tears the old Rick put into his career.

The new Rick could be happy with a comfortable chair, a pair of sweats, and a good book. Technology was only being allowed for him in controlled, supervised intervals. The old Rick had detoxed from drugs and technology at the same time. If ever there was a perk to this episode of amnesia, this was it.

Emily came home with her new nanny, Jada. Susan, after the accident, had chosen just to focus on school. Marissa freed her of her guilt and offered to keep her on. Susan thanked her, offered to return the summer money (which Marissa did not accept), and focused on school. However, Sherry came here at least once a week, and filled them in on how Susan was doing.

"Hi, Daddy," Emily whispers, shyly, smiling at him.

"Hi, Emily. Thank you for all of the cards. They are hanging in my room at the place that's helping me get better."

Emily's smile widened. "You remember me?"

Swallowing the lump in his throat and his eyes glistening with tears, Rick replied in a soft voice. "Yes, Emily, I do. I am starting to have lots of amazing memories with you in them."

"Oh, Daddy!" Emily squealed, and ran into his arms, where Rick gave her the biggest hug his heart full.

This was truly the therapy he needed. Marissa stood off to the side with a smile. Her heart was racing. After a few moments, she left the room to pull herself together and check in with the doctor.

Chapter 66

Chad stood at a campaign rally in downtown Manhattan. Harding and Jillian had arranged for it to be in Gramercy Park. It's a pretty populated area, filled with a combination of businesses and residential apartments. Chad was speaking to an outraged group from the Queens neighborhood today about tenant rights. The people there had been dealing with some lousy treatment. Many went without heat on the frigid days and working air conditioners on the hot days.

Chad did his speech drawing the attention of the residents and the press when he proclaimed, "You will not walk alone in solving this. I will walk with you."

His words led to a burst of cheers from the audience, and then suddenly Chad heard some familiar voices singing, "Praise the Lord, our angel has come...amen."

Chad looked into the crowd and saw about seven members of the gospel choir he and Hailey had been rescued by. Chad smiled, clapping for their singing.

"My friends are here, I see," Chad stated into the microphone. "Please, come up to the podium." He gestured to them, waving them over. Turning back to the crowd, he gestured to the people approaching, announcing, "Ladies and gentlemen, these are some of the heroes who rescued Hailey and I when we were stranded upstate during the rescue of Emily Lynch. These are the real heroes who stopped to help two dehydrated strangers."

The crowd laughed and clapped as the seven made their way to the stage, each one shaking hands with Chad as they stepped forward.

"I won't let you down," he stated to each of them.

They clapped Chad on the back. "Great job!" the first stated.

Followed by, "You are the man for the job." Each one looked at him with awe and pride. He has their votes.

Chad knew he needed to work hard to convince the rest of the crowd he was a man who was honorable, ethical and could get the job done with their best interests in mind. He's up for the challenge.

Chad took questions from the crowd. "What will you be doing about crime in our neighborhood?" a woman asks.

"Great question," Chad answers. "I will be working very carefully with the police commissioner to create a localized crime prevention team and implement an active neighborhood watch." The crowd clapped in response to his statement.

Chad continued to answer questions on his plans for seniors, helping with affordable housing and rallying for the construction of a neighborhood park. He finally felt like this was where he belonged and what he wanted to do. Surprising himself, Chad wanted this with all his heart and soul. He knew he could be the voice of change.

Chapter 67

Sherry came over to the Lynch's house on Sunday and was baking chocolate chunk cookies with Emily. The first night having Rick home had gone well. He slept in the guest room, but he understood why. Marissa was getting to know him again, and he was getting to know her. Although there was definitely still an attraction, both of them needed to take it slow, especially Marissa.

Rick had a few breakthrough memories of Emily learning to crawl and playing soccer when she was three. Emily was thrilled he was having the memories. They were a signal to them all that his brain was beginning to heal. She kept hugging him and saying how nice he was. So many people were saying that to him. He felt humbled by their reactions and a bit puzzled.

He really wondered what he was like before, and yet, he was almost afraid to know. Marissa still seemed cautious with him, again giving him the feeling he hurt her very badly. He wondered what he did. Everyone still seemed to be treading lightly with him. He understood but wished for some normalcy.

Sherry looked over at him sitting in the chair in the living room. Rick was going through photo albums filled with pictures of Emily. "Mr. Lynch, can I get you a cup of coffee or tea?"

Rick looked up and smiled at Sherry and Emily baking cookies. "Coffee would be wonderful. Thank you," he said appreciatively.

Sherry seemed very kind and Emily was so happy to be with her, she didn't stop smiling. He had been told her daughter used to be Emily's nanny, and Sherry had been good to Emily. No one broached the subject of the kidnapping with Rick. That would be a story for another day.

Rick liked the smell of the cookies and loved listening to the chatter between Sherry and Emily. He enjoyed his coffee and company. This was much better than rehab. He had to go back in a few hours. Marissa was out shopping for some more sweats for him before he had to go back. The weekend had gone well, and he did find many things familiar again giving him some comfort. He hoped he would be back to himself again soon.

Lana joined Marissa for a girls' day out. They headed to the outlets to shop for sweats for Rick and baby clothes. Marissa didn't need to hide her pregnancy anymore from Rick, but he didn't seem to notice or even question her on her changing shape. They slept in separate rooms, and she wore bulky sweaters and a bathrobe. She wasn't ready for anything else just yet.

Understandably, she didn't talk about that with Lana at all. Lana asked, "How is Rick doing?" Marissa filled her in. "Progressing at his own pace, I guess," she simply stated, thankful to put an end to the conversation.

To Lana, the affair was a thing of the past, and her future was Trevor and the baby. Marissa was a different, stronger Marissa and she was not letting the past influence her future., it certainly wasn't easy, as she didn't go into things too deeply with Rick for that reason. Why dredge up the past when there was a future out there for them.

Was it odd she had become good friends with her husband's mistress? Probably, but it was working for them both as a business arrangement and now friendship. Lana had been with him for so long, it felt more like she was an ex -wife to Rick.

Her therapist had been incredibly proud of her and referred to her as his miracle patient to his colleagues. Not many wives would be this forgiving. Marissa wasn't sure where her future lay regarding Rick, but she liked her future having a career and a friend. Two things she was not entitled to with the old Rick. Could this new Rick be what she needed?

Chapter 68

Election Day was upon them sooner than anyone anticipated. Chad had given it his all, and regardless of the outcome, he was proud of his efforts, and grateful for everyone who helped and supported him throughout the whole process.

His mom and dad had flown in, and Cecelia had her hair done and of course purchased a Dior dress for the event. Cecelia beamed with pride at Chad. She believed he lived up to the family name and campaigned with dignity. She was certain he would win and keep the legacy alive.

Hailey stayed by his side the entire day. She was off from school that day, and knew Chad needed her for support. He was nervous and excited. He went early to vote and found the press there waiting for him. They snapped pictures of him at the polls.

The voter turnout appeared great! It was a beautiful fall day and people came out in droves, okay with waiting in the long lines.

Harding and Jillian took Chad and Hailey to lunch at the Japanese steakhouse down the road from the polling place. He didn't want to go too far but needed the distraction for an hour or two.

"How does this feel?" Jillian asked her brother between bites of her steaming Hibachi chicken.

"Surreal," Chad admitted. "Tomorrow I am either a senator or I'll be back to being Chad the lawyer."

Hailey looked at him lovingly and squeezed his hand. "You gave it your all, and you already helped so many."

Chad smiled at her and reached for his iced tea and took a drink. "I also met you along the way," he emphasized as he set his glass down, looking back at her.

Hailey blushed and they smiled, staring into each other's eyes.

"Barf," exclaimed Harding, barely hiding his smirk. "Listen, lovebirds, we are trying to eat here."

Jillian narrowed her eyes and playfully gave Harding a light punch, making all of them burst out laughing. "Oh, Harding, I remember a time when you were a romantic man who swept me off my feet," Jillian playfully taunts.

Harding laughs. "Oh, you want to be swept off your feet, do you?" He looks over at Jillian and gives her his Groucho Marx eyebrows.

Jillian pretends to swoon Hollywood style as he plants a dramatic kiss on her lips. Everyone bursts into laughter.

As they settled down and caught their breath, Hailey exchanged a loving look with Chad who smiled back. Life felt good, for the moment and Chad was grateful, and excited for what lay ahead. He was happy to have his family, friends, and most of all his beautiful Hailey. be here to support him. Whatever the results end up being tonight, he was ready.

Chapter 69

There was just no hiding her pregnancy now, Marissa had popped. At her last appointment, she found out the baby was a boy. He's a kicker, definitely a soccer player.

She hadn't visited Rick for three days since she has been so busy with her events with Lana. The work was good for her, but Marissa felt incredibly guilty for the time spent away from him and hopes it hasn't been detrimental to his recovery.

They had to organize and implement two corporate lunches and one dental conference. Fortunately, they were both a big success.

Sherry volunteered to visit Rick on the days Marissa couldn't, and she brought Emily with her. Emily was thrilled to see her dad, and they were forging a special relationship. Emily shared her artwork with him and even left a box of crayons for him. "Daddy, drawing makes me happy, it will make you happy too," she exclaimed, hugging him tight. Rick's face lit up and he held Emily tight. He was so happy to see her. She was his special angel who brought him so much joy.

Rick was making tremendous progress. The doctors scheduled him to finally come home next week. He's so ecstatic. He feels immense relief at being out of the hospital shortly and hopes he can return to some normalcy in his life, whatever that may be. Although he had no idea what the future would be with Marissa, he couldn't wait to go home and be with his family again. He felt he was ready. He hoped and prayed that Marissa would give him another chance and open her heart again to him.

Marissa was nervous about Rick coming home. She pondered what it would be like with him back home every day and if he would return to the old Rick. More than anything, she wondered how Rick would react to the pregnancy. There was definitely no way of hiding it now. Marissa was so nervous, the old Rick wanted only one child, and he had his prize in Emily. How would he feel about this baby? Marissa felt anxious and nervous about the big reveal.

To distract herself with thoughts of Rick, she texted Hailey, wishing Chad luck. Chad was a good man, and Marissa was glad her sister landed in his arms.

Wishing Chad much success, she texted and sent it with a smile. Marissa couldn't wait to see the results. Chad deserved the win. She believed he was the kind of man who would always be 'in the right place at the right time.'

Chapter 70

"And there is much excitement tonight over the race for Senator of the seventh district. It is a close race, but it looks like Chadwick Harper is going to be declared the winner." The news reporter from Channel 8 was reporting from the party headquarters in downtown Manhattan.

The red, white, and blue decorated room was filled with hundreds of party supporters. It was an extremely festive atmosphere with music playing as well as drinks and hors d'oeuvre flowing. Chad was surrounded by his parents, grandmother, and Hailey.

"It's looking good, son," Thad stated, patting him on the back.

Chad nodded, taking it all in. It had been quite the ride and he was exhausted but excited. He's proud of the campaign he ran and the road he traveled. He saw this election night event and his campaign supporters being there as an honor. He received his concession phone call from his opponent Jed Henderson, and Chad accepted it with grace and congratulated him on running a very classy campaign.

At 11:02 p.m. that night, Chad was officially declared the winner. He felt his eyes well with tears that he fought to hold back as Cecelia gave him a hug and his dad shook his hand. Hailey met his eyes and wiped away her own proud tears as Chad was led to the stage.

At 11:05 p.m. Chad made his acceptance speech, thanking his supporters and campaign volunteers. "It is with tremendous gratitude that I stand before you, accepting the senatorial position. I am honored to represent the 23rd district in the great city of New York."

"My adversary ran a good race. He is a good man who will still do much for the city."

"I will do everything in my power to listen to the people of this community and strive to give you all the quality of life that you so deserve." The crowd went wild after his speech and knowing they voted a good man into office.

At 11:20 p.m. Hailey was escorted onto the stage by Harding. "He wants you beside him," Harding states, smiling at Hailey.

The press continued snapping away as Hailey tentatively approached Chad. He smiled at Hailey and pulled her into an embrace. The press went wild, cameras flashing, live reports taking place. Chad suddenly looks at Hailey and proclaims, "You are beautiful, I am a lucky man."

Hailey smiles and responds with a loving look, "I am the lucky one, and I couldn't be more proud of you."

The room erupts in applause at her reply, and then a hush settles over the crowd as Chad gets down on one knee and presents her with a two-carat diamond ring surrounded by stones from his grandmother's ring. Cecelia had given it to him on the day she met Hailey. Chad wanted to buy Hailey a ring, but this one had so much sentiment and she knew that Hailey had forged a bond with Cecelia and would be thrilled.

"Hailey, I love you. Will you be my wife? You help make me the man I am and the husband who I want to be. I would be honored if you would marry me."

Hailey looked beautiful, her green eyes glistening with tears and her chestnut highlights sparkling in the bright lights. She couldn't love him more, and she couldn't have asked for a more spectacular night. Hailey put her hand in Chad's as he placed the gorgeous ring on her finger, pulling her into a loving embrace. She kissed him with a kiss that displayed her love for him while the press happily snapped away.

Marissa saw the proposal live on the air, her heart clenching. She couldn't have been happier for her sister. Chad had told Marissa the plan and she helped Chad call their parents and asked to be able to fly them out to meet him. He told their parents how much he loved Hailey and that he called to ask their permission. Everyone could see his authenticity and love for Hailey.

Marissa turned off the TV with a smile. She remembered being in love like that. Rick had truly swept her off her feet. Could she have that kind of love with him again? She was still working through her resentment of him possibly drugging her, having an affair for a decade, and just having that erratic side to him, and now finding out he had been self-medicating. It's a lot to process.

Yet, the new Rick seemed to be everything she would want in a man. She talked endlessly to her therapist and wanted to really give it a chance with him.

He was due to come home for good tomorrow. He had been here for two weekends in a row, and it had gone well. He had memories now of buying the home, going to law school, his first car and many, many with Emily and now even some wonderful memories of the early romantic years with Marissa. Although, he still had no recollection of the mugging, or Emily's attempted kidnapping.

He also wanted to try to do a little work. Trevor had been taking on the brunt of the responsibility at the law firm during Rick's six-month absence. Trying to help, he put together files on a few cases for Rick to work on from home. It sounded like a good start.

For now, Rick would stay in the spare bedroom. Marissa needed to build trust and proof he wouldn't show his monster side. She was grateful for the second chance and willing to give it a try, hoping for the best.

Emily ran a fever that night. Although Marissa didn't like seeing her sick, she wasn't too concerned, as kids often got sick. She called the doctor and alternated Tylenol and Motrin through the night as directed.

The doctor vocalized his concern for Marissa because she was pregnant, advising her to be super careful. Marissa agreed, but she was more concerned because Rick was due to come home tomorrow. Why couldn't anything be easy?

Marissa took Emily's temperature with the forehead digital thermometer and saw that it was close to normal on the medication. She exhaled a sigh of relief, gave her sleeping daughter a kiss on the forehead and went to bed for the night.

Chapter 71

Rick stood at the door of his room toying with the straps of his duffle bag and whistling quietly, excited to be going home. He packed his toiletries and personal items into the black gym bag that Marissa had bought him. She was coming to pick him up in a few minutes. He packed and then began pacing the room filled with nervous anticipation.

She mentioned Emily was running a fever, and he would need to keep his distance for a few days, but he planned on doing the opposite. He wanted to bring her soup and read her books, the way a father should. Rick was determined to be a good father, a good man, a changed man. He wants to be present in her life, to be there for all of her school plays and field trips. He's determined to be a wonderful role model who she can be proud of. He didn't want to be that Rick Lynch who everyone who loved him feared.

He had been warned it was leaked to the press that he was being released. The press only knew he had been in the accident. Fortunately, they didn't know about the partial amnesia, the drug detoxification, and the troubles with Marissa. They only knew he almost died, literally died, on the table and was brought back. They didn't know the extent of what he'd been through. He only hoped they would leave him alone. He needed time.

Rick's phone was loaded with the numbers of his doctors. Two had given him their personal cell phone numbers. They had grown to like him, despite his harsh reputation and they wanted to see him land on his feet. He's now on the right combination of drugs for his condition, and he should not feel the need to self-medicate any longer. Rick had everyone he needed in his corner, and hopefully his future and his health was looking bright for him. He's a smart thirty-eight-year-old man who had a beautiful wife, daughter, and home. He could do this.

Marissa stood in the doorway. "Ready?" she prompted, arching her eyebrows.

He caught a glimpse of her side profile as she entered, his eyes widening in surprise. Was she? Was Marissa pregnant?

She caught his eyes and smiled. "Yes," she confirmed. "Our son is due in four months."

Rick looked like it was Christmas Day. His eyes were twinkling, and his smile was huge. He shyly asked Marissa, "May I hug you?"

She nodded with tears in her eyes, overwhelmed by his reaction. They ran into each other's arms and embraced.

"Oh, Marissa, thank you," he whispered just loudly enough for her to hear "Thank you for giving us this chance."

Marissa looked at him, her eyes filling with tears, and her voice cracking with emotion as she spoke. "Rick, the man I am getting to know now has all the good parts of the old Rick, and the good parts of the new Rick. It is going to take some time to trust this, trust us again. But I am willing to take it slow and give it a try."

Rick locked eyes with her. His blue ones staring straight into her turquoise ones. He gently placed his hands on her shoulders and noticed that she didn't pull away. That was a good sign. "Marissa, I love you. A chance is all that I am asking for. You owe me nothing and have given me more than I can ever thank you for. I need to prove to you that I can be a good man, a good husband, a father that Emily admires, and a chance for a fresh start with our son." Marissa fell into his arms and welcomed his embrace.

"Rick, I am willing to give it a try," she whispered, stroking his neck with her hand. "I want this for us, I want this for our children."

"I love you Marissa," Rick reiterated in a deep voice choked with emotion. "Thank you."

They both felt extremely happy, at peace with their fresh start as they left the rehab center hand in hand and headed home.

Chapter 72

Two weeks later…

Hailey and Chad strolled hand in hand through Central Park. It was a cold November Saturday, and they had been busy looking at apartments all day. They finally decided on a place on Columbus Circle with a view of Central Park. Both Chad and Hailey would have a fifteen-minute subway ride to work, and it was close to everything they loved, museums, parks, shops and more. They were so excited for their future.

She and Chad were both so excited for the new place, his new position, and their bright future. They were happily planning their wedding for springtime on Cecelia's sprawling Hampton property. Things couldn't be more perfect for Hailey and Chad.

Hailey couldn't stay too long; her theater group was putting on their holiday show in a few weeks and she had to lead the rehearsal. But they enjoyed taking advantage of any time they could spend together. "I love you," she whispered as they parted at the subway stop.

"I love you, too," he proclaimed, giving her a sweet kiss. The press was there photographing them, but this time they didn't care.

Rick was running a fever again, 101. He thought he caught Emily's virus, but that had come and gone a week ago and now he was running one again. He also noticed some odd bruises popping up and made a doctor's appointment for tomorrow. For now, he'd do his best to rest and stay in his room.

Things had been going so well at home with him, Emily, and Marissa. There was a joy for all of them in everyday things. They loved painting and reading stories together. Emily was excited about having her daddy home and overjoyed at being a big sister.

Rick started working on a few of the cases and loved having his mind busy. More memories continued coming back slowly. He still remained a calmer, less intense version of his old self, but a few of his memories agitated him. Rick shook his head and rubbed his temple at the memories of the old him.

He remembered being on the news and putting the commentator down. He cringed when he remembered how he verbally sliced an adversary over a case he shouldn't have won. But due to his theatrics and skills, he did. He was also starting to recall how he treated Marissa at times. He was verbally cruel and controlling. He felt horribly over the memories and told her so. Could he blame the drugs, or was it really who he was? Rick grappled over this with his doctor at his therapy sessions.

"Listen, the drugs fueled you to be like that to some extent," his therapist began. "But remember, the choices are always yours to own up to."

Rick nodded in acknowledgement and vowed to change. His only major challenge that was thrown at him occurred when Lana came over. He hadn't seen her since her one visit to his hospital room. He had no idea who she was, only that she had said she was a friend.

She came over last week after Emily was deemed healthy. "Hello, Rick," she commented, stepping into the house. "Nice to see you again."

Rick looked at her, trying to remember who she was. He knew her name was Lana, that she said she was a friend of his, and she was now being introduced as his wife's business partner. But he had this nagging feeling he knew her from somewhere else.

"Hi, Lana" he said. "Nice to see you again, too."

Marissa watched their interaction from the doorway. They acted like complete strangers. She was glad his memories of their affair had been wiped out and would like it if they stayed that way.

Rick headed off to the library to do some work and left them alone to plan their next event. He noticed Lana was pregnant, too. She appeared to be as pregnant as Marissa. They had that in common. Rick didn't give it much thought as he went to do his work.

He spent the night in Marissa's room last night. She had invited him in. They only spent the night holding each other and he felt the baby kick. It was enough for him to be able to hold her and feel that life inside her. Marissa was letting him in slowly, but it's a wonderful start. Rick was incredibly grateful.

Now he was running a fever again. Marissa was the one who noticed the odd bruises on his leg and told him to make an appointment right away. He felt very tired all of a sudden and laid down to go to sleep.

A few hours later he woke up to intense night sweats that soaked through his pajamas along with an extremely high fever. Marissa heard him moan in his sleep. She tried to wake him, but he was so out of it. She couldn't get him up and frantically called for an ambulance.

The ambulance arrived and when they realized their patient was Rick Lynch, they moved quickly, rushing him to the hospital. He was admitted and being seen by doctors within twenty minutes, while his bloodwork and scans were done within the hour.

Marissa called Hailey for help. She and Chad rushed over and scooped up a sleeping Emily, but Emily woke up and excitedly packed a bag to stay a few days with Aunt Hailey and Uncle Chad.

224

Chapter 73

Marissa was eight months pregnant, exhausted, and scared for Rick. He didn't look well, and his fever was still high. He complained of being dizzy, too. Marissa sat there with a surgical mask on, holding his hand.

"It'll be okay," she murmured, trying to calm him and herself at the same time.

He looked very pale and seemed agitated, constantly going in and out of consciousness.

The doctor finally came in. "Mrs. Lynch, I am afraid we have some troubling findings on Rick's bloodwork. His white blood cell count is extremely high. We are recommending you see an oncologist. He will be in shortly to speak with you."

Marissa took a moment to process this information, an oncologist. She felt as if she had been punched. They were recommending a cancer specialist see Rick? She started to cry. Marissa leaned against the wall, using it for support. This was all too much.

"Mrs. Lynch, please sit down. We will know more when Dr. Steiner runs his tests. He is in the best hands. You need to take care of yourself and the baby."

Marissa felt a contraction at this point and winced but just ignored it. She's tense and she'd been having Braxton Hicks contractions for a while. The doctor had a nurse come in and sit with her until the oncologist came in.

With the nurse by her side, Marissa called Hailey to fill her in. She was sending Chad down to be with her while she watched Emily. "He's on his way," she informs Marissa. Chad knew a lot of the hospital higher ups and Hailey knew he would be able to guide and help Marissa get what she needed.

The oncologist walked into the room at the same time Chad arrived. He hugged Marissa and informed her, "I am here for you and Rick." He was soon to be their brother-in-law and despite Rick Lynch's former reputation, he wanted to help.

Marissa squeezed his hand and mumbled, "Thank you."

With his eyebrows drawn down, looking serious, the doctor pulled their attention to him, asking, "Is it okay to speak with both of you outside?" He gestures to the door.

Marissa and Chad both nod and follow him out the door without a word.

"Mrs. Lynch, we can't be sure until we run more scans and tests, but we suspect Rick has Leukemia. His body has been through so much, and his immune system took a beating. If it is what we think, there are treatments that can help."

Marissa started to cry again, big heaping sobs. Chad wrapped his arms around her and held her while the doctor looked on sympathetically. Unfortunately, he was used to this reaction. It was part of his job, and in the end, he sought to give this hard news but save as many lives as he could.

"We are going to have him transferred to the oncology floor," he informed them.

Between sobs Marissa stammered, "Th..thank you." Then, Chad guided her to a chair and sat her down. She was shaking. How could she tell Rick? Things were just starting to look better.

In the end it was Chad who broke the news to Rick. His fever had thankfully come down, and he'd been moved to Unit 10 in Oncology. He sat in his bed awake, glassy eyed, and fatigued.

"Hey, Rick," Chad murmured, bringing him a glass of water.

"Thank you," Rick replied as he took the glass, gulping down the water. "I'm back here again?" he inquired, looking defeated as his eyes roamed around the hospital room.

"Yup," Chad said in a lighthearted tone. "You liked this place so much, you couldn't stay away."

Rick smiled. "What's wrong with me? I feel like I've been hit by a truck."

Chad cleared his throat. This was going to be rough, but Marissa had asked him to tell Rick the truth. She was having some more contractions and the doctor ordered for her to lay down in another room and be monitored. She wanted to be there for him, but the stress on the baby was prohibiting it.

"Listen, they ran some tests," Chad began, but paused.

Rick instantly picked up on the pause. "Not good, huh?" Rick looks at his hands which began nervously trembling before focusing back on Chad. He forced Chad to look him in the eye for his next words. He may have been the new Rick, but he still had some nuances of the old Rick in him.

"Not the best," Chad replied, trying to contain his emotions. His voice dropped an octave filled with emotion. "They suspect Leukemia."

Rick took a deep breath, and exhaled, taking a moment. "What do I do now?" he asked, his voice barely above a whisper.

Chad looked at him, this man who had been a wrecking ball only eight months ago, now looked like he was a child in need of his mom.

"What you do now," proclaimed Chad, "is fight."

Chapter 74

Rick remained in the hospital for two weeks. During that time, he started an aggressive chemotherapy regimen. The doctors refused to talk of survival odds with him. They wanted to continue to focus on the positives with him. The same team of doctors who had taken care of him during his two previous episodes stayed on, and they added an oncology team to the mix. Rick truly was receiving the best care.

Chemotherapy hit him hard. He was nauseous, dizzy, and losing hair almost immediately. After the two weeks, the doctors felt it was best for him both mentally and physically to be at home. Marissa set him up in the guest room with a team of nurses staying with them. She had a day nurse with him as a one-to-one nurse, and she was relieved by a night nurse who came by at 6 p.m. and stayed for the night. There were a few hours gap between shifts and Marissa took care of Rick then.

She was nine months pregnant at this point, emotionally stressed, and exhausted. The doctors informed them that Rick wouldn't be able to be in the delivery room due to his fragile state, so Hailey offered to step in and record the birth for Rick. They planned to FaceTime him, too.

Marissa had fallen very much in love with Rick again. More than anything, she wanted him to recover and be a part of the baby's life for a long time to come.

Hailey and Chad had been going to Lamaze classes with Marissa and filming them for Rick. He felt incredibly frustrated with being weak and unable to be there, but he was giving it his all and giving it his best fight. He read a lot on the days he felt strong as well as continued to work on cases. He played with Emily, both wearing surgical masks when they did. Rick was trying to still be the man he wanted to be despite every obstacle placed in his path.

Chad and Hailey were getting ready to go to Hailey's theater group's holiday concert. Hailey had been preparing for months and the children were beyond excited to be able to perform for their parents. The pageant was scheduled to start at 7 p.m. and end at 9 p.m. The kids were due to arrive at 6 p.m. Hailey and Chad ordered pizza for everyone to enjoy after the show, and they were looking forward to seeing everyone arrive.

The theater had been saved and surprisingly Cecilia donated money to have it restored. So far, the auditorium where they'd been performing in had been updated. The seats were all covered in new navy fabric, the stage had been enlarged, and new lights added. Hailey had been going out weekly to have lunch with Cecelia even before she did this, but when she found out about what she was doing for the theater, she was so grateful. She's touched by her gesture of supporting something so near and dear to her heart.

Chad was shocked by Cecelia's generosity, but incredibly pleased she and Hailey hit it off. It felt like a dream for him to have two very important women in his life get along so well.

Chad carried the pizzas into the back room when they arrived. Hailey was having the kids take their seats in the order they stood on the bleachers. Chad looked over and noticed one little boy was very fidgety. He was squirming in his seat.

"Something wrong?" Chad squatted down to ask him.

He looked about six or seven years old and had slicked back hair and expressive eyes. He was dressed in a navy suit. "Yeah," the little boy said, looking at Chad with a toothless smile. "I can't do my tie. It came off." He handed Chad a bright red holiday decorated tie scrunched in a ball.

"I can fix that," Chad remarked, smiling as he helped the boy with his tie. "What's your name?"

"Dylan. "What's yours?"

"Chad," he replied chuckling.

Hailey watched from her seat at the piano, smiling. She couldn't wait to have kids with Chad. He was so sweet and nurturing to children, she could imagine how he would be with his own. She felt like she was living a dream. After he finished with Dylan, he turned to Hailey and smiled.

Hailey handed Chad her pocketbook. "Hold this for me please."

"But it doesn't match my shoes," Chad joked, awkwardly holding the bag, while Hailey ushered the kids on stage.

He laughed, carried her pocketbook like a football, and took a seat a few rows back from the stage to enjoy the show. He smiled at the people around him as they all recognized him as the senator-elect and fiancé of Hailey. Many complimented Hailey to him, saying how incredible she was with the kids.

The show soon began, the chorus started singing, "It's A Small World." The children's faces lit up as they sang, standing tall with pride, their voices angelic.

In the middle of the song, Chad suddenly felt Hailey's phone vibrate in her pocketbook. He ignored it and continued watching the show, but he couldn't ignore it when his own phone started to vibrate wildly with both a text message and then a voicemail. Chad discreetly looked down at his phone. He saw a message from Marissa.

"I'm in labor. Contractions coming fast. Reeve came over to drive me to the hospital. I need Hailey."

Looking up at the stage, Chad saw Hailey happily conducting the concert. He looked at the time and realized there was another hour of performances, not sure what to do.

Chad's phone vibrated with another text. Looking down, he reads a frantic text from Rick, "It is killing me not to be there with her. Please, Chad, take my place and go to her."

Chad looked at the stage, then his phone. Standing, he exited the row as quickly as possible, mumbling his apologies. Quickly, he made his way backstage. Once backstage, he found a piece of cardboard, and a marker. Writing swiftly, but clearly, he wrote, "Marissa in labor, heading to the hospital. Rick wants me there." He waited until he saw Hailey's eyes look over. Then, he held up the sign.

She smiled and nodded. "Go," she mouthed before returning her attention back to the kids for their final numbers. He knows she will meet him there right after the show.

Chad left her pocketbook in the hands of a parent volunteer, briefly explaining the situation, and rushed out. He hopped in the car and veered towards the hospital.

Chapter 75

Chad had arrived at the hospital a few minutes after Reeve and Marissa. Reeve had already checked her in. "I'm an old pro at this," he joked laughing. His wife delivered their second son only two months before.

Marissa had been invited to the baby shower with Emily. They had become lifelong friends. Reeve now had two country music, race car loving sons, and he couldn't have been happier. They named their second baby Luke for Luke Bryan.

Reeve turned to Chad informing him, "Rick didn't look so good."

Chad nodded. "He's running out of options. We will all meet with the doctors next week."

"Prayers coming his way. You better get in there," Reeve advised, urging Chad inside. "Those contractions are coming pretty darn fast. I reckon Marissa is delivering a future Indy 500 driver."

Chad smiled. "Thank you, Reeve." Then he was led by the nurse into Marissa's private room.

"Oh!" Marissa exclaimed. "That's a big one." Glancing over at Chad, relief washes over her face. "Oh, thank goodness you are here. Where is Hailey?"

Marissa looked wiped out already. Chad had never seen someone give birth. He saw the videos in the Lamaze classes he and Hailey went to with Marissa, but the actual live giving birth felt surreal.

"Hailey is at her show," he revealed to the frantic Marissa who was panting her contractions away. "She is coming right after."

Marissa answered with, "Oh! Oh! They are coming so fast! They didn't come this quickly with Emily!"

Chad looked around frantically for something to give Marissa something to do. He felt so helpless watching her stomach contract and hear her yelling in pain. He pushed the button for the nurse. She came right in.

"She's in a lot of pain," he advised.

"The doctor is on his way," the nurse informed him with a polite nod. "She's already dilated and about to crown."

Chad looked at her wide-eyed, like she was speaking a foreign language.

"Mr. Harper," the nurse prompted calmly. "Get your phone out and Face-

Time Mr. Lynch, his son is on his way."

"Oh," stated Chad helplessly. This was all a bit much, but amazing at the same time. He quickly dialed in to Rick. "Hey," he commented to a tired and thin looking Rick. "Your son is on his way."

Rick teared up and exclaimed, "I wish I could be there."

Chad's words caught in his throat. "You are here. I won't let you miss a minute."

Chad did everything he could to film the birth and not pass out at the same time. He watched as Richard Lynch Jr. made his appearance into the world with a loud cry and then happily gurgled as he lay contently against Marissa's chest. He had black hair just like Rick, with a trace of auburn. He was 21 inches and 8 lbs. of cuteness.

Rick Lynch was happier and prouder than he had ever been. Each day he woke up feeling valued and loved. He found so much joy in his time with Emily. Now, he smiled all the time, despite what he'd been through. He was going to live for this baby.

Hailey arrived a few minutes later, flushed and out of breath from rushing to get there. She rushed over and hugged her sister. "I am so sorry I wasn't here."

Marissa smiled and spoke softly with the sleeping child across her chest. "Chad was wonderful and filmed the whole thing with the iPad and FaceTimed Rick." She turned and smiled at Chad, incredibly grateful. "Thank you."

Chad looked at Hailey. "It was scary as hell and wonderful at the same time. I need to go now and buy this kid some Matchbox cars and a Hess Truck. Oh, and he needs a baseball glove. And I have to get Emily a doll."

Marissa and Hailey laughed. They both thought Chad was a rare breed of man. Marissa was so happy for her sister and to know she would be welcoming him into their family.

Chapter 76

Marissa left the hospital the next day. Chad and Hailey brought her and Rick Jr. home. Emily and a thin, weak but happy looking Rick greeted them at the door. He couldn't wait to hold his son. He vowed to do everything in his power to live to see him grow up.

Three days later Lana went into labor. Trevor was ready and calmer than Lana. Trevor could not wait to be a dad. This had been the best nine months of their marriage. They felt like they had a fresh start. They were so excited to be parents together.

Lana's labor was long and exhausting. Twenty-two hours later and after being given Pitocin, a drug that speeds up pregnancy, Alex Robert Drysdale was born. He let out a cry and had a full head of dark hair with auburn highlights. Trevor fell in love right from the start and claimed that he looked like his grandfather. Lana was in love and tried to deny in her mind that he looked like Rick.

. . . .

Rick wasn't doing well. The doctors were using words like, "Clinical trials," and, "Stem cell transplants." The chemo and radiation were doing nothing but making him sicker and weaker. The only times he got out of bed was to be with the kids for a few hours or spend a little time with Marissa. Most of the time he slept.

Marissa had a nanny to help her, and her parents had flown in for a week. They offered to stay longer, but Marissa knew they were older now and missed their home and routine. She appreciated their visit and knew how badly they felt about Rick. They all did. The press didn't even bother them anymore. No one had interest in a dying man, and he was dying.

His memory returning had plateaued, and he kept fighting the fight for his kids. The doctors asked him to let them know when he felt he had enough. He was almost there.

Emily came into his room one night and asked to cuddle with him and watch a Disney movie. She had been afraid to do that for a while. He always seemed so weak, or he was sleeping. "Daddy," she asked meekly, "can I come up?" Rick patted the bed and motioned for her to hop up. Emily looked at him, and he met her eyes. She melted into his outstretched arms. They both needed this moment.

"Daddy, don't die, we need you," she declared, and burst into tears curling into him. Rick pulled her tighter into his embrace, overwhelmed with emotion. Emily meant the world to him. He stroked her hair and tried to soothe her the best he could.

He realized they really did need him, and he needed to continue to fight for his kids, for his wife, and for his life. Rick made an appointment for the next day to find out about the clinical trial. Luckily, he qualified and began taking the medicine within a week. This was his last hope, his last chance, but he was ready to go another round in his fight. He had his family to live for, so much to live for.

Chapter 77

Spring came with some beautiful blooms on the Cherry Trees. Rick was stronger now, strong enough to take Rick Junior on walks and push Emily on the swings. He started working again from home, and Marissa was back working with Lana planning the events.

Lana continued working with Marissa; a kinship had been forged. She and Trevor were doing wonderfully enjoying baby Alex. Life seemed good for the two families. It was simply amazing that everyone was able to move past all that had happened between them.

Like her sister, Hailey was happy and kept busy planning their wedding for the next month. Cecelia, of course, had gone all out hiring a wedding planner. She was bringing in tents, an orchestra for the cocktail hour, a band for the reception, and one of the finest caterers in the Hamptons. She loved Hailey and Chad, and she was incredibly proud of her Senator grandson and his beautiful bride to be.

Cecelia invited Hailey over for lunch many times to discuss the wedding. In reality, Cecelia loved having Hailey over, and Hailey loved spending time with Cecelia. Hailey learned that Cecelia was a pianist in her youth and played for many theater companies. There was a Steinway in the living room, but Hailey had never inquired who in the family played. She longed to sit down and run her fingers over the keys but had been too shy to ask.

"Who plays piano?" she asked, her curiosity finally winning out one day while having tea with Cecelia in the living room. The bright sun was shining in from the skylight and it truly looked like a spotlight on the piano.

"It is me," Cecelia boasted, smiling at the memory "In my youth I had many piano recitals and was trained by a concert pianist." She smiled widely at the memory, the pure joy reaching her eyes. She loved spending time with Hailey. "Some days when the arthritis isn't kicking in, I like to sit down and play a good concerto."

Hailey's mouth dropped open at this surprise tidbit of information. "That is incredible," she replied. "I would love to hear you play."

With Hailey's encouragement, Cecelia, wearing her trademark linen skirt, button down and pearls, walked slowly to the Steinway. She extended her fingers and massaged them. "Working out the kinks," she commented laughing. Hailey smiled at her, encouraging her to play.

Cecelia focused, her eyes planted on the keys and became trancelike as she played the most beautiful Beethoven Concerto No. 2 that Hailey had ever heard. Cecelia's fingers glided over the keys with surprising ease as she closed her eyes and played the piece from memory. Cecelia smiled as she played, lost totally in the music. Hailey stood up, eyes wide and mouth open, while Ingrid, who was doing laundry, popped her head out and tears filled her eyes seeing Cecelia play with such passion. Cecelia hadn't played in so long, the piano had been collecting dust. Hailey brought music back into Cecelia's world without even realizing it. When she stopped playing, she went silent, a single tear fell from her eyes.

"That was simply beautiful," Hailey praised, striding over, and giving Cecelia a hug. "Amazing. Why have you been hiding this from everyone?"

"I needed to focus on my children, my grandchildren," Cecelia claimed, staring into Hailey's green eyes. "Now that they are happy, maybe I can play again. Would you sit down and play with me?"

"Absolutely." Hailey happily joined Cecelia at the piano. They played some Bach and more Beethoven together. Cecelia had found her soulmate in Hailey, and Hailey had found a grandmother in Cecelia.

Beyond the music revelation, Cecelia was showing her happiness more and more now that all her children and grandchildren had reached her goals for them. She proudly displayed everyone's picture on the wall over her Steinway, her judge son in his black robe, her Senator son being sworn in, her other son in his robe and her daughter at her desk. Under those pictures were ones of her successful grandchildren. She had just recently and proudly added Chad's picture to the row. He was standing next to Hailey and making his acceptance speech.

Hailey tried to stop by Cecelia's house at least once a week after school. She would take the train out to Westhampton and Cecelia's driver would pick her up. Cecelia delighted in each and every visit as they played piano together and spoke about the wedding.

"I am just so excited, my dear," Cecelia announced, smiling at Hailey as they ate chicken salad sandwiches four months out from the wedding day. "I can only imagine that all eyes will be on you my dear, as you will be gorgeous, but I plan to give you a little competition in a stunning gown."

Hailey smiled in delight as Cecelia showed her the gown that she had selected, and of course she planned to wear her pearls. Hailey was truly enjoying this special relationship that she had forged with Cecelia. Every moment they spent together was becoming precious to both of them. They were always laughing, and Ingrid joined in. She even brought out Cecelia's wedding album, and they admired her beautiful ornate gown. She had lost Martin, her husband twenty years prior. He had been the true love of her life. Cecelia reminisced about her love for him.

"Chad reminds me of Martin," she explained. "I think that is why I have such an affinity for him and pushed him to reach his full potential. Martin was a bit of a do-gooder too and needed my pushing."

Hailey laughed knowing that Martin was a former three-time senator prior to Thad and then Chad. Hailey understood why the legacy was important to Cecelia. Hailey also had a new appreciation for the multi-generational bonds. Family was so important, hers and now Chad's.

Hailey cherished her time with Emily now more than ever. She was slated to be a flower girl in their wedding. They had chosen a beautiful lavender dress for her to wear, and she would be tossing flower petals from a white wicker basket.

She was so excited when Hailey and Chad had asked her to be in their wedding. One Saturday in December they took her to Serendipity, ordered her a Foot Long Hot Dog and a Frozen Hot Chocolate. Her eyes were huge as she took in the giant food items. They had the waiter come over with a pink balloon, attached to it was a note that read, Will you be our flower girl at our wedding?

Emily cheered so loudly that everyone in the place turned around. She couldn't wait. "I get to be in a wedding," she squealed, "and wear a purple dress." Chad and Hailey laughed as they both gave her a big hug. The wedding was really going to happen. They were all so excited. The storms of the past year had hopefully come to an end. They all hoped for rainbows ahead.

Marissa carefully designed the invitations, placing them in gold sealed envelopes emblazoned with a delicate lace design. She was so happy for her sister and was eager to celebrate their union. Love was in the air for her as well. She and Rick had created a wonderful new, equal relationship born out of honesty and renewed trust. She once again believed that happiness was possible. She prayed for continued progress in his health. They were due to go for scans next week and that always made her nervous, but she was trying to stay positive. Positivity and strength are what have gotten her through all of the hurdles so far.

She wasn't the same Marissa, much as Rick wasn't the same Rick. Renewal could often be beautiful, and she felt like a butterfly released from her cocoon. Her transformation had not been without emotional bloodshed and tears, but she was looking forward instead of backward. The future, although often un-predictable, was starting to look bright. Focusing on the wedding and her sister made her so happy. Marissa took on her maid of honor duties with zest.

The wedding would be spectacular. Everyone would work together to make it spectacular for Hailey and Chad. Chad asked Harding, Reeve, and Rick to be his best men and they were all honored and flattered. Hailey asked Jillian, Maris-sa, and her best friend Brianna to be her bridesmaids. Chad's niece and nephew were in the wedding party as well. Chad's niece would walk beside Emily as another flower girl and his nephew was the ring bearer. It would be a memora-ble event.

Cecilia was in her glory, she was giddy with excitement and fluttering around socializing, while the press was buzzing around. She was also planning a surprise for them and had been practicing every day. Music and love filled Cecelia's heart and she couldn't wait for this celebration. Hailey had become so special to her, and Chad was her world.

To prepare for the big day, Cecelia hired a security team and Rick had insist-ed on having some of his former security team be part of it. His memory was coming back more consistently now. He had wiped out a lot from the trauma, but he had some great memories of his family and that's what was most im-portant to him. The meds he was on kept him mentally stable while his physical body suffered a punch. But for now, he's doing well, and looking forward to the wedding.

Rick reached a point in his life where he felt content. He had everything he wanted in his wife, two kids, and home. He even found peace in one of his past mistakes, receiving an email from the actress he had been with and paid off to disappear. She wished him well and informed him that going off to Las Ve-gas and leaving New York had been a wonderful thing for her in the end. Her brother had relocated with her, giving them both a fresh start. She wished him good health and congratulated him on the baby. At first, he'd been confused about who sent him the email, then he remembered. He felt relieved this was in his past.

It was a spectacular day in May, the day of the wedding. The sun shined bright, the temperature a mild 72 degrees. Reeve promised them a good weath-er day and it had come true. They went back and forth between two dates. Reeve used his models and weather charts and advised them which one to pick. They're glad they listened, especially because their alternate date was last week, and it had poured rain all day.

Hailey was excitedly getting ready, not able to wipe the smile off her face.

The last ten months with Chad had been a wonderful whirlwind, and she couldn't wait to spend the rest of her days with him. He's everything she wanted and more.

Chad looked like he stepped out of a modeling ad in his black tux. Hailey's gown was designed just for her by a friend who was a wedding gown designer. It was fitted and strapless with thousands of crystals sewn from the bodice to the train in an intricate pattern. She wore her chestnut hair down with a side comb of delicate flowers. Her diamond earrings shimmered. She looked stunning.

Chad was blown away the moment he saw her walk down the aisle on her father's arm. He stood there proudly at the podium decorated in hundreds of fresh flowers. The bridesmaids and groomsmen had already walked down the aisle to the strains of Cannon, the women wearing lilac and champagne and the men wearing black tuxes.

Chad saw Hailey from a distance, the veil covering her face and he inhaled. "Beautiful," he exclaimed to no one in particular, "simply beautiful." The priest and the wedding party couldn't agree more. Hailey was spectacular.

Hailey walked down the aisle tearing up as she got closer to Chad. Everyone felt her intense emotion, and many were already dabbing their eyes. Chad shook her father's hand, took Hailey's hand in his and whispered, "I love you," as he helped her up onto the podium. Marissa came up behind her and smoothed out her stunning five-foot train. The crystals shimmered in the light.

The ceremony began and they stared into each other's eyes like no one else was in the room. They had written their own vows. Hers were filled with love and promise for the days ahead, while Chad's were equally as heartfelt.

Hailey looked deeply into Chad's eyes and proclaimed her love for him. "Chad, from the moment that I met you, you have made me feel special. You show your love for me every day in a million ways. I love coming home to you each night, and often finding roses in a vase, or wildflowers cut from our garden. You helped me save the theater and are my hero every single day. I love you, Chad with all of my heart and soul."

Chad wiped a tear from Hailey's eye and went on to say his vows locking her beautiful green eyes with his own. "Hailey, you make me want to just be a better man. I came alive, truly alive when I met you. I didn't know a woman as wonderful as you existed until you were placed in my path and will be forever in my heart. I come home each night to so much love, and a hug from you makes my day complete. I am looking forward to many adventures with you, and quiet nights sitting on the porch swing at grandmas and looking at the stars. I love you, Hailey."

Chad whispered the final few words of his vows. Both he and Hailey were tearing up as he finished, and many were in tears after hearing their heartfelt exchange. Cecelia, dressed in a light blue gown with her pearls, even wiped away a tear at the mention of them sitting on her porch swing. They were a beautiful, thoughtful couple and she was so proud. She didn't want to admit it to anyone, but they had in fact risen up the ranks to be her favorites.

Chad was so in love with Hailey, he wasn't sure if there were enough words in the English language to express it. They exchanged rings and kissed. Just as they were about to step off the podium, they were stopped by the priest. They looked at him in surprise, but he just winked.

Cecelia carefully stood up from her seat in the front and smoothed her gown. She smiled and walked slowly up to the podium, exchanged looks with a surprised Chad, and winked at Hailey. All eyes were on her as she was escorted over to the Steinway located to the left of the podium. Cecelia looked a little nervous as she stretched out her fingers and announced, "This is for my handsome grandson and his beautiful wife, may you be blessed always. I wrote this for you."

Cecelia played a harmonious piece of music that had the family and the guest in tears. Everyone watched her fingers move effortlessly across the keys and her body sway to the music with her eyes closed. The music reflected her joy, her confidence, her passion, and her love for the family. It was a priceless gift. When she was done, the whole room stood on their feet cheering and clapping while Hailey and Chad ran over and hugged her and helped her back to her seat. They all now knew that Cecelia was immensely talented and full of surprises.

It's a gorgeous wedding and wedding party. Chad surprised Hailey and had her children's choir and the gospel choir that rescued them join together on the grounds and sing, "Hallelujah" while Hailey and Chad came back down the aisle as man and wife. Hailey was moved to tears, as were most of the guests. It took a lot of work to make that happen and Chad was thrilled he pulled it off. There wasn't a dry eye in the place after the wedding.

"You are amazing," whispered Hailey, kissing Chad. "I am so lucky." He smiled and vowed to do anything and everything for her.

Marissa and Rick joined them on the dance floor for the song September by Earth, Wind and Fire. Rick held her in his arms. Marissa savored the moment. It was a night of romance. She moved in closer to Rick, and it felt so nice.

"Marissa," he began halfway into the dance, "I don't feel so well…" His voice trailed off as he collapsed on the dance floor, Marissa felt his weight on her as he fell.

She screamed, and the band stopped playing. All eyes were on Rick Lynch as he lay there with his eyes closed barely breathing on the floor.

Chapter 78

"I am sorry, Mrs. Lynch, the news is not good, and we need to discuss keeping him comfortable. We think hospice may be a good idea at this point." The doctor stands in front of Marissa with the same somber look that Marissa grew to dread. She heard the hopelessness in his voice and the practiced look in his eyes. He held her stare as he delivered the bad news. This was truly the worst part of his job.

Marissa burst into tears. She was still in her bridesmaid dress with Rick's tux jacket thrown over it. She had just been told after five hours, multiple scans, and blood tests that Rick's clinical trial meds had stopped working, and in fact had the opposite effect, accelerating the cancer. Rick was down to a two percent chance of survival. This was such devastating news that even his oncologist was near tears when he saw him. Rick was his miracle patient, and the clinical trial was going so well on other patients. They had held out so much hope that it would work for Rick.

Marissa stood in shock. He had been doing so well. What happened? Questions ran through her mind as she stood there alone. She didn't even have Hailey with her. Marissa insisted that she and Chad go on their Hawaiian honeymoon. She thought this was just a blip in his treatment and not the end. Her parents were with the guests. Marissa wrapped her arms around herself, feeling all alone. She wished someone was there by her side.

Reeve and his wife came by for a few hours, but they had to get home to their kids. Marissa put her head between her legs and cried. There had to be something they could do. After she was able to pull herself together enough to ask questions, she paged the doctor again and he returned to the room.

"Tell me something...anything that we can try. I am not ready to let him go."

The doctor saw the pain in her eyes and her desperation to keep her husband alive. The mighty Rick Lynch had taken quite the fall from the top and he was coming down hard. Everyone felt badly and helpless. Rick Lynch was a changed man. Life had thrown him a few brutal curveballs, and he was now unfortunately paying for all the damage he had done to his body from the years and years of drug use.

The irony now is that he was clean and doing well in all other aspects of his life. This just didn't seem fair. There had to be something that could be done in this final hour to save this man. This was Rick, Marissa's Rick.

"Please, doctor, please," Marissa begged, her eyes welling with tears. She felt beaten down, alone, desperate.

He looked at her and despite his stoic presence, he felt her pain, he too wanted to save Rick and remarked, "Let me make some calls."

They soon found that there was one doctor in New York willing to try a bone marrow stem cell transplant on Rick, even at this late stage. He came to the hospital within the hour and explained the procedure to Rick while he was laying in the hospital bed on oxygen, struggling to breathe. He informed them of the risks, as well as the slim chance of success. Marissa was praying for any chance they had. Rick nodded, and Marissa as his medical proxy signed the forms for him giving permission for this procedure. It was their nugget of hope, and they needed to hang on to it.

The doctor explained that they needed to test Emily and the baby to see if they were a match. He requested for all Rick's relatives to go to their nearest hospital and get tested. They needed the closest DNA match to Rick to give him the best chance of survival.

Over the next few days everyone was tested, and they found the closest match was Emily. Marissa cringed at putting her daughter through this process, but Emily wanted to do this for her dad.

"I need to help daddy," she cried after being told that she would need to go to the hospital for the procedure.

"She will be hooked up to an IV," the doctor explained, "and a machine will separate and collect her stem cells from her blood. After that, they will be transferred in an isolated setting to Rick." Marissa nodded and agreed. Rick in the meantime was being kept alive by machines. He was so weak that they were feeding him through a tube while he remained mostly in a state of unconsciousness.

On the day they were scheduled to do the extraction, Emily ran a fever, a high one, making it impossible to do the procedure. Emily was heartbroken and cried herself to sleep.

"It's not your fault, honey," Marissa and Sherry took turns saying to her, attempting to sooth an inconsolable Emily. "You can't help it if you are sick. They will find another way, for now, all we can do is pray."

The social worker came in and spoke to the family and prepared hospice for Rick as he declined more interventions or treatments.

"I am done," Rick announced, taking a deep breath. "It gets to a point when you have to say when. This is it." His eyes were flat, and he was having trouble catching his breath.

"Marissa," he continued gasping for air, "please don't let Emily blame herself. I love you all, and I am sorry I wasn't a better man. I paid for my funeral, arrangements have been made for you and the kids and I just want you to go on and be happy. You deserve to be happy." He lost consciousness right after that. It was looking pretty bleak.

Marissa held him and cried for their past, present, and future that wouldn't be. The man of steel was brought down by his own personal kryptonite. He was ending it in a bed, hooked up to tubes, and gasping for air.

At that moment, Lana, trembling, walked into the hospital and paged the doctor.

Epilogue

Six months later

It was a beautiful sunny summer day when Cecelia summoned everyone to her Hampton home. It was her 86th birthday and she wanted her family to be there to celebrate. So much has happened this past year. Her sons had long since retired, and her daughter spent much more time with her now as she was starting to become a little frail. Chad was elected to the senate making her exceptionally proud.

This birthday meant so much to her, and she wanted everyone in attendance. She extended the invitation to Marissa and Rick as well; they were family now that Hailey was married to Chad.

It's a true miracle that Rick was even alive. He slowly regained his strength and a dose of chemo put him in remission. He's immensely grateful for this chance and told Marissa how he loved and cherished her every chance he had.

Marissa was so in love with this new Rick. Her favorite times were when they were all together as a family in the park or just taking a walk. Rick was always smiling now, and not taking anything for granted. Marissa felt for the first time in a long time that they had a bright future.

They also came to terms with Lana and Trevor. Trevor and Lana had struggled for a bit but pulled their marriage back together. It was a rough road for him finding out that Alex was not his biological child, but his partner Rick's.

When the baby was born, Lana invested in saving the cord blood. She knew she may need it someday, knowing Rick's medical state and knowing Leukemia could be inherited.

Knowing her husband had been told he would have difficulty conceiving, she believed Alex was Rick's baby from the start, although she always hoped otherwise. She had taken hair from Emily's brush the day she snuck up to the camp in case she ever had to prove paternity. She prayed she never had to, and in her heart, the baby was Trevor's.

Marissa learned about what Lana had done when the doctor paged her and informed her they tested the cord blood, and it was the strongest match, even stronger than Emily. Marissa was shocked, but grateful to Lana for stepping up. She had no choice but to forgive and move on. It was the right choice. Her son had been born to save Rick. She knew that now.

Trevor and Rick dissolved the firm but remained cordial for the sake of the children. Trevor, in Lana's eyes, was Alex's dad. One day they would sit down and explain it all, but for now, the four of them had resolved it enough to be civil for the sake of the children. It wasn't their fault; they shouldn't suffer for their parent's actions.

Marissa held Rick's hand as Emily pushed her baby brother in his stroller up Cecelia's gravel driveway. Chad and Hailey walked hand in hand behind them laughing with each other. They were just a happy couple and had so many wonderful things to celebrate since being together. Jillian followed a few minutes later with Harding and their children, who were blowing bubbles and running ahead of their parents. Chad's parents had flown up from Florida for the event, and Cecelia's other children Zane, Damian, Elana, and their spouses, as well as each of their children flew in. Zane had two grown children, Damian had one and Elana had three.

Cecelia greeted everyone with warm smiles and hugs and kisses. Her hair was in a neat bun, and she was wearing a lilac skirt, white collared shirt, and her trademark pearls. She looked lovely and radiant. This was the type of day she loved the most, having her family around her. She may have been a tad bit more frail than last year, but her blue eyes still sparkled with fire and mischief. She had a little secret and she couldn't wait to have it revealed. But first, she wanted everyone to have lunch and relax.

The caterers had set up an array of food under a red tent on Cecelia's sprawling grounds. There were trays of meats and cheeses, vegetable and dips, shrimp, lobster, and steaks, and for the kids, macaroni and cheese and chicken fingers. The dessert table was laden with heaping trays of bakery cookies, small cakes decorated in bright icing and cannoli filled to the brim with cream. It looked like quite a spread, and Cecelia was quite pleased.

She watched with her matriarch's eyes as everyone mingled and took their plates to the table. Cecelia sat next to Chad on one side and Hailey on the other. She had taken extreme care in arranging the seating. Marissa and Rick were seated at the head of the table, near Hailey and Chad. The four of them had become her new favorite people, they're over often on the weekends to spend time with her and take her to the theater. She enjoyed their company immensely. Emily sat at the children's table, and the baby was being watched by the nanny who Cecelia hired for the occasion. All the children were being catered to and given bubbles, lawn toys and remote-control cars keeping them happy and occupied. Cecelia thought of every detail. This was her event and she spent months planning it.

While everyone was lunching and enjoying conversations with one another, Thad stood up and clinked his glass. "May I please have everyone's attention?" Everyone stopped talking and all eyes went to Thad, standing there smiling in his khakis and light blue golf shirt. He appeared relaxed and happy to be there; retirement in Florida agreed with him. "I would just like to wish our beautiful mother Cecelia a very happy 86th! Mom, you have cared about us, supported us, and given us your heart. We would all like to do something for you. We are sending you and Ingrid on a cruise to Europe in December, and we have arranged for your book club to be on that same fourteen-day cruise. Happy birthday, Mom."

Everyone cheered as they all knew about the surprise and had chipped in. Everyone turned to watch Cecelia's reaction, although it wasn't what they expected. She looked sad and forlorn, her eyes lost their twinkle and she blurted, "But I can't go in December. Chad and Hailey will be having their baby then."

Everyone turned and looked at each other. Harding's mouth dropped open and Jillian started to tear up. Thad prompted, "What?"

Marissa looked at Hailey wide eyed and commented, "Oh, that makes sense now why you didn't have wine last night."

Chad looked from Hailey to Cecelia. Cecelia covered her mouth in shocked realization at what she had done. She wasn't supposed to say anything.

Chad furrowed his brow for just a moment, he's a little upset the cat is out of the bag. They hadn't told anyone but Cecelia and asked her to keep it a secret until they were ready to tell.

Hailey touched both Cecelia's and Chad's arms. "It's okay, it's okay. They were all going to find out soon anyway, I can't hide it much longer."

Chad smiled at that, relief evident on his face and squeezed Hailey's hands. Hailey stood up. "Well, since the cat is out of the bag, let me tell you more news. We're having twin girls."

The group went wild with congratulations and hugs. When all had settled down, they agreed to change the cruise to February, and then fell back into easy conversation.

Hailey turned to Marissa and conspiratorially whispered, "What if they are like us?"

Marissa started laughing, her laughter could be heard by everyone. "If they are like us," Marissa exclaimed, "Run!" Elated, she turned and gave her sister a hug.

The End

Author Jessica Gold's love of writing began when her story, The Animals in Africa, won honorable mention in the local county writing contest. Gold's dream of writing and publishing a book came true when she signed with traditional publisher, Pen It! Publications, LLC to publish several of her works. She has been an educator, a freelance magazine journalist and website writer for twenty-five years. She writes many of her articles and books on her phone while listening to Top 40 songs and drinking her favorite beverage; unsweetened iced tea.

Jessica is a busy mom of two active children; she spends many hours bringing them to sports and music events. She credits her husband of twenty-one years for inspiring her to keep writing and to let her creativity flow. When she is not writing, she loves the beach, spending time with her family and friends and making a good lasagna.

CPSIA information can be obtained
at www.ICGtesting.com
Printed in the USA
LVHW081522191222
735534LV00027B/521

9 781639 843688